UP TO ME

"Scorching hot . . . insanely intense . . . and it is shocking. *Shocking!*"
—*The Bookish Babe*

"I definitely did NOT see the twists coming."
—*The Book List Reviews*

"You know those first books in a series that totally blow you away and you just think, wow, this just can't get any better than this? I mean, how can you make perfection better after all? Well, no worries here. Not only did [Leighton] completely blow *Down to You* out of the water with *Up to Me*, but she took it even further."
—*My Guilty Obsession*

"Brilliant . . . Cash is seriously one of my most favorite characters ever. He's a true alpha male, and you know how much I love those! He's just one sexy beast."
—*The Book Goddess*

"Leighton never gives the reader a chance to catch her breath . . . The plot has so many unexpected twists and turns that my heart was racing along . . . fast-paced, edge of your seat thrills. Yes, there is sex, OMG tongue hanging out of mouth, scorching sex."
—*Literati Literature Lovers*

"Well, I drank this one down in one huge gulp . . . and it was delicious. How . . . hot is Cash? Oh my god, and the sex. The sex in this book is seriously *scandalicious*."
—*Scandalicious Book Reviews*

"With twists happening faster than you can turn the page, Leighton continues her epic action and romance with characters that just keep getting hotter and hotter." —*A Life Bound by Books*

"Delicious . . . I stopped reading in order to grab a cold beer and cool off . . . the twists and turns on the plot line are brilliant."
—*Review Enthusiast*

"[*Down to You*] was such a shock . . . *Up to Me* has even more shockers in store!" —Examiner.com

EVERYTHING FOR US

The Bad Boys, Book 3

M. LEIGHTON

HODDER

First published in the United States of America in 2013
by The Berkley Publishing Group

First published in Great Britain in 2013 by Hodder & Stoughton
An Hachette UK company

1

Copyright © M. Leighton 2013

A CIP catalogue record for this title is available from the British Library.

ISBN 978 1 444 78034 5

Printed and bound by CPI Group (UK) Ltd, Croydon, CR0 4YY

Hodder & Stoughton policy is to use papers that are natural, renewable
and recyclable products and made from wood grown in sustainable forests.
The logging and manufacturing processes are expected to conform
to the environmental regulations of the country of origin.

To my God,
without you there is no inspiration
and no Davenport boys.

EVERYTHING FOR US

ONE

Nash

It's always the same. The dream starts out with the feeling of a weight being lifted from my arms. That's how I know what's coming, that I'll look down at my feet and see my hands pulling away from the box of supplies I was carrying, the box that now rests on the faded planks of the dock.

I straighten and take my cell phone from my pocket, flicking my thumb over the button that brings the screen to glowing life. I hit the camera app and raise the phone until I see the girl framed perfectly inside the lighted square.

She's lying on the top deck of a yacht across the way. It's swaying gently against the dock at the marina. It's a great boat, but it's not the boat that I'm interested in. Not at all. I'm interested in the girl. She's young, she's blond, and she's topless.

Her skin is shiny with tanning oil and the sun glints off the firm, round globes of her tits. They're the perfect handful, the kind that begs to be squeezed until she moans. The breeze picks up and, although it's warm, her nipples pucker against it. They're pouty and pink and they make my dick throb.

Damn, I love the marina!

Someone bumps my shoulder and I lose the girl in my view-finder. I turn and glare at the old man who's ambling off down the pier. I bite back the snide comment that's hanging on the tip of my tongue. Cash wouldn't bother. He doesn't hold his tongue for anybody. But I'm not Cash.

Ignoring the old man, I turn back toward the yacht, back toward the topless girl with the great rack. But before I can find her again, something else catches my attention.

There's a man standing at the end of the walkway, at the edge of the shore. He's lounging against the back wall of the little shack that sells basic grocery items and gas for the various watercraft that use the marina. He looks casual enough, but there's something about the way he's dressed that seems . . . off. He's wearing slacks. Like, dress slacks. And he's pulling a thin rectangle out of his pocket. For the most part it looks like a cell phone. Only it's not. With the magnification of my camera, I can see that it's just a plain black box with a little red button on top.

I see his thumb slide easily over the button just before something slams into me so hard it knocks me off my feet and into the water behind me.

Then there's nothing.

I don't know how many minutes, or hours, or even days have passed when I wake up in the water. I'm floating face up as my head bumps repeatedly against the nubby, barnacle-covered pier.

Achy, I urge my muscles into motion and roll onto my stomach. Stiffly, I ease into a slow swim toward one of the several ladders that dot the length of the dock. I climb, dripping wet, out of the water and look around for whatever caused the loud explosion I heard just before I was thrown into the water.

When I turn toward where my family's schooner was tethered, I see a cluster of people gathered there. It takes a full thirty seconds for my mind to interpret what I'm seeing—an empty boat slip, pieces of flaming wood peppering the dock, bits of splintered furniture scattered throughout the water. And smoke. Lots of smoke. And whispers, too. And, in the distance, growing closer, sirens.

I come awake from the nightmare with a start, just like I always do. I'm sweating and breathing hard, just like I always am. My face is wet with tears, just like it always is. It's been so long since I've had the dream, I forget how devastated and empty and . . . *angry* it leaves me feeling.

But now I remember. I remember with perfect clarity. And today, it's like pouring gasoline onto a raging fire.

I sit up in the bed to catch my breath. My side twinges in pain, reminding me of what happened last night. All of it comes rushing back, further fueling my fury.

Until a small, cool hand touches my shoulder.

I turn to see Marissa sitting up behind me, leaning on her elbow, looking at me through sleepy, sexy blue eyes. Before I can even think about what I'm doing, all the bitterness, all the anger, all the pent-up aggression gets channeled into pure lust. The need to devour something, to lose myself in something overwhelms everything else and I dive in. To her.

Spinning, I roll onto Marissa, pressing her warm body into the mattress. I hear her soft gasp as I crush her lips beneath mine. I swallow it—the sound, the fear, the hesitant desire—taking it in and letting it feed the animal inside me.

My tongue slips easily into her mouth. She tastes sweet, like honey. I push my knee between her thighs and they part, allowing me to settle my hips against hers.

It's not until I push my hand under the edge of her shirt that I realize she's stiff. I lift my head to look down at her. She's staring at me with wide, surprised, slightly terrified eyes.

TWO

Marissa

Nash stops kissing me just as I was about to lose myself to him. That would've been a disaster.

Wouldn't it?

I hold my breath as he stares down at me. Even in the low light, I can see the awareness come back into his black eyes. Something else had hold of him. And something in me liked it, which is totally *not* like me at all. But, then again, nothing seems to be the same since I was abducted. Why should I expect this to be any different?

I wonder absently if my life will ever be the same again. And if I even want it to be.

I feel slightly bereft when Nash moves off me and flops back onto the bed, flinging his arm over his eyes.

"You should probably stay away from me." His voice is a low rumble in the quiet darkness.

"I know," I reply in a moment of bald honesty. And I *do* know.

He's right. I *should* stay away from him. But I also know, deep down in some newly unearthed part of me, that I won't. That I can't. I'm drawn to him like I'm drawn to water or air. I don't know why and I'm not entirely comfortable with it, but I'm smart enough and rational enough to admit it, to recognize and to realize that I need to deal with it. The question is: How?

After a few seconds of silence, Nash jerks his arm away from his face and turns his head to glare at me. "Then what the hell are you still doing here?"

I stare into the fiery, furious depths of his eyes and still, despite the danger I *know* lurks within them, within *him*, I can't bring myself to get up and walk away. To distance myself from him. I can't. Not just yet.

"Because I need you," I say simply. And I do. To make me feel protected. Safe.

Nash opens his mouth as if he's going to reply, but no words come out. He just looks at me, looks *into me* with those cold-and-hot-at-the-same-time eyes of his. They're so much like Cash's, like the Nash I thought I knew, but they're also nothing like them. Nothing like anything I've ever seen before.

Seen or felt.

After a long pause, he finally speaks. "I'm trouble."

"I know."

Another pause.

"You'll probably get hurt."

I gulp. I know it's true, but hearing the words, out loud, acknowledging them, is something else entirely. "I know," I admit.

"Then you can't say I didn't warn you."

"I know," I say again, wondering if I've lost my mind as well as my vocabulary.

After a few more seconds of staring at me, Nash turns gingerly onto his unwounded side. "Roll over," he says gruffly.

I'm not sure why, but I do as he says without asking questions. It makes me pretty certain that yes, I *have* lost my mind.

On my side, facing away from him, I fold my hands under my cheek. My mind races with questions that have no answers and images that haunt me from the darkness. Just as a sense of panic starts to creep up from my chest and lodge in my throat, Nash drapes his arm over my waist, pulling me toward him, snugging me up into the curve of his body. He does it roughly, almost grudgingly. I don't get the feeling that he's giving me comfort so much as giving in and getting some for himself. It's almost as though he resists the help, the emotion of other people. He's a loner, stranded on an island of anger and bitterness. He needs rescuing. He just doesn't know it yet.

Regardless of his motives, the effect is still the same. In fact, the thought that he might need me as much as I feel like I need him intensifies it. Instantly, my mind stills and the panic quiets. That's the moment I realize that yes, he *is* trouble. And that no, it won't keep me away from him. Nothing will.

And I don't know why.

When next I open my eyes, I can see streaks of daylight peeking beneath the edge of my curtains. I listen to the sounds around me.

Nash's breathing is deep and even where it fans the side of my neck. A chill runs through me at the feel of his hard body pressed against my back.

I don't know what has gotten into me. I've never reacted to a man this way. Not even close. And I dated his brother, for God's sake! But it was nothing like this. This is something more, something wild. Something . . . different.

I hear the click of a door shutting. It sounded like it came from Olivia's room. One of them must be up.

Olivia.

Guilt washes through me when I think of her. How in the world she could be so kind to me, to risk so much to save me when I've treated her so badly, is truly beyond my comprehension. It makes me want to be worthy of that generosity and sincerity, although I doubt I ever could be.

An idea strikes me, so I move slowly away from Nash and slip out of the bed, padding quietly to the kitchen. I'm pleased to see that Olivia kept the fridge stocked while I was gone. Pulling eggs from the cubby inside the door, I open the freezer, too, taking out sausage patties and hash browns and laying it all on the counter. I grab a bowl and three skillets of varying sizes from the cabinet and set them on the stove. Looking proudly at my progress thus far, I push up my sleeves, ready to dig in and make a great breakfast for everyone. I jump, startled, when I hear a throat clear behind me.

I turn around, a big smile in place, fully expecting to see Olivia standing in the doorway. The voltage of the gesture, as well as the sincerity, dims considerably when I see Cash poised there instead.

"What are you doing?"

"Making breakfast," I respond, trying hard to rid my tone of sarcasm as I turn back to the food. "What's it look like?"

"You don't cook," Cash says flatly.

"It's never too late to start." I don't bother to look at him; I keep my attention focused on the eggs I'm cracking into a mixing bowl.

"You can drop the act, Marissa. It's just us. You don't have to pretend for me. You forget, I *know* you."

"Maybe you *used to* know me, as much as two people like us could've known each other, but that's in the past. Things are different now."

"Oh really?" There's no doubt he feels that's completely impossible. And that makes me angry.

I whirl to face him, pointing my whisk like an accusing weapon. "Don't act like you were any better than me. You lied to everyone in your life, everyone you called a friend or coworker. You used me for my position, to get close to my father, to keep your job at the firm. You were more than happy to do whatever you had to do to achieve your goals. Don't you dare get all pious and spit your righteous indignation at me. Don't *you* forget that I know *you*, too."

It only makes me angrier that he looks completely unflustered. "True. But that wasn't the real me. You never knew the real me. Only the person I let you see, the act I put on for everyone else's benefit."

"Judge all you want. Justify your actions all you want. I don't really care what you think, and I don't have to prove anything to you. I owe Olivia. As long as I can prove myself to her, I don't give a damn what you think."

With that, I turn back to my bowl full of raw eggs, diving in with my whisk and beating the crap out of them.

The thing that makes me angriest is that Cash is right. I don't deserve a second chance. I don't deserve anybody's trust or confidence. They've all seen what I was like. I've made an impression that I may well never be able to live down.

But that doesn't mean I'll stop trying. At this point, there are few opinions I actually care about. I'll just have to focus on those and put the rest out of my mind.

I hear the shuffle of Cash's bare feet as he leaves the kitchen. They stop at the last minute, so I stop whisking to listen.

"I'm sorry for what happened, Marissa. Not even someone like you deserved to be dragged into the shitstorm of my life."

I say nothing, just listen to the quiet as he waits for a response, gets none, and then walks away. I try to ignore how his obvious distaste for me stings. I don't really care what he thinks, but it's disturbing to think anyone feels that way about me. Was I really that bad?

Before I can start down the horrible road of self-loathing, I hear another voice.

"Ignore him, Marissa." This time it *is* Olivia standing in the doorway when I turn. She looks tousled and sleepy and sweet, as always. I'm a little embarrassed that she heard what he said. "He's like a bear with a thorn in his paw this morning. I don't know what his problem is." Her grin is kind. I know she's trying to excuse his behavior, but somehow that just makes me feel worse. Has she always come to my defense this way? And have I always been this undeserving of it?

My stomach curls into a sick knot. I know the answer to that question.

Yes.

"You don't have to cover for him, Liv. I can only imagine how hard it would be to believe someone can have a change of heart overnight."

She eases on into the kitchen and perches on one of the bar stools at the island. "That might be true if something so . . . drastic weren't involved. But Marissa, you were kidnapped. I mean, you had no idea what was going on, that you were even in danger.

None of us did. No one thought you might get hurt. Or grabbed. That's enough to change anyone's perspective."

I smile at her before I turn back to the eggs. I give them a few more strokes before pouring them into the hot, buttery skillet. "I guess it's one of those things that I'll have to prove with time."

She says nothing at first, but then she appears at my side, leaning over the stove until I meet her eyes. "You don't have to prove anything to anybody. You've been through a lot. You should be concentrating on getting your life back in order."

"It's not out of order."

"You came home early from a trip, then disappeared for a couple of days. Um, yeah. I'm pretty sure you'll have some questions to answer."

I shrug. "Maybe. But I don't owe anyone answers. Not one of the people in my life really cares about me. Not really." Just saying the words aloud is like holding a searing hot branding iron to my heart. Because it's true. "Besides, I'm still supposed to be out of town, so . . ."

"Marissa, I care about you. I hope you know that. And your father cares about you. Your mother. I'm sure you have friends who care about what happens to you. It might not seem like it right now, but—"

"Liv, you're so sweet for trying to make me feel better, but you've seen the people I've surrounded myself with. You went to that art exhibition. I know and work with and spend time with most of the people there. And they're horrible, Liv. Horrible! You saw that."

I see her start to say something, see her *want* to say something, but there's nothing to say. She knows I'm right.

"Look, Marissa. You're in the unique position of getting a second chance, a chance to make different choices and live life in a better way. Everybody has . . . unsavory people they have to deal with, but you can't hide from them. You just have to tolerate them the best you can."

"I know I can't hide. Not forever, anyway. But I don't think I'm ready to get back out there just yet. Maybe in a few days . . ."

"So you're not going to work today?"

"Nah. I think I'll call and let them know I'm taking a couple of weeks off. I am sort of in between projects, too. Daddy was 'grooming me,'" I say, holding up air quotes and rolling my eyes.

"I thought you liked that?"

I feel the frown pinch my eyebrows together as I give the eggs a stir. "I did. But I'm not sure what I want anymore."

That's not entirely true. There is something that I want, something that's been plaguing me since I was drugged, manhandled, and kept against my will. But it's something that would mean a huge life change for me, something that would be frowned on by practically everyone I know. Everyone except Liv. And probably Nash. The thing is, I'm just not sure I'm that brave yet. But I'm also not sure there's another way forward. It certainly doesn't *feel* like I have a choice.

Nash

The smell of cooking meat wakes me. I'm nothing if not a ravenous carnivore.

I open my eyes to an empty bed, which is probably best. Even though I wouldn't mind losing myself in Marissa for a little while, now's not the time. Her tenderness last night made me feel comforted, and that's a very dangerous place to find myself. I have no desire to get involved with a woman. Any woman. That's why I can say that her absence is a good thing all the way around.

I roll onto my back and feel a twinge of pain in my side. It's not nearly as bad as it could be, but I don't like that it still hurts *at all*. I'm sure the doc's medicines helped, but I'm an extremely fast healer, so even the small amount of pain I'm feeling now is a surprise. A very unwelcome one.

Ignoring it as though there weren't a gash in my side, I sit up and throw my legs over the side of the bed. My head swims a little and I stay put until it settles.

What the hell did that bastard have on that knife? Did he dip it in just enough poison to piss me off, but not kill me?

Standing, I make my way unsteadily to the bathroom to take a piss before facing a house full of people I don't trust. I need to be at my best, and it irritates the shit out of me that I'm still hurting and that I'm dizzy. That means weakness, and weakness of any kind is something I don't tolerate. At all.

I feel a little more like myself after I splash some water on my face and let my body adjust to being in an upright position. As I meet the reflection of my eyes in the mirror, I will myself to feel better. I don't have time to be sick or hurt or sore. Therefore I will not. Still, the dull ache in my side ensures that I'm as surly as ever when my nose leads me to the kitchen.

I feel like growling when I see Marissa in front of the stove, putting pieces of sausage on a paper towel to drain. She's so damn sexy, even doing something as mundane and domestic as cooking. But that's not what bothers me. It's the fact that I *like* seeing her doing such a simple caretaking activity. I've been away for a long time—away from civilization as I always knew it, away from home and love and life as I knew it. I learned not to miss it.

Until now.

I steel myself against feeling anything other than the desire to tear her pants off, put her up on the counter, and eat *her* for breakfast before the toast pops up. I remind myself that Marissa's obvious interest in me is all fine and good as long as it stays purely physical. On my end, anyway. I don't care what happens on her end. I can't.

But me? I have to care about how involved I get. And the instant I start feeling anything . . . deeper, I'm out the door. I haven't needed a woman in my life for years. Other than in the most physical, carnal way possible, that is. And I don't ever plan to let one drag me into feeling *anything* other than lust.

She looks over her shoulder and laughs at something, and I notice Olivia sitting at the island. As Marissa turns back toward the stove, her eyes stumble to a stop on me. Her smile climbs a notch on the brilliance scale and she greets me. "Good morning."

I grunt at her and walk to the fridge. I open it and make a show of looking around inside before I close it. Channeling everything into anger, like I've done for the last seven years, I lean my hip against the counter and give Marissa my full attention.

"So why the ass-kissing?"

Her smile wavers for a second before she returns to the sausage. It's so quiet in the kitchen, the sizzle of the last few pieces of sausage in the still-hot skillet is almost deafening.

"Nash, that's completely unfair. You—"

Marissa cuts Olivia off. "Olivia, it's all right."

After a long pause, during which Olivia obviously has to swallow some angry comments she was about to foist on me, she clears her throat. "Well, I guess I'll go change and get Cash, then I'll come set the table, 'kay?"

She doesn't wait for an answer; she just gets up and walks out. She's stiff as a board when she passes me and I imagine if she looked up, I'd see sparks shooting from her eyes.

Fiery little thing.

And I like fiery. To a point.

Fiery can be irrational and unstable, though, which really does nothing for me in a woman. I guess that's one of the few things I've retained of my former self. I value an intelligent woman who knows what she wants. Except in bed. I like fiery in bed. Fiery and willing. There's nothing better than a woman who's game for anything.

The clatter of the spatula draws my attention back to Marissa. Her lips are set into a thin, tight line, which makes me think she's got something to say.

And I'm right.

"You don't know the kind of person I used to be," she states quietly. "You don't know what was expected of me, who and how my father expected me to be."

"You don't think I kept an eye on my brother when I came into town? I know *exactly* the kind of person you were."

She glances up at me and I see a multitude of emotions play across her face, the last one being shame.

"Then you know I've got a lot to make up for."

"And you think kissing ass will accomplish that?"

"No, I . . . I . . . I guess I feel the need to make amends, especially to Olivia."

"And that'll make it all better? The way you treated her? The way you treated everyone?"

She whips her head toward me, a little temper flashing in her bright blue eyes. "Of course not! But consistently showing her that I care can't hurt."

I nod. I guess she's right. "Why go to that much trouble? Who cares what she thinks? Who cares what *anybody* thinks?"

She looks me square in the eye and her chin tips up a notch. "I do. Very much."

"But, then again, you always have, right? Isn't that your Achilles' heel? Perception? Gotta keep up appearances?"

Her mouth opens and closes like she wants to argue. Only she doesn't. She can't. Because I'm right.

Much faster than I would've liked, Olivia chooses this moment to return with Cash.

"We'll see how long that lasts after you get back in the real world," I whisper to Marissa.

"It smells wonderful, Marissa. And I'm starving, so I know these big cavemen are, too," Olivia says a little too brightly. I watch Marissa collect herself and return Olivia's overly ambitious smile. It's starting to look like I'm in a room of many pretenders. Until my eyes meet Cash's. He looks bothered. And he should. With guys like Duffy out there running loose, violent men and murderers, none of us are safe. The sooner Cash realizes that, the sooner he'll agree with me that we have to take care of some business.

My way.

We stare silently at each other as the women get breakfast on the table. When we sit and I look around at everyone putting napkins in their lap and keeping their elbows off the table, I feel even further removed from civilization. It's been a long time since I've shared a meal with people who aren't in a band of high seas criminals. I haven't forgotten how to comport myself; it's just an unwelcome reminder of the life I've missed out on. The life that Cash has been living in my absence.

"So, Nash, what are your plans now that you're back in the land of the living?" Olivia asks me in a conversational tone.

"Apparently I've got a really nice condo uptown. I was thinking of moving back in," I say pointedly, daring Cash to challenge me.

"Really? I thought you might stay here for a little while. At least until all this is resolved. I mean, Marissa could still be in danger. I thought . . ."

"You thought because she was stupid enough to date my

brother, who was masquerading as me, and get herself into trouble, that I ought to stay and clean up the mess?"

I know nobody likes my comment, but it's true and no one can argue it. I think that pisses them off more than anything. I don't lie. I don't pretend. I don't treat them with kid gloves. I tell it like it is. It's not my fault they don't like hearing the harsh truth. But they'd better get used to it when I'm around. I've had to live with that razor-sharp bitch called reality for a lot of years. Yeah, it sucked. Hell yeah, it sucked! But at least I was always prepared. Nothing good ever comes from hiding from the truth. Nothing. Ever.

"I'm fine by myself," Marissa chimes in before the tension can ratchet up any higher.

I look at her stunning face, at the tightness of her features, at the obvious discomfort reflected there, and I feel bad for being so . . . blunt when she's trying so hard to be considerate.

"I guess I could stay here for a few days. You never know. If they come after you, I might get a chance to right a few wrongs without Dear Brother here's permission."

I slide a smug smile over at Cash. I know he doesn't like the thought of me taking matters into my own hands any more than I like the thought of letting these psychopaths live. But, regardless of preference, we see who's making the compromise. They're not dead yet and I'm still here, playing by Cash's rules. Why, I'm not sure. Maybe there's some small part of the nice guy I used to be left inside me, some tiny wedge that's holding me back. But that won't always be the case. I'll play along for a little while longer, but Cash is crazy if he thinks I won't have my revenge. Because I will. Duffy, as well as the bastards who commissioned him to blow up my family's boat, will pay dearly for what they cost me. It's just a matter of time.

"Hopefully that won't happen until we can talk to Dad and get some more information, get another plan together."

"I've got a gash in my side that says they're far from patient and far from finished, so you'd better make it fast," I remind him, rubbing lightly over my aching wound.

"Then we need to get to Dad fast."

"Agreed. So what are we waiting for? Let's go today, get the ball rolling."

"I've got a few things to do this morning, but my early afternoon is free. I just need to be back in time to pick up Olivia from school."

"I told you I'm—" Olivia begins to argue, but Cash cuts her off.

"I know what you said, but I told you there's nothing more important than making sure you're safe. You better be glad I'm not going to class with you."

He leans over to kiss the side of her neck and she grins. "I wouldn't learn a thing if you were in my class."

"I could make up for that later. I'm sure I could teach you a few things."

She giggles and he nips playfully at her ear. Again, it gnaws at me that he's been living this perfect life while I've been in exile. I've missed out on . . . everything.

Biting back all the snide comments I could make, I clear my throat and continue as if they're not practically devouring each other in their heads.

"Obviously, I'm wide open, so . . ." I happen to glance over at Marissa and see that she looks more than a little uncomfortable. I'm not sure if it's because her ex-boyfriend is gushing all over her cousin or if it's something else. "Unless you have something you need to do today, Marissa. I can tag along and keep an eye on you."

"You don't need to do that," she says graciously. Her expression still appears . . . bothered, though. "I'm not sure what I'm going to do, anyway."

"What, no work?"

"Everyone but my father thinks I'm still out of town, so I still have a few days off."

"And do what?"

I've never been a fan of idle time.

She shrugs. "Maybe do a little research."

"On . . ." I prompt.

Marissa clears her throat. For whatever reason, I get the feeling she's uncomfortable with my questioning. "Criminal law."

"Ahh," I say, leaning back in my chair. "So I'm not the only one who wants revenge, then."

She looks up at me. "I didn't say that."

"You didn't have to."

"Like Cash, I think there's a way to do it legally and achieve all our goals."

"All *our* goals?"

Twin pink spots appear on the apples of her cheeks. "Like it or not, we're all in this together."

"Exactly!" Olivia says emphatically. "Which is why we need to stick together."

"Believe it or not, Nash is actually the brains in the family. He could probably be a huge help with research. Of course, you'd have to explain that to all the people at your father's law firm."

"I was thinking of going to the county library. You know, avoid . . . everybody."

Oh yeah, Marissa's definitely hiding from something. Or someone. For whatever reason, that intrigues me. She doesn't seem like the type to run or hide. And, from what little I saw of her with my brother, she always seemed in control, so it surprises me to see her at such a loss. Of course, she *did* just get kidnapped. And dumped. All in a couple days' time.

Damn, that's one shitty week!

"Even better," Cash says. "They'll probably think Nash is some kind of criminal working on his case. No offense, man, but you do look kinda rough."

He cringes and I laugh. "Luckily, I have no desire to please or deceive anyone about who and what I am, so . . ."

Cash sobers at my blatant reminder of the life of lies he's lived. I know that was a low blow, but my temper is on a short fuse. Has been for about seven years.

After the last couple of days, my mood seems to be even darker than usual. Maybe I just need some tension relief.

I need to get laid.

My eyes and my thoughts go straight to Marissa. I'll have her before it's over with. And she'll be begging me for it before I'm through. I just hope she can keep it physical. She's been through enough without adding heartbreak to the mix. But then again, that's not my problem.

Cash is right. You really are an asshole, man.

The problem is, I just can't seem to find a reason to care.

FOUR

Marissa

I examine my reflection in the mirror for the tenth time, and then I wonder for the tenth time why I care what I look like today. I'm going to the county law library. No big deal. But for the tenth time, only an image goes through my mind in answer.

Nash.

He's under my skin. I don't know why. And I don't know why I'm letting it go on. It's totally unlike me to let *anything* get beyond my control. And yet I'm jumping in headfirst with this . . . this . . . attraction, or whatever it is.

I sigh as I take in my long hair, brushed into a shiny, platinum wave; my deep blue eyes, lined with smoky gray shadow; and my pouty lips, glistening with dark pink gloss. To me, I look better than I have in months. Maybe years. I can't imagine the reason for that. At this point, all I *do* know is that it feels good, whatever is happening to me. It feels good to focus on Nash, to focus on things that aren't familiar to me. It feels good to hide away from my life and the people who have filled it for so many years. I almost want to throw away all things old and find the new. That might be the most bizarre thing of all.

To a pragmatist like me, it makes no sense to even consider doing something so rash. But maybe that's the most appealing thing about it—it's nothing like the me I've always been, the me I used to know. Maybe this is the new me. And maybe I want to embrace her completely and leave the old me behind.

That's a lot of maybes, but I feel like I don't have any answers right now. And, in the absence of answers, I'll take all the maybes I can get. They're far better than complete oblivion.

Tugging on the hem of my casual black skirt and straightening the neckline of the nearly sheer red blouse I coupled it with, I slip my feet into black heels and head for the living room.

"Ready when you are," I announce as I come to a stop in front of the small table near the door where my purse always sits.

"Wow," Nash says from behind me. I turn to find him standing in front of the couch, his arms crossed over his chest as though he'd been waiting somewhat impatiently. "Is this how you dress for a casual day at the library?"

I glance down at the outfit I agonized over. "What's wrong with what I'm wearing?"

He walks slowly toward me. For some reason, the mental image of a lion stalking his prey comes to mind, and chills spread down my back.

"Nothing's 'wrong' with it. I'm just wondering how you expect anyone to concentrate." He stops when he's within a few inches of me. He's close enough that I can feel his body heat, but still far enough away that I can breathe somewhat naturally. Part of that might have something to do with the fact that he's looking me up and down rather than staring into my eyes with that sexy black gaze of his. "I can just make out the shadow of your nipples through that shirt. The material is like the perfect tease. Makes me want to peel it off you. And that skirt cups your ass the way I'd like to. Makes me wanna dig my fingers into it, then my teeth. And those shoes—they make your legs look like they go on forever." He drops his voice down to a whisper when he glances back up to my face, to my eyes. "Makes me wanna wrap them around my waist and show you how good I can make you feel."

Now my breath is coming in short, shallow bursts and my fingers are curled so tightly around my purse strap that my knuckles ache. My mouth is bone-dry and I'm torn between leaning closer to him and standing absolutely still, waiting.

Not by conscious choice, I remain motionless in my anticipation, waiting while a battle rages inside me—the angel on one shoulder, the devil on the other. The question is, which is which?

You're making a mistake by letting him talk to you like that. Only a whore would put up with that.

No, by taking charge, you'd simply be showing him you're a woman who knows what she wants. And isn't afraid to go after it.

Or that you're a slut, an easy slut who's fine with being used until the need is satisfied.

And what's wrong with that? Everyone has needs. Can't you both get what you want and not quibble over the details?

Show some self-respect!

Show some fire!

Back and forth, the opposing viewpoints duel. It keeps me occupied until the moment passes and there's no longer a choice to make.

"You want to give in to it, but propriety says that's not what a lady does, right?" He doesn't give me time to answer. "How 'bout this? I'll give you time to feel comfortable with enjoying what I do to you. Just don't make me wait too long."

With that, Nash leans in close, reaching to the table behind me to grab my car keys. My breath lodges in my throat when his lips stop within an inch of mine. Up close, his eyes seem even darker than his brother's. They're so dark, in fact, I can't even see where the iris stops and the pupil begins. They're black. They're fathomless. They're consuming. It would be all too easy to get lost in them. Forget everything and everyone else. The lure to do exactly that is extremely compelling.

"Let's go," he says quietly, meaningfully, just before he leans away to open the door and hold it for me.

I can't help but notice that my first few steps forward are on legs that feel like rubber.

I'm more than a little surprised by how relaxed I feel when Nash guides my car into a spot outside the courthouse, inside which is the Fulton County Law Library. The ride over has been as revelatory as it was stimulating. Nash is sharp. Very sharp.

I guess it was erroneous on my part to expect him to be . . . less than his brother, intellectually speaking. At this point, I think I would go so far as to say that Nash is the smarter of the two, which says a lot because I always found Cash to be brilliant. And so did my father, which was why it was a no-brainer for him to hire Cash (then Nash) on at the firm.

While Nash was away, he stayed on top of pretty much everything that went on in the civilized world, especially the South and

Atlanta in particular. I'm sure that was easiest since he was watching Cash. And me.

I shiver.

The thought of him watching me from a distance, without my knowledge, gives me a little thrill. Even though he wasn't watching me in a perverted kind of way, it's still somewhat intrusive. But a part of me doesn't mind him intruding on my privacy. In fact, on some level, I crave it. I crave everything he represents. He feels like rebellion. And freedom. Like a salvation of sorts. I just didn't know until recently that I needed saving.

As I suspected, the parking lot outside the library entrance is devoid of any cars that I recognize. Our firm practices the type of corporate law that seldom requires trips to the local courthouse. On top of that, none of my coworkers would have a need to visit the county law library when there is an extensively stocked one in our office downtown. Unless, of course, they are like me—hiding.

Nash and I walk in silence to an empty table among the stacks and stacks of books. I've been here only a handful of times, and even then, I was never concentrating on criminal law, so my expertise in this area is virtually nil. But that's what I'm here to change.

I set down my things at the table and start digging back through my law school days for helpful memories like precedents and effective ways to construct a criminal case. The wheels spin, but for the most part, they're ineffective. I'm just not well versed in this kind of thing.

"Maybe we should at least look into racketeering, since that's what Cash has worked so long on proving. Maybe there's a way we can still make a case," Nash offers.

Yes, anyone would be a fool to underestimate Nash simply because he looks like a felon. There's an incredibly sharp, obser-

vant mind behind his attractively unkempt façade. It's an intoxicating combination.

"I guess that's as good a place to start as any."

He smiles down at me. It's a genuine smile, one I don't think
I've seen him wear. He looks more boyish and less harmful with
it in place. It's very deceptive, as I know he's neither.

"I figured you might need a place to dig in. This isn't exactly
your specialty, right?"

I laugh uneasily as I return his smile. I feel a bit off-kilter from
his ability to continually surprise me with his perceptiveness. "No,
not exactly."

"Let's get on with this, then."

His eyes are sparkling when they meet mine. Not only do I
think he means much more than just the research, but now I can
add "charming" to his list of deadly attributes.

FIVE

Nash

I bring back the first armload of books and set them on our table. A couple of them contain direct references to the Gambino crime family case. Marissa thinks it will be most helpful, as it details the successful prosecution and imprisonment of a crime family based on the RICO (Racketeer Influenced and Corrupt Organizations) Act.

I don't mind researching case law to keep myself busy for a while, but it's not nearly the distraction Marissa will be. Pursuing her will give me something to focus my . . . intensity on until all of this mess is settled. She's just the sort of release I need.

I could take care of things my own way, Cash be damned. But despite the lingering resentment over him taking over my identity, I still care about him. He's my twin, for God's sake. And I know he was misled, that Dad didn't tell him I was alive. In his way, Dad was trying to protect us both. And I guess we both did the best we could in a bad situation.

It's still hard to sit back and wait rather than act, though. That's why Marissa's presence is so timely. I'll have something to do in the meantime. She'll be a challenge. She's used to a certain kind of man, a man that's nothing like me, so she's in unfamiliar territory. And I'm just asshole enough to take full advantage of that before she changes her mind and runs back to the life she had before she met the Davenports.

When I find Marissa within the stacks again, she's four aisles over, at the back of the room. She's holding three more books in her arms. But she's not alone.

An impeccably dressed blond guy has cornered her. He's nearly as tall as me, just not as muscular. He's dressed in a dark blue suit. It's custom cut, I'm sure. He's smiling down at Marissa. And she's smiling back.

I stop a few feet behind them and clear my throat.

Marissa looks at me. "Oh, Jensen, this is, um . . . this is . . ." The guy, Jensen, turns toward me and smiles politely. I can see that his eyes are a startling blue and his skin is tan. And not *too* tan, either. Or too even. Nothing like what he might get in a tanning bed, which I'm convinced is for pussies. No, his color makes me think he spends a good bit of his time outdoors.

Probably playing polo or some hoity-toity shit like that.

Marissa is still stammering, so I step forward and offer my hand. "Cash Davenport." It makes sense that since there's already a Nash Davenport in this "circle" that I be the rebellious brother.

I'm surprised that I don't trip over the name. In fact, it comes out a little bit *too* easily. I guess that's how Cash felt the first time he tried to pass himself off as me.

Marissa falls right in line with my deception. "Yes, you remember

Nash Davenport, right? This is his twin brother, Cash. He owns a club across town."

Jensen extends his hand. "Jensen Strong. I work at the DA's office. Met your brother once or twice around at some functions, I think. So, a club, huh?" He nods his head appreciatively. "Nice."

"It pays the bills," I say simply.

We fall into an easy silence for a few seconds before Jensen speaks again. "Well, I guess I'd better run. I'm actually in court today. An unexpected witness gave me an idea, so I thought I'd come over and check on something during recess." He nods to me and then turns his full attention to Marissa. "It was great seeing you again. Let me know if I can help with what you're working on. Prosecution is kinda my thing," he says charmingly. Marissa smiles and he continues. "Maybe we can do dinner sometime soon. Catch up."

I'm a guy, so I know what he's *really* saying is that he wants to get in her pants as soon as possible. I also know by Marissa's reaction that she isn't exactly saying no.

"That sounds great," she replies. Her smile widens. It's both flattered and maybe a little interested, which pisses me off. I can't have her attention divided until I'm done with her. I'm not jealous by any far stretch of the imagination. I couldn't care less who she sleeps with or who she's interested in. I just want her to wait for a few days. Until I'm gone. Right now, I need her to focus on me so that I don't go apeshit while I'm waiting on the go-ahead to tear someone a new ass.

I have no doubt I can give her more than enough to keep her mind and her body busy, but another guy in the picture just complicates things. And I'm dealing with too many complications already. I don't need bullshit from my biggest source of stress relief, too.

"I'll call your office, then."

"Okay. See you later."

With a nod as he passes me, Jensen leaves the aisle. I wait until he's around the corner and out of earshot before I speak. "Looks like they're lining up already."

"What's that supposed to mean?"

"It was no secret you and 'Nash' were an item, right? And it's probably no secret that he dumped you. I mean, shit like that spreads like wildfire. One secretary finds out and suddenly it's common knowledge."

"And you think they're coming out of the woodwork to console me?" Her laugh is wryly amused. "I don't think so. I'm sure anyone who knows about it knows I'm far from devastated. I can hardly be crushed when 'something' that was never anything is over."

I eye her skeptically. Could she really have such a . . . a . . . guy-like attitude about it?

"So you didn't really give a damn about my brother?"

Marissa shrugs. On her face is uncertainty, but I think it's more that she doesn't know how to respond.

"It's not that I want to see him hurt or anything. I'm not a monster. I don't wish him ill. I guess I'm more . . . ambivalent than anything else. The only emotion I felt over the breakup was wounded pride. Feelings like that go away very quickly. The bottom line is: Cash and I were convenient and useful for each other. That's pretty much it."

I can't help but laugh. I wonder what Cash would say if he knew that the whole time he was with Marissa, he was getting played as much as she was. I suspect there might be some wounded pride on his end, too. But then again, he's so head over heels for Olivia, he might not give a damn.

"Good God, you're like all the best parts of a woman without all the annoying parts."

Her laugh is light. "Um, o-kay. I guess I should thank you?"

"Oh, it was definitely a compliment. It makes me that much more anxious to uncover *all* your parts."

I step in closer to her. She doesn't move away; she stands her ground, which is a huge turn-on for me. I like that she's willing, openly interested. I like that she doesn't try to pretend otherwise, like so many women do. It's boring and childish. And it's false. Most women want to be talked into it, eased into it, as if they're being coerced. It soothes their conscience, I guess. God forbid they take the situation by the balls and have fun with it. But I think Marissa will. She'll give in. And she'll like it. And I'd say she's woman enough that she won't make any excuses for wanting it.

"They're just parts, like any other woman's," she replies breathily, trying to be casual.

"I'd be willing to bet your parts are exceptional. In fact, now might be a good time to warn you that if we come back to this library, I'll find out for myself. In this very spot. I'll push you up against the books in the corner and I'll put my hands on you. I'll do things to you. In the quiet. And you won't be able to make a sound. Not a whimper, not a moan. You'll have to bite your lip to keep it all inside. And you know what?" I ask, reaching up to trace my index finger along her full, trembling lower lip.

"What?" she whispers, her pupils two dilated dots of excitement.

"You'll love every second of it."

With a wicked grin, I take the books from her arms and turn to walk back the way I came.

SIX

Marissa

As I watch Cash pull away from the curb with Nash in the passenger seat, I can't help but feel a bit breathless when his eyes meet mine through the glass of the window. He doesn't smile. Or wink. Or flirt. He just watches me, intently. I feel like I'm snapping out of a hot, sticky spell when Olivia speaks from behind me.

"So, how'd the research go?"

I turn to look at her. She kicked off her shoes and poured us each a Coke as soon as she came through the door from school. Now she's curled up on the couch, watching me with the hint of a smile lurking around her lips.

"Very well, actually," I respond, walking over to sit on the opposite end of the couch.

And it did. Despite the rising sexual tension between us, Nash was helpful. He's so sharp and catches on so quickly, it makes me wonder if he didn't do some light law-book reading while he was . . . wherever he was.

"What'd you find out?"

"Even though we had to give up the original accounting ledgers, there might still be a RICO case against them. This might be a way around them, so we don't have to worry about Duffy helping us get the ledgers back. If we could get Duffy to testify, we might really have a shot. Of course, I'd want someone who knows a lot more about this type of case than me to go over everything before we show our hand."

"Do you know someone you can trust with something this big?"

I smile when I think how handy it was that I ran into Jensen at the library. He might be just the person I could go to for help. "As a matter of fact, I do."

"Oooh, that smile looks juicy. Can I get some details?"

I wave my hand dismissively. "Oh, it's nothing like that. It's just that I ran into a guy I know at the library. He works for the DA. He sort of asked me out. Pretty amazing coincidence, don't you think?"

"Sure is." Olivia nods but says nothing else for a few seconds. She clears her throat. "So, did, uh, Nash meet this guy?"

"Yes."

"And?"

"And what? I tried to introduce him, but I started to bungle it, so he took care of it. Introduced himself as Cash. He had to since he couldn't be sure at the time that Jensen didn't know Cash as Nash. Good call on his part."

"And he's okay with all this?"

I shrug. "I don't know. I just now thought of it. But why wouldn't he be?"

It's Olivia's turn to shrug. "I just get the impression that he might find you . . . interesting. I didn't know how he'd view competition."

A little thrill races down my spine that Olivia picked up on it. *I* know it's there, but for some reason I like that he's not able to completely hide it from everyone else. Because I know he tries. It makes me feel like his control might not be bulletproof. I guess it's every girl's dream to be a man's one true weakness. But that's just an egotistical dream because, in reality, I doubt *any* woman will *ever* be a weakness for a guy like Nash. The destruction of someone like him usually comes from within.

"I don't think Nash sees anyone as competition."

Olivia laughs. "That's probably true. He's pretty confident, even though he's got that . . . rough edge."

"Yes, he certainly is. And yes, he's definitely . . . rough."

And I'm just crazy enough to be completely and utterly drawn to it.

"Cash has had some big blows over the years, but I can definitely see why Nash would be bitter, why he had to develop those rough edges. I mean the guy was practically exiled. As a teenager. And after witnessing the murder of his mother, no less."

"And that seems so strange to me."

"What does?"

"That their father would send Nash away like that, but let Cash pretend to be him. What possible purpose could that serve? It sounds just plain *mean*."

"Well, at the time that he sent Nash away, Cash playing both boys wasn't part of the plan. He sent Nash away to protect him. And the evidence. Not only was he an eyewitness, but he had a very valuable piece of the puzzle on his phone. I guess their dad was doing his best to play it safe until he could figure out what to do. But then he went to prison. And Cash ended up playing both brothers so that his father wouldn't go down for the murder of his mother *and* his brother. And by the time Cash started the deception, he couldn't really talk to his father about it in prison. All those conversations are monitored."

"Do you think Cash was ever in any real danger?"

Olivia shrugs. "I don't know, but it sounds like these . . . people never knew Nash witnessed the crime or had the video, so I'd say not. But I guess he could've been, had they ever found out somehow. I can see how things got so crazy. There was so much going on, and so many questions. I guess their father just did the best he could for his family, and they all had to live with the consequences. It's hard to tell what any of us would do in a situation like that. Cash finds out his mother and brother were killed and the murder was being blamed on his father, who is then carted off to prison. For Nash, he was nearly blown to bits and was the only real witness to the murder of his mother. He got banished from everything and everyone he's ever known. And for their father, he lost his wife, got framed for her murder, and had to send one of his sons away in an effort to keep him safe. Or so he thought at the time. It's like a comedy of errors. Only there's nothing funny about it."

I sigh. There are so many complex sides to Nash. The more I learn about him and his past, the more questions I have. "It sounds like Nash has a legitimate reason to be upset, then. His father surely could've let him come home before now, once he realized there was no danger."

"I think he was keeping as many aces up his sleeve as he could until all this played out."

My head is beginning to hurt as I chase these thoughts round and round. "Well, maybe being back, being able to live his life and be with his family, will help smooth out those rough edges a little."

"Maybe," Olivia says, but I think she believes that's possible just about as much as I do. Which is *not possible at all*. I think Nash is the way he is, and not much will change it at this point.

SEVEN

Nash

I let the silence in the car stretch on until I feel like Cash might be getting uncomfortable. That's when I make my move. I want him off balance, unprepared. I want his knee-jerk reaction. I want honesty. I won't settle for anything else, even if I have to beat it out of him.

"Who were you talking to on the phone this morning?"

At least he has the good sense not to bother trying to deny it. Or cover it up.

"Duffy."

"Were you going to tell me about it? Or just keep that little detail to yourself?"

I feel my temper rising just talking about it, reliving the conversation I overheard and how angry it made me.

"*Did you do this?*" Cash had asked, obviously referring to someone wrecking me on his bike. But that wasn't what made me so mad; it was that he immediately started making plans, taking matters into his own hands. Without even mentioning it to me.

"What the hell are we gonna do now? I have to make adjustments to protect the people I love."

"There's nothing to tell. I wanted to know if he had something to do with the hit on you. He said he didn't."

Even now, he's not being totally straight with me. "And?"

"And nothing. That's it. I believe him."

"Really?" I say dryly, crossing my arms over my chest to keep from wrapping my hands around his throat and squeezing. I can't remember if I've always found him this irritating and infuriating. If I did, it's a wonder I didn't kill him when we were younger. "You believe what the guy who killed our mother said? Just like that?"

"No, not 'just like that.' I just think it makes more sense that he *wasn't* involved. Obviously, he's still loyal to Dad. Why else would he have responded to the ad? And if Dad didn't trust him, why would he have brought him to us? Duffy would have to be a freakin' moron to go to all the trouble of responding to the ad, coming out to meet us, confessing all the shit he did, and then turn on us. He doesn't strike me as *that much* of a dumbass."

I guess he makes a good point. That would be pretty stupid. But that doesn't make me feel any better about Duffy. "Even if he didn't have something to do with it, I still think he's a slimy bastard the world would be better off without."

I hear Cash sigh. "Look, it's not that I don't agree with you. I mean, the guy killed Mom and would've kidnapped and killed Olivia. He's a lowlife, no question. But if he can help us *in any way* to get rid of the whole problem, or at least most of it, I'm okay with keeping him around until after all is said and done."

I glance over at Cash. I know my surprise registers on my face.

"You sneaky son of a bitch. You're gonna use him to help us and *then* kill him."

"*I'm* not killing anybody," is his only response. To me, that says he's got someone else in mind to do it. Probably that monster of a friend of his, Gavin. That guy reminds me of some of the smugglers I've met over the years. Not men to be messed with. Some of them even put a little unease in me, which is saying a lot. There are some scary bastards out there!

I'm impressed and admittedly pleased to see a little of the old Cash showing through. Finally. In a way, we've almost switched places and it's somehow comforting to see a glimpse of the reckless brother I used to know. Reckless and hotheaded. I'd be willing to bet Cash was like a wild animal right after the accident.

"How was it after Mom died?"

Between the abrupt change in subject *and* the new subject matter, I think I put Cash off balance again. And made him angry, too.

"How the hell do you think it was? It was awful."

"I know that," I say, exercising my patience. "I meant, how was it *for you*? You were kind of a loose cannon. I can't imagine that you took it well. Did you go ballistic on some poor bastard you met at the bar?"

I see the muscle in his jaw clench as he thinks back. "Surprisingly, I didn't. With all the buzz about Dad, it was like a circus for a while. It was like losing one parent and then watching the other one slowly dying. Then there were the accounting books, of course. I felt like I was holding plutonium for the first few weeks. And then there was your supposed death. I guess it was sort of a good thing that I had to pretend to be you. It kept me busy with . . . life until the trial was over and Dad was in prison. By then, I knew what I had to do and I focused on getting through school. And researching. I did lots and lots of research. Any big blowup I was going to have was just . . . over." He falls quiet, and so do I. I'm trying to imagine what he went through, how it felt to lose almost everything. Put myself in his shoes. It's not all that hard. In a way, I lost more than he did.

"You know, Nash, I never enjoyed pretending to be you, pretending to be the brother I could never compare to, never live up to. The person I missed like a . . . a . . . like my damn arm. Despite the accomplishments, I never once got any peace or pleasure from being you. Not once."

"I'm not surprised. You were always the cool one, the one who got to have all the fun. I'd say pretending to be me was a lot like being in prison."

"I didn't say that," he snaps. "I didn't mean it like that. Look, man, I'm just saying that it wasn't the picnic out here that you seem to think it was."

"I don't doubt it," I say, deadpan. Cash's head whips toward me, like he's expecting to see sarcasm or bitterness on my face. And he's ready for it. When he sees that I'm serious, that I'm sincere, he looks at first confused, then deflated.

After a few miles of silence, during which we both have time to think and calm down, to get our bearings again, he asks me the same question. I'm sure he's curious and I'm sure he's wanted to ask before now, but considering how mad I was at first, he probably didn't want to stir up that shit and make it stink any worse.

"What about you? How was it for you after the accident?"

"A lot like it was for you, I guess. When I woke up, I was floating under the dock with my head banging up against one of the pilings. I doubt anyone even saw me. The cavalry was just on their way by the time I got out of the water.

"I had no idea what the hell had happened, so I called Dad. Took me a few minutes to find my phone. I guess it flew out of my hand when the bomb went off and knocked me into the water. It was lying on the dock a few dozen feet from where I was standing. Thank God it didn't go in the water with me or we'd be screwed. Without those books, that video is all the leverage we've got to get Dad out of prison."

Cash nods in agreement. "No shit."

"Anyway, I took off to call Dad. I was the lucky one who got to tell him his wife had been killed." There's no keeping the bitterness from my voice on that point. "But the upside was that it gave him time to think. And to prepare a little, I guess. I told him about the video. That's when he told me I had to leave, that it wasn't safe for any of us anymore, especially me since I had the video. Too many unknowns. And I was the only witness. Well, you get the idea. So he told me where he'd stashed his getaway . . . stuff, had me go there to get the money and the passports, and told me to disappear."

"How'd you end up on a smuggler's ship, then?"

"I told you before that he sent me to his contact. Are you gonna let me finish?"

Cash nods, but says nothing. Makes me feel like a piece of shit for being so short-tempered, but I just can't seem to help myself. It's hard to give a damn after so long. And I'm not entirely sure I even want to. Caring just gets you in trouble. That's how I've managed to survive all this time—the only thing I cared about was getting to the day I'd finally take my revenge.

"Sorry. Continue," he says.

I sigh. "Along with the money and passports, there was a cell phone with a few contacts already loaded into it. There were also a couple of notes. One was to Mom. I guess it was his plan B, in case something happened to him. Just him telling her he loved her, and that he was sorry, and to do exactly what they'd talked about. I guess she knew what to do with everything, who to call. But then there was another note. It was to us in the event something happened to both Mom and Dad. It just said to call Dmitry. He'd know what to do. So I did. He told me to get to Savannah right away. Told me to hole up in a motel there and not leave it until midnight on the following Saturday. He gave me the address of a dive down near the wharf. Told me to meet him there, that he'd know me. And he did. Said I looked a lot like Dad."

"Is he the one you . . . worked with?"

I smirk at his attempt to so delicately state that I was a gun runner. It's nothing less than ironic that the more straitlaced of the two of us, the most likely to succeed in the corporate world, turned out to be the criminal. To this day, it leaves a bitter taste in my mouth.

"No, he's just the one who set it all up. Evidently, if something had happened to Dad, he was supposed to get us out of the country, but only Mom knew what to do after that. If there was a place to go or money or whatever. All I had was the little bit of money that was in the bag and the clothes on my back. He did the only thing he could do, I guess. He got me a job."

I know Cash wants to ask questions about what I was involved in, but his social skills have so much improved since we were younger that he shows restraint and keeps his mouth shut. Which is a good thing. I don't want to talk about it. Not with him, not with anybody. I'm not exactly proud of the way I've spent my time over the last seven years.

"You had to do what you had to do, man. No one blames you. You were just a kid."

My laugh is bitter. "Listen to you, trying to make your big brother feel better about giving in to the family curse."

"You're only older than me by four minutes, so don't get too hung up on the 'big brother' thing. And what's that supposed to mean? 'The family curse'?"

"We have criminal blood. I always thought it was a choice, but I don't think it ever was. I think it's what we're destined for. As a family."

"I'm not a criminal. Don't ever plan to be one, either."

"Oh really?" I can't keep the sarcasm from my tone. "And the shit you and Gavin were involved in to save Olivia, that was all perfectly legal, right?" I see his fingers tighten on the steering wheel. "Guess you just overlooked that little incident, is that it?"

He says nothing. Because there's nothing he can say. I'm right and he knows it.

It's miles and miles later when Cash finally speaks again. "Let's just get through this so we can move on and live decent lives. Both of us. *All* of us."

"If that's even possible," I reply pessimistically. But deep down, against everything I know to be probable, I feel a little glimmer of hope that something as preposterous as that just might happen.

EIGHT

Marissa

I'm just gathering up my clothes to take to the cleaner when the doorbell rings. Even though it's broad daylight and Olivia's just on the other side of the condo, my stomach turns a nervous flip.

I chastise myself all the way to the door, where I lean against it to look through the peephole. My stomach reacts anxiously again, but this time for a different reason.

On the other side of the door, looking impatient as ever, is my father, David Townsend. He looks much like Olivia and her father, with his dark hair and greenish hazel eyes. But his demeanor gives him an elegance (and an arrogance) that shows in every smooth line of his entire body.

Even though he's related to me, he's still one of the most intimidating men I've ever known. He's the reason I can hold my own with practically anyone in the corporate, legal, and judicial worlds.

Cutting one's teeth on David Townsend results in fangs. Long, sharp fangs.

I take a deep breath and throw the deadbolt, swinging the door open on my fake smile. "Daddy. What are you doing here?"

Without a word, he brushes past me in his thousand-dollar suit, carrying with him the faint scent of his nearly as expensive cologne.

He walks to the edge of the living room and turns toward me, his brow set in a line as stern and unyielding as his mouth. "Just what is it you think you're doing, young lady?"

"I don't know what you mean," I say calmly, closing the door behind him. I learned long ago to bury everything I feel beneath a calm exterior. It's the ultimate weapon in my world. Well, the world that used to feel like mine, but now feels more like just his.

"First, you leave to come home early, giving me no choice but to follow."

"You didn't have to cut your trip short, Daddy."

"How would that have looked? My daughter has some sort of emergency she has to return to the States for and I continue working?"

Of course it would all boil down to appearances. That's what it always boils down to. It's the way my life, my family, my whole world has always been.

"I'm sorry it inconvenienced you."

"No you're not. You weren't thinking of anyone but yourself. And then to show up at my house with some . . . some . . . criminal in tow. What were you thinking?"

I hadn't told my father what happened when Nash brought me home. I told him it was personal and left it at that. Evidently, that was some sort of trigger. He backed off immediately. But not before he lectured me about the importance of keeping my personal life strictly aboveboard unless I could keep it discreet and forever hidden from public knowledge. I have no idea what he thinks I'm up to, but I suspect he thinks it's deviant.

"I'm sorry, Daddy. I'll be more thoughtful next time."

I've done this all my life—cater to Daddy, pander to Daddy, yield to Daddy. It's always come naturally. He's the type of man who demands it, without ever really having to ask for it. But today, for the first time that I can ever remember, I choke a little bit on the words.

"You're a Townsend, Marissa. Mistakes like these can't happen. One slipup can have lasting consequences on your career and your reputation. You know to protect them at all costs. I've taught you better than this." I nod obediently, keeping my eyes cast down so he won't see the change in me, so he won't see the struggle. "Now, the cat's out of the bag about our early return. There's a fund-raiser you'll be expected to attend tonight. I think it would be a good idea for you to bring Nash. I think that would go a long way toward dispelling any rumors that might be circulating."

"Nash and I broke up, Daddy."

"You think I don't know that?"

It's never worried me before that he keeps such a close eye on me. It doesn't worry me now, per se. But it makes me very uncomfortable.

A curious thought pops into my head before he continues, a thought about how he might've known I was unaccounted for over a thirty-some-hour period. But I don't have time to finish the disturbing notion before he speaks again.

"Do what you need to do to make up. He's a rising star, as you well know. I wouldn't waste my time on anything less. A match with him is a good move for you, for the family and the firm."

"Even though his father's in prison for murder?"

"That just makes him more relatable to constituents. Makes him seem more human. He's the boy from the streets who overcame his humble beginnings. A man of the people."

Constituents?

"And why does that matter? It's not like he's—"

I stop abruptly, for the first time recognizing my father's big-picture plan for me. I always thought it had to do with him grooming me to take my place as a partner in the firm one day, but it didn't. It never did. He never had plans like that for me. He was simply grooming me to be the wife of a powerful man. A very powerful man. Like a man in politics.

He has plans for Nash in politics.

"Oh my God! How did I never see this before?"

His lips thin, confirming my suspicion. He doesn't even bother to deny it. He knows exactly what I'm talking about. "I knew you'd catch on one day and see how perfectly this could all work out." He takes a step toward me, narrowing his eyes on mine. "As long as you don't screw it up."

My mouth drops open. I can't help it. Has he always treated me like nothing more than a pawn and I've just never noticed it? Is it possible for someone to be so wrapped up in an identity that she'd never notice she was living in such a twisted, narcissistic, superficial world?

Apparently so.

"Close your mouth. And don't act like this is a foreign concept to you. You've been more than happy to go along with my plans up until now." He walks to me and puts his hands on my upper arms, bending slightly to look into my eyes. It's his version of tenderness. I recognize it. I've just never realized how cold, calculated, and practiced it is. "I only want what's best for you, sweetheart."

I close my mouth, but only to keep the words that are lodged in my throat from spilling off my tongue. I nod robotically and give him my best attempt at a smile. I need to keep up pretenses as much as I can until I have some time to think. And plan. And figure out how to live, how to make a life for myself, outside of everything and everyone I've ever known.

In a town that my father practically owns.

It doesn't look very promising for me.

NINE

Nash

Visiting my father in prison, with all the security checks, thick bars, uniformed men, and violent-looking criminals at every turn, is a harsh reality check. It marks the first time I'm able to have a little sympathy for what Cash must've felt the first time he'd visited Dad all those years ago. As a lost kid, no less. That slap in the face must've hurt like a bitch.

"Sign in, please," the guard says automatically. It's the second time we've had to do this, which makes me wonder what kind of incompetent asshole is keeping the records when you have to sign in two different times, on the same day at the same prison, for the same inmate.

Good God, people! It's not that hard.

I'm grouchy. I'll admit it. None of this—from seeing Cash again, to finally finding the man who killed Mom, to how I'd spend my first few days "alive," so to speak—is anything like I'd imagined it would be. It makes me wonder if the rest of my life will be as disappointing. Maybe this is the way everything will turn out—shitty.

I'll be damned, I think rebelliously. I refuse to let a cascade of events that was beyond my control and perpetrated by people other than me ruin my life.

I just need to get this figured out, get past this part, and move the hell on!

My head aches from the scowl I know is plastered across my face. It's been a constant companion for about seven years now. I know the feeling well.

Because there are two of us, they put us in a small room to await Dad. It reminds me of an interrogation room from one of those cheesy law shows on TV. All that's missing is a bright light swinging over the table.

I sit in one of the cold, plastic chairs and lean back to cross my arms over my chest. I feel impatient. And on edge. I'm mulling over all the negativity that's swirling around inside me when the door opens again and a guard escorts my cuffed and shackled father into the room.

My headache and every bad thing I've been thinking of melt away the instant his eyes meet mine. Like waves crashing against the shore, a thousand feelings collide, sending a spray of emotion through me. At once, I experience a dozen states and stages of my life in the blink of an eye. I'm the scared kid I was when I left seven years ago. I'm the confident, determined teenager I was before my mother was killed. I'm the angry boy growing up and butting heads with his father. I'm the child basking in the comfort of his parent. And I'm the man who's been in exile, away from what's left of his family, returned.

I see the tears well in his eyes and, before the guard can reach me, I'm on my feet and across the room, wrapping my arms around my father. I feel his bound hands rise to touch my shoulder on one side. He can't embrace me, but he would if he could.

The few seconds I got to reunite with my father are worth the few minutes of restraint I get when two other guards burst through the door and physically remove me from the vicinity of my father and plant me back in the chair I just left. Not for one second do Dad and I break eye contact.

Once the guards are reasonably comfortable with my willingness to cooperate, they leave Inept Guard Number One in charge of the room again. I should feel guilty for making the guy look bad, but I don't. He can kiss my ass. This is the dad I haven't seen in seven years.

When the room is quiet, Dad speaks. "For seven years I've prayed that I'd see both my boys again, alive and healthy." His voice breaks on the last and my chest gets tight with emotion. He takes a minute to collect himself before he continues. "How have you been, son?"

There are an ass-ton of complaints I could give, but not one of them seems relevant at the moment. "I'm fine. Alive. Back. Ready to get all this over with."

He nods, his eyes flickering back and forth over my face like he's memorizing my features. Granted, Cash and I are twins, but he and Mom could always tell us apart. And now, what with my "look," which is nearly the polar opposite of the one he last saw, I'm sure he's noticing even more differences.

"It's like you and your brother switched places," he says casually.

I feel the sting of resentment, like salt in a raw wound that never gets a chance to heal. "For the most part, I guess we have. He's everything you wanted me to be. And I'm everything you were afraid he'd become."

His smile is sad. "No, I could never be more proud of either of you. You've shown a strength I only wish I had. You're both just like your mother."

My heart twists painfully inside my chest. "I guess there's no greater compliment."

A barrage of imagery flits through my mind, every one involving my mother—her sitting on the edge of my bed; her dark blue eyes smiling down at me as she pushes my hair back; her laughing at me and Cash as we flex our childish muscles for her; her shaking her head at the mess I made in the kitchen; her crying over a plaque I made her in shop class; her cheering me on from the stands of the stadium; her telling me she's proud of me for staying sober so I could drive my friends home.

She was the glue that held our family together. When she died, we fell apart. Went our separate ways. Became people she wouldn't approve of, doing things she'd be ashamed of.

Animosity and anger swell inside me like an old friend. The desire to lash out, to hurt the people who *hurt me* rises up to choke me. Like it has for seven long years. But thoughts of what she would say, how she would chastise me for sinking to their level, war with those feelings, making me feel torn and lost, stealing the purpose that has brought me this far.

With an internal shake of my head, I push those thoughts away. There will be time to torture myself over them later. Right now, I have time with my father. And there are questions. Hundreds of questions.

But he preempts me.

"I'll never forgive myself for what I've done to you boys, to our family. That's a regret I'll take to the grave. That and a dozen others. I was young. And stupid. Something neither of you boys is. You won't make a mess of things like I did. I know that. I trust you both to do the right thing. Always."

He pauses before he continues. His face wrinkles into a cringe. I'm sure he's beating himself up over his choices. Probably like he's done hundreds of times over the last many, many years.

"I hope you can forgive me one day. In the end, I thought I was doing what was best. For you. For our family. Cash," he says, turning his attention toward my brother, who has been sitting beside me, quietly observing. "I know it seems unfair that I didn't tell you about your brother, but you were such a hothead. I knew what you'd do. Pretending to be him, learning some self-control and having a healthy focus for all your anger seemed like a good way to help you turn your life in a different direction. I never meant to hurt you. I hope you can see that."

Cash says nothing. His face is a blank, unreadable mask. Even to me, his twin.

And then Dad turns to me. "And Nash, I knew you'd make it. I've never met a person more determined to succeed. You were born driven. And you were always a good kid. I knew you'd do what I asked you to do, without question." He looks down at the table, like he can't bear to look me in the eye. I see his throat work as he swallows hard before glancing up at me again. "I didn't realize you had so much of your brother in you. But I should've. I should've known you'd be angry, that you wouldn't be able to let it go. By sending you away, I turned you into something you hate. But don't you ever think for one second that I'm not proud of you. You survived. You made a way for yourself without . . . anything or anyone. So few people could do that as adults and you were just a kid. I relied on you more than any parent has a right to. I only hope that one day you'll see what that means. What it meant to me and your brother, what it would've meant to your mother. What it should mean to you as a man. And I also hope you can see your way clear of these years. Forgive yourself. Find a way to get back the life you gave up. Losing it would be the biggest tragedy of all. If your mother were alive, it would kill her to see you give up."

Guiltily, he looks back and forth between me and Cash.

"You boys were like two halves of the same person from the day you were born. Like night and day, north and south. Up and down. I always hoped you could find a little bit of each other. It was all you ever needed, just a touch of what the other had. I would never have wished for this, though. I was proud of you both, regardless. I never wanted this for you—this pain, this hard life, this much regret and anger. I only ever wanted what was best for you. I did the best I could, with what information I had. It may not seem like it, but I always put you first. I just made a lot of bad decisions along the way."

"We're gettin' ready to make at least a few wrongs right, Dad. We've got—"

Dad cuts off Cash, shaking his head. "Let this go, son. I'm paying for my sins. Maybe not what they *think* I'm paying for, but I'm paying nonetheless. I've lived my life. You two have so much ahead of you. Don't let the past dictate your future. Move on. Find a job worth working, a wife worth having, and a life worth living. Don't keep making mistakes that'll keep boxing you in. Do the right thing. Let it go and move on."

"And what? Forget that our father was wrongly imprisoned? That he was blamed for a heinous crime he didn't commit?"

"I don't expect you to forget. I'm just asking you to let it go. It's what your mother would want. It would break her heart to see you boys giving up your present and risking your future for my mistakes. It's like piling more casualties on top of her grave, God rest her soul."

Guilt. I feel it, piling on top of me like the casualties he's talking about.

Cash says nothing, which makes me feel a little better about my own silence. I don't know what to say. I know Dad feels guilty and responsible, which he is in many ways, and that he wants us to understand. But I also feel like he's trying to take away from me the one thing I've held on to all this time. My anger and my thirst for revenge have been like air to me for the last seven years. It's the only reason I didn't give up when I found myself in situations that were so abhorrent to me that I could barely sleep at night. I've done things—awful things—that would eat me alive if not for the anger that I've built a life inside. It's like an impenetrable armor that shields my conscience from the damning pricks of reality. And if I listen to what he's saying, if I give up everything that's kept me going for seven hard, unforgiving, torturous years, what will I have?

One word rings through my head, like a ghostly echo of the emptiness I feel.

Nothing. Nothing. Nothing.

The earsplitting honking of some sort of internal alarm has us all covering our ears. All except the guard, however, who springs into action. Maybe he's not so inept after all.

Immediately, he hauls Dad roughly out of his chair and toward the door, where he opens it and hands him off to another guard who's waiting there. They disappear around the corner as another guard comes in, and he, along with the original one, order Cash and me to make our way to the exit.

Now.

"What the hell is going on?" I demand.

"Sir, all alarms in the prison are for the safety of prisoners as well as visitors. Keep moving."

The two guards shuffle us quickly back the way we'd come less than thirty minutes earlier. Never once do they offer any information by way of explanation.

As we move from area to area, passing other visitors being herded to the exit just as we are, I see more than just flashing lights and hear more than just a deafening alarm. There are guards scrambling through barred doors, many of whom are dressed in black padded clothing and face shields. There are commands being shouted, something about cell blocks and lockdowns and weapons. One word stands out, though, and the fact that I hear it more than once gives me some clue as to what's happening.

Riot. There's a riot in the prison. And there's a protocol that's being followed. And our presence isn't a desirable part of it. So they want us out. Right now.

Once Cash and I, along with a couple dozen other startled, disgruntled visitors, are back where we started at the main entrance, they push us past the last set of secured doors. I hear them click shut and lock behind us.

The guard who was sitting behind the sheet of glass near the front door is still sitting there. He still looks as old and unconcerned as he did when we arrived.

"What the hell is going on?" I repeat, not really expecting anything more from him than I'd gotten from Guard Number One.

He shrugs his thin shoulders. "Riot. Must've started down on D block. Those mean bastards have been a pain in the ass for almost a year now." He chuckles like he said something funny. Which he didn't. I expect to see more teeth than I can count on one hand. But I don't. Looking at his frail frame and kinda-crazy eyes, it becomes clear that this is probably the only post an old fart like this guy can man. That and he's probably related to the warden, because he's got to be long past retirement age.

I nod to the old man and he smiles his nearly toothless grin at me. I turn back toward Cash and I hear him say, "Come back and see us." And then he cackles.

I just shake my head as I walk past Cash toward the glass door that leads outside, out to freedom. I don't look back to see if my brother is following me. I need air. I have to get out of here.

I step out into the sunshine and take several deep breaths. Even in the wide open space of the area in front of the prison, with only the parking lot and a long expanse of road in front of me, I feel trapped. By life.

My father's words resonate in my head. He's asking us to let it go, asking *me* to let it go. He's asking me to forget about the people responsible for destroying my family, for destroying my life and the future I thought I had. And he's asking it for my dead mother's sake.

I run my fingers through my hair. I feel the tug of strands being pulled out from under the elastic band that keeps it neat at my nape, but I don't care. I feel like pulling it all out, like screaming at the world, at the unfairness of it all.

He wants me to let it go!

I keep coming back to that. And to the fact that he's right; it *is* what Mom would want. And on top of that, seeing Dad waste away in prison gives me a clear picture of the one thing that could be worse than living with the status quo—living in prison for the rest of my days.

So where does that leave me?

I pace back and forth across the short stretch of sidewalk. Curling my fingers into tight fists and relaxing them over and over, I pay no attention to the people around me, to what they think. I don't give a shit. I haven't given a shit about anybody or anything much in seven years, and I can't imagine starting now.

Just the thought of watching everything I've ever planned, everything I've ever thought I knew vanish right before my eyes makes me feel impotent and exasperated and enraged and . . . lost. Trapped and lost.

I grit my teeth so hard my jaws ache and it's all I can do not to turn around swinging when Cash grabs my arm.

"You ready, man, or you gonna stand here and act like a deranged lunatic for the rest of the day?"

I want to plant my fist in the middle of his smug face until I feel bones crunch beneath my knuckles. I want to hurt him, and I'm not really sure why. I just know that I do. I want to lash out at everybody.

But something in me feels deflated, like purpose has been stolen from me. And concern over that overrides my desire to inflict pain. For the moment, anyway.

"We're not gonna let him stop us from pursuing this."

It doesn't really matter to me what Cash does. I'll go my own way, regardless. I guess I just want him to ignore Dad's advice, too. Make me feel better about holding on to the rage and vengeful spirit I've nurtured all these years.

"Hell no! I think his conscience is bothering him, seeing what your life is like now. I think it would make him feel better to be the martyr. But he'll get over it. We need to see this through. We need to bring Mom's killers to justice."

"Good," I say, more relieved than I care to admit. "I'm glad you're not pussin' out on me."

"Look, Nash, just because we got off to a rough start and we approach this in two different ways doesn't mean we both don't want the same thing. Because we do. I wanna rip some heads off just as much as you. But I won't. That would only make things worse. I'd feel great for about a second and then I'd spend my life either on the run, in a nonextradition country, or in prison. Or dead. I choose to take my revenge the smart way. The way you would've done it once upon a time."

His chin tips up in challenge and I feel my hackles rise. "Maybe I'm not that guy anymore."

"Yeah, you are. I can see it. You've just gotta dump this chip on your shoulder. Mark my words, it'll ruin your life if you don't."

"My life is already ruined."

"No, you just got your life back. What you choose to do with it from this point on is up to you. If you ruin it, you'll have nobody to blame but yourself."

I clench my teeth again. Mainly because I know he's right. I can admit that. But only on the inside. Beneath all the anger.

And there's a lot of that—anger.

TEN

Marissa

"I'm sure he'd do it if you need him to. He doesn't hate you, Marissa." She's trying to persuade me to ask Cash to go with me to the fund-raiser.

I know that the look I send Olivia is full of all the skepticism I feel. "You're so sweet for saying so, but you and I both know that's just not true."

"He *doesn't* hate you," she emphasizes.

"Okay, maybe *hate* is a strong word. Let's just say he has trouble tolerating me. Does that go down a little easier?"

Olivia cocks her head. "I'm not having trouble swallowing anything. I just really don't believe he hates you. You two had a . . . rough relationship. You were a different person then. And in a lot of ways, so was he. You just have to find a way to put all that behind you and move forward. As friends. Or at the very least friendly acquaintances."

I stare into my cousin's jewel-green eyes. She wants us to get along so badly. But why?

"I know this is probably not something I should bring up, but it bothers me wondering if it bothers *you*. I don't want it to."

"Wondering if what bothers me?"

I hesitate, giving myself one last opportunity to change the subject before I bring up something that could change her feelings toward me. But I need to clear the air. The time for being selfish is over. If I'm going to be *this* person, I have to take all the bumps and scrapes that go along with moving beyond my past. It's time to grow up and pay the piper, all that jazz.

"The fact that Cash and I used to . . . date."

Olivia shrugs. I don't think she feels as casual about it as the gesture implies, but I don't see any real distress on her face, either, which is the main thing.

"It's not something I want to sit around and think about, but it's not like it eats at me constantly, either. I know Cash loves me. And I know you both had your reasons for carrying on the relationship. Now, if you'd been in love, that would be different. But you weren't. You each had a purpose for using the other. I can live with that. Because it's over."

You each had a purpose for using the other. How nasty that sounds. But, sadly, how true. We did use each other. And that makes me feel like a dirty whore. Which, by most definitions, I was. Technically. I had sex with someone who meant very little to me. He was a means to an end. Just because there was no money changing hands doesn't alter the fact that I was with him for gain—to please my father. And that's sick. Sick, sick, sick.

My smile is tremulous at best. I can feel it wavering and I try to bolster it. "I'm so glad. I don't want something like that between us, bothering you. I wanted to make sure you knew it was nothing. And that it's over."

Her smile is genuine. "I do. And thank you for worrying about it."

It's my turn to shrug. I feel a little embarrassed. And very unworthy of her easy forgiveness. I feel the need to prove to her that her "investment" in me, her faith in me isn't wasted.

"So now you know that I mean it when I say that if he needs to go with you, it's totally fine," she says.

I shake my head, more determined than ever to not do things that might make her uncomfortable. I've given her enough trouble already.

"Nope. I can go alone."

"Go where alone?"

Chills break out down my arms at Nash's voice. The strange thing is, I know it's him without even turning toward the door. Even though he sounds almost exactly like his brother, I can tell the difference. His voice is a little harder, a little more gruff. Nothing too obvious. But something I recognize on a visceral level. And my reaction is instant.

I turn to see him standing in the doorway of my condo. His expression is similar to a scowl, much as it seems always to be. But I see something just beneath the surface, just beneath the angst and bitterness. I hope I'm not imagining it, that it's really there and that there's something inside him that's worth saving, that's worth the risk.

I roll my eyes and exaggerate the insignificance of the event with a wave of my hand. "Meh, just a fund-raiser my father is convinced that I *must* attend."

"With Nash," Olivia chimes in. "The Nash *they* know."

"But he'll get over it. He needs to get it through his head that the Nash he knew is no longer . . . with us. Or with me."

I avoid Cash's eyes when he pushes past Nash and heads toward Olivia. I cast my eyes down, examining my fingernails, which have suddenly become very interesting. From the corner of my eye, I see him bend to cup her face and kiss her. Like he's eradicating the image of us from her mind. When I glance back up, my eyes crash into Nash's dark ones.

"Well, if you're that anxious to prove yourself to your father, then take me. If you're brave enough, that is." The challenge is there in his eyes. He doesn't believe I'll do it. That I *can* do it. But why should he? I've wondered the very same thing myself. Am I strong enough to go against everything and everyone I've ever known? To abandon the only life I've ever lived? To thumb my nose at some of the most powerful people in Georgia law?

At this moment, proving a point to them doesn't feel nearly as important as proving a point to Nash. The doubt in his eyes, the expression that says he thinks I'm full of crap . . .

"That sounds like a great idea," I say impulsively, my stomach turning a flip at the thought of what I just agreed to. By not showing up with the Davenport they might expect to see me with, I'm proving three things: To Olivia, I'm proving that I'll put her comfort (even though she says it doesn't bother her) above my own; to my father and practically everyone I know, I'm proving that I no longer put society and my father's wants ahead of my own; and to myself, I'm proving that I'm strong. Stronger than I was. Strong enough to go against the grain.

"I'm sure the old Nash has something appropriate for the *real* Nash to wear, right?" he asks. His eyes stay locked on mine, even as he addresses his brother. Cash answers from my left.

"Yeah, but you can't go as Nash. We need to keep things under wraps for a little while longer, until we can get this shit straightened out and get some bastards thrown in jail."

"So what, go as Cash? Masquerade as the devil-may-care, wild-card owner of a nightclub? Out for a night with the decent folks, like a charity case, on the arm of his plastic trophy girlfriend? This should be fun."

Although I know his venom stems from his inability to get past the life he feels like his brother stole, still, his words hurt. Does he really think I'm plastic? Or that I'm a trophy girlfriend? Some mindless piece of fluff?

"Don't think that's permission for you to go and make me into a spectacle. You still have to act like you've got some sense. Stirring up a public shitstorm won't exactly do us any favors."

"I'm not an idiot, *brother*. Hell, I'm even potty-trained. I won't fu—screw it up," he amends. He catches himself before he finishes the thought. I've noticed him doing that—curbing his colorful language. I can't imagine why, but it seems almost in deference to the females in the room. Like a gentlemanly gesture. It's incongruous, such thoughtful and nearly *tender* respect coming from someone who appears to be anything *but* thoughtful and tender. Against my will, another seed of hope takes root in my heart. No doubt it's dangerous territory I'm in, but . . . I'm helpless to stop now. Helpless. "I won't screw it up. Don't forget I used to be the sensible, responsible one. Just because you—"

"I know, I know," Cash interrupts testily. "I wasn't saying you aren't. It was just a reminder. That's all."

The tension between the two brothers makes me nervous. I feel like, at any moment, they might tear into each other in a very physical way. And there would be nothing I could do, of course.

I mean, they're both humongous. There was a reason Cash never needed a bouncer at his club when he was working. He never came across anyone he couldn't handle. Or any two or three he couldn't handle. He told me that himself. As Nash, of course, but still . . .

I'm relieved and strangely encouraged when Nash bites his tongue and ignores Cash's sharp response.

"So what time are we talking about here?" Nash asks, turning his attention back to me.

"I'll have to find out the details, but last year I attended this same charity event and they structured it like an auction. Kind of a fun, gimmicky thing. It started with bidding on hors d'oeuvres then on to seats around tables featuring certain local celebrities. It started at seven thirty, I think, so I'm guessing somewhere along those lines this year, too."

Nash takes his cell phone out of his pocket and looks at the screen, presumably to find out what time it is. He nods and looks back up at me. "That'll be fine. I've got some things to do in the meantime. Pick you up at seven?"

"That sounds good. If you'll give me your number, I can text you if the time is different."

He punches some numbers into his phone and I hear mine buzz an alert a few seconds later. He doesn't look at me again as I reach for my phone but addresses Cash instead.

"Can I borrow your car again?"

"Can you drop us back at the club?"

"Yes."

"You'll be okay the rest of the afternoon?" Olivia asks me.

"Of course. I'm going to go through my closet for a dress and then give myself a spa day, I think. You know, decompress before I have to deal with Daddy and all his cronies."

Olivia doesn't look entirely convinced. "If you're sure . . ."

"I'm positive. You two go. Enjoy your day."

"I'll be back here to stay tonight."

"Olivia," Cash begins in warning.

She tosses him a withering look, and he sighs and turns away, shaking his head.

"We'll be back here tonight. I don't want you staying by yourself until this is over."

"I told you I'd stay," Nash growls from his spot near the front door. He didn't move very far into the room. "Don't you people listen?"

"See?" Cash says to Olivia.

Olivia turns her skeptical gaze to me. "That's up to Marissa."

A quiver works its way through the lowest part of my stomach when I think of the way Nash woke this morning. Of course, he'll likely sleep in Olivia's bed if they aren't in it.

Likely . . .

"That's fine. We'll be fine. I'm sure no one would dare come through that door with him in the house."

I say it in jest, but it's probably ninety percent true. Only the scariest of criminals might not give Nash a second thought. Of course, those are the ones we're all worried about.

"Damn straight," Nash murmurs from his spot.

I grin at Olivia when she rolls her eyes. "See?"

"Well, I'll check back in with you later, anyway. I won't be working a shift. I've got some homework I need to get done, so . . ."

"Please stop worrying about me," I plead earnestly. The more compassion and kindness she shows me, the worse I feel about the way I've always treated her. And I already feel like a steaming pile of poo. "You've got your own troubles to deal with. And your own happiness to bask in. I'll be fine. I promise."

Her smile is reluctant, but it comes. And I feel better for having helped put it there. It feels good to be this person, this pleasant, thoughtful person rather than the scathing bitch I was before. The girl no one really wanted to be around unless they had something to gain from it.

"Yeah, we have basking to do," Cash reiterates huskily as he pulls Olivia to her feet and into his arms. He nuzzles her throat and she giggles, wrapping her arms around his neck.

"Okay, okay."

"Good. It's all worked out then. Let's go," Cash says, taking Olivia by the hand and towing her toward the door. As she passes me, she impulsively bends down and winds one arm around my shoulders, hugging me to her.

"I'm glad you're back," she whispers in my ear, giving me a light squeeze. I reach up to return her hug, feeling the warmth of her personality more than ever.

And to think, if it weren't for a case of being in the wrong place at the wrong time, I could've gone the rest of my life missing out on someone as wonderful as Liv. That would've been the biggest tragedy of all.

"I am, too," I whisper back. From the couch, I watch the trio leave. The last thing I see is the black pools of Nash's eyes when they meet mine as he's shutting the door.

I feel the complex heat of them long after he's gone.

ELEVEN

Nash

I thought when I finally got to come out of hiding, when I finally got to *live*, I'd never have a reason to go back. Ever. To any part of the life I've had for these last seven years.

But I was wrong.

Of course, I never imagined that Dad would want us to give up the fight, that he'd be content to rot in prison and let Mom's killer go free. But then again, he's known who killed her all along.

My stomach clenches at the thought of Duffy. My fingers ache with the remembered desire to wrap my hands around his throat and look him in the eye as I squeeze the life out of him.

But Duffy's just one man. Even though he's technically the one who killed my mother with that bomb, whether he intended to or not, he's just one of several who were ultimately behind Mom's death and all the hell that followed. My thirst for revenge won't be satisfied until they're all dead or in prison. Maybe Dad knows that. Maybe that's why he wants us to give it up. Maybe it's a lifelong pursuit, trying to get to the bottom. Or the top, rather.

Either way, it doesn't matter. I'm not giving it up. Not ever. I can't. It would kill too much of me, of who I was and who I am, to let it go. So I'll see it through. No matter what it takes or how long I have to fight, I'll see it through.

After dropping Cash and Olivia back at Dual, I drive the quick trip across town to the train station. I stopped there on my way into town and got myself a locker. Having no roots to speak of makes it a little more difficult to keep important things safe. Even some people *with* roots choose locations such as these to keep valuable things out of harm's way. Like Dad, for instance. It was at this very train station that he'd stashed his bag of goodies.

My smile is wry and a little hostile when I think to myself that it's probably a good thing only one of us boys followed so closely in Dad's footsteps. I just always assumed if either of us turned out to be a criminal or turned out to possess criminal tendencies, it would be Cash. I think everyone assumed that. In a way, I guess Nash really *did* die the day of the explosion. The guy he was and the guy he would've grown to be are dead. Both of them. Gone forever. The question is: Who am I? Who rose to take their place?

Pushing those troubling thoughts aside, I find a place to park in the lot outside the station. Glancing casually over my shoulder, a habit I doubt I'll ever break, I make my way into the building and over to the small stand of lockers to the left. I'd picked a locker number I'd remember easily. Number four thirteen. Mom's birthday. April thirteenth.

As always, when I think of her birthday, I think of the day she died. As if that's ever far from my mind. But sometimes it's more . . . poignant. The guilt of surviving when I should've died, of being the douche on the dock filming a topless girl rather than on the boat where he should've been, eats at me. She shouldn't have been alone. She shouldn't have died alone. I should've been with her. But I wasn't. I was spared. And look what's become of me. The world would be a much better place if she'd lived and I'd been the one blown to bits that day.

But that's not the way it worked out. So the least I can do is bring the culprits to justice. One way or the other.

I pull a small key with an orange top out of my boot. It's non-descript. If someone were to ever find it, they'd never know where it came from or, if they happened to figure it out somehow, what locker it fits.

It slides easily into the lock and I turn it until the door pops open. Inside is a black bag with a few emergency supplies and a couple of phones. One of them is very important. Like the one Dad had left us, it has all sorts of numbers that I might need at some point. I had hoped I'd never have to use any of them, but I kept them for a reason. Because things rarely go as planned. Dammit.

It also contains another copy of the footage from the dock. There are a few other odds and ends stored on it. Things that could easily get me killed. Things about weapons and smugglers and routes I should know nothing about. But I do. There's enough insurance here to save my life a dozen times over. Or cost it. Depends on who has the phone. And who knows what's on it. Right now, it's only me. And that's how I plan to keep it. Trust no one. I've survived a long time on that motto. It's kept me safe. Alive.

I power the phone up and scroll through the list of contacts until I find Dmitry's number. I text it to a second phone, that of a burner that also resides in the locker. One of several burner phones, actually. Someone in my line of work and with my family history can never have too many. I get them with no GPS and very limited . . . everything. I can use them, then trash them, leaving no trace that could ever lead back to me.

After another casual assessment of my surroundings, I secure the locker and drop the key back in my boot. I take the burner phone to an empty bench and hit the send button.

It rings several times before a familiar gruff voice says three short, heavily accented words.

"Leave me message." A beep follows.

"It's Nikolai," I begin. It's the name Dmitry gave me from the moment we met. I had to be someone other than Greg Davenport's son, Nash. I had to be someone else entirely. "I, uh, I need to talk to you. It's really something I'd rather discuss in person, though. If you can make it to the place I first met you, about the same time, in two days, I'd really appreciate it. Thanks, Dmitry."

I hang up, knowing he'll understand my message perfectly. And I know in two days, he'll be there if at all possible. The boat shouldn't be pulling out for another week or so, so it should be no problem for him to get there.

Punching a few keys to erase all traces of the text and the call, I get up and walk toward the exit, nonchalantly dropping the phone in a trash can as I pass.

As I make my way back to Cash's car, my mind flickers back over the past seven years' worth of conversations with Dmitry. He told me dozens of stories involving him and Dad. Nothing too scandalous; just mischief they got into in the early years. Evidently they both got into the business about the same time.

They made their way through the ranks, my father eventually going into the money-laundering side, Dmitry into the smuggling side. They remained friends and confidants, which is why Dad had

Dmitry as an emergency exit strategy. It's not that he would've risked our safety with a smuggler; it's just that he trusted Dmitry above all others.

And now I'm about to trust Dmitry. And I'm about to ask for his help. It's a big favor, one that he might not be willing to grant, but it's worth asking. Things might've degraded to where he's one of three or four linchpins on which our only shot of making this right depends. Only time will tell, but I have to start somewhere. I have to do something. I need a plan A and a plan B. I can't let this go. And even though Cash said he has no intention of letting it go, I don't trust that it's as important to him to see this through. At least not as important as it is to me. I just don't trust anyone that much. Not even family. I've been on my own too long for that to change. Maybe one day. But I doubt it.

My conscience prickles. Here I am, hesitating to fully trust anyone when I myself would be considered by most to be untrustworthy. I've become so driven, I let very little get in my way, especially if it's a matter of something like "right" standing in the path of what I want or need. The life that I was forced into is one of survival of the fittest with a take-no-prisoners kind of attitude. It's hard to shake those habits and make a smooth return to the civilized world.

A pair of bright blue eyes watches me from the back of my mind. My conscience stabs me again. I wonder what she'd think if she knew everything. Everything I've done.

Especially the things that involve her.

Unlocking the car, I slide behind the wheel and put all such deep, bothersome thoughts out of my head. Some things aren't good to dwell on. This is one of them.

Pushing the start button on Cash's BMW, I pull out of the parking lot and turn back toward his condo. I need to work out two plans, down to the last detail. I can't afford surprises. One of them *has to* succeed.

After a few hours spent researching on the computer, I'm very ready for a break, even if that break involves a tuxedo and a bunch of rich assholes. I don't give a shit about them; it's Marissa I'm looking forward to spending time with. And I'm not even going to pretend my motives aren't one hundred percent selfish.

I need a delicious, feminine body to lose myself in, to bury my troubles in. Even if it's just for a little while. And although I could probably find any number of willing partners, she's the one I want. For many reasons, one of which, I'm sure, is the fact that she's a spoiled little rich girl.

I know I could probably go there right now and have sex with her, but I'm enjoying this little game we've got going on that's leading up to it. It's another form of distraction, and I welcome it. I don't mind getting all dressed up to continue playing just as long as she doesn't start expecting more. I've already warned her about me. I hope she's not fool enough to ignore that warning.

I tug at the snug collar of my crisp, white shirt. I've worn a tuxedo exactly one time in my life. My junior prom. I don't remember it feeling nearly so constrictive. As I shrug my shoulders inside the perfectly cut material, I realize it's not the suit that's suffocating me; it's life.

I'm not adjusting nearly as well as I'd imagined I would. I had this vision of landing back in real life as if no time had passed, as if nothing had happened and I was the same guy I was when I left. I couldn't have been more wrong.

That, ladies and gentlemen, is called denial. Ain't she a bitch?

I'm a few minutes early when I reach Marissa's door. I try the knob, but it's locked.

At least she's got some *kind of brain!*

I could use the key on Cash's set, but I don't. I ring the bell instead.

It takes her a couple of minutes to answer. I guess beauty like hers takes time. And when she flips the lock and appears in the open doorway, I realize it's worth every second.

Damn, she's gorgeous.

Marissa's tall, lean body is wrapped in a black dress that was made to hug her. From where the strap sits on only one shoulder to where the material loosens just past her knees and falls to the floor, it fits her like a second skin. Every sleek curve is perfectly delineated, and the strappy heels she's wearing make her legs look that much longer.

Her blond hair looks like a platinum wave gushing over her one bare shoulder, and her skin glows like liquid gold. But it's those damn eyes that get me. Vivid blue orbs that look both innocent and seductive all at the same time. And she's always watching me with them. Curiously. Intently. I can't help but wonder what she's thinking, what she's imagining. If she's remembering . . .

I know it's probably just my conscience playing tricks again. After what I've done. Surely she can't know. But still, I wonder.

"You look stunning," I say in a moment of honesty.

Her lips part in an even more stunning smile. "Thank you. And you look very handsome. As always."

I'll admit I cleaned up a little. But not much. I could've gone all out and cut my hair and shaved my face. But I didn't. And I won't. I'm still too much of a bastard to do anything drastic like that just to pretend to be Cash (when he's pretending to be me). Nobody's that important. Including her. But I did comb my hair back neatly and tuck it behind my ears. And I trimmed my goatee and shaved around it. I'm sure I still look like someone who should never be allowed into a high-society function, tuxedo or not. But they can all kiss my ass. I'm going anyway.

My motives aren't totally selfish, I guess. By doing this, by going with her, I'll be proving a point to Marissa about how strong she is. Or isn't. Taking someone like me to an event like this will push her further one way or the other. Which way is hard to tell.

I refuse to think about any other reasons, deep-seated ones, that might have played a role in my attendance tonight. I can't afford to let myself feel anything for a damn woman. And that's that.

At least that's what I tell myself.

TWELVE

Marissa

How twins can look so much alike yet so different is beyond me. Maybe it's just his personality that makes him seem so different, but to me, Nash is nothing like Cash. Not at all. I always thought Cash (when I thought he was Nash) was good looking, but he doesn't hold a candle to the real Nash. He's breathtaking. I don't think I've ever seen a sexier man. And even in his tuxedo you can see that he belongs in a black leather jacket, perched on the back of a motorcycle. It's who he is, right down to his bones.

Dangerous.

"Let me get my things and we can go," I say quickly, turning to head back to my room. My fingers are shaking anxiously when I throw a lipstick, my keys, a compact, and my debit card into a black sequined clutch and snap it shut.

I pause in front of the mirror and take a deep breath. Why do

I feel like I'm walking into an inferno? A moth drawn inexplicably to the brutal flame?

I have no illusions about him. I can't blame it on any lack of understanding. I know Nash is just that—brutal. But I can't stay away. Despite the danger, I don't even want to. It doesn't make any sense, and I'm not going to try to make it. I'm just gonna run with it. For once in my life, I'm jumping.

Closing my eyes against my troubling thoughts, I make my way back out to Nash. Back out to the flame.

I think the valet is actually afraid to take the tip Nash hands him. His eyes flit nervously to me, to Nash, and then quickly away before he reaches hesitantly for the folded bill. With a shy nod, he stuffs it in his pocket, hops in the car, and drives very slowly to the parking lot. I hide my smile behind my hand. I bet he makes sure the car is in perfect condition when he brings it back.

Nash joins me at the curb and offers me his arm, a gesture that shows me he knows how to comport himself in company like the people he's getting ready to meet. And that he's not going to be totally obtuse.

"Shall we?"

His brow is raised in mockery. I smile and tip my head at him, slipping my hand under his elbow.

My stomach jumps around anxiously. Part of it is the close proximity to Nash. But that's nothing new. If he's anywhere around, my focus is almost entirely centered on him. The other part of it is something that has nothing to do with Nash or his effect on me.

I acknowledge with more than a little disappointment that it's worry, worry that he will do or say something to make a fool of himself. Or me. Or, worse, Daddy.

I remind myself that the new me shouldn't even care about that. Olivia wouldn't give something so superficial a second thought. And neither should I.

But old habits die hard. And mine have been in the grave for only a few hours. I don't want any parts of that woman to be resurrected. I desperately want the old me to stay dead.

Putting on my most confident smile, I glance at Nash, walking cockily at my side, and we make our way toward the lectern to sign in.

The first person to spot us when we walk into the main room is Millicent Strobe, quite possibly one of *the* most vapid "friends" I have. Evidently she was in the process of exiting one conversation and moving to another, one with a couple situated more in my direction. She rudely abandons them, however, and changes course for, you guessed it, *me*.

"Well, look what the cat dragged in," she says in her sugary-sweet way. Her smile is too wide and her eyes too curious as she looks at Nash. She leans in for air kisses to both my cheeks. "A kitty and her chew toy." She laughs her tinkling, fake laugh and lays her red-nailed hand on Nash's arm. "Kidding."

Only she wasn't. Kidding, that is. The look she gives Nash, from the top of his head to the tip of his toes, is full of disdain.

"Who's this? Nash's career-criminal brother?" She laughs her fake laugh again, and I feel the blood rush to my cheeks. I shouldn't have worried about Nash embarrassing anybody; I should've worried about the people I already knew embarrassing *us*.

"As a matter of fact . . ." Nash says quietly from my side. At first I think I misunderstood him, but when I glance up at him, I see that his expression is stoic, serious. He's willfully provoking her.

"Now *he's* kidding, Leese," I interject lightly, laughing as well and using the pet name her close friends have used for years. "This is, um, Cash, Nash's brother."

My heart is a jackhammer inside my chest, determined to beat ruthlessly through the wall of my ribs. We didn't discuss what we'd tell people. I assumed we'd still go with him being Cash, but . . . not like this.

"Yes. Nash. I remember him well. The question is: Do you? Why would you leave him at home on a night like tonight?" Left unspoken is what she really means—*and bring* this guy *instead*.

My father never bothered to hide his fondness for Nash and his desire to make him part of the Townsend empire. We live a very public life in some ways, which means that most everyone knows we broke up, too. The thing is, not one of them probably expected me to disregard my father's wishes. They would expect me to appear here with Nash on my arm by whatever means. Because no one defies a man with my father's kind of influence.

No one.

I hear the first syllable of Nash's rebuttal. With my eyes on Millicent, I swallow hard, fix my smile in place, and dig my nails into Nash's arm, a silent plea for him not to say whatever he's thinking of saying. I hear the angry huff of his breath, but he doesn't utter another sound, not a single word. I can practically feel the cool air emanating from him, though. He doesn't like being muzzled.

"This was last-minute and Nash had something else planned. *Technically*, I'm not even supposed to be back in the country," I say conspiratorially.

"Then why are you?"

"Some, um, some personal things came up that needed my attention."

"Personal things, huh?" I know that look in her eye. It's the same look a shark gets when it scents blood in the water.

Damn you, why didn't you think of how to handle all this before *you got here?* I chastise myself, albeit far too late.

"Yes, you remember what those are, right? Before we were suddenly expected to live our life in public?"

"When was that? When we were two years old?"

"Exactly." I laugh again, feeling more and more uncomfortable by the minute.

Millicent grew up in a privileged family, much as I did, with certain . . . expectations. She knows exactly what I mean. The problem is, she hasn't realized that it's a crappy way to live. Mainly because she hasn't been shown how awful of a life it is, what awful people it's made us. But I have. I have no excuse to act like that anymore, to act like her.

"As daughters of some of the most influential men and women in this state, we have certain responsibilities and . . . appearances to uphold. Or have you forgotten that as well?"

Is she really going to do this? Could I ever have called someone like *this* a friend?

It horrifies me to think that things were even worse than I'd suspected.

"I could never disgrace my family," she adds scathingly.

I can't decide if she's insinuating that arriving with *this* Nash, as Cash, is disgracing my family or if it's just my oversensitivity. Am I making more of the undertones than what she's intending? I've known Millicent most of my adult life. I can't imagine her being this person. Maybe I'm projecting. Maybe my guilty conscience is making me see things that aren't really there.

But then another part of me speaks up, asking if I *am*, in fact, being incredibly disrespectful and inconsiderate of my family by showing up like this with "Cash." I knew Daddy wanted me to bring Nash, but I also knew he would undoubtedly rather I come alone than with someone whose . . . questionable nature might bring him shame.

It's ridiculous that it would even be a consideration, but it's just part of the world in which we live. Isn't it?

My heart pumps with guilt, but over what? Daddy? Nash? That I'm actually having to *think* about what's right here?

But then something else kicks in. Something foreign. And scary. But something welcome. And right.

I give Millicent my sweetest smile. "Well, I hardly think disgracing people who don't even have the common decency to be polite is something I'll lose sleep over." Her mouth drops open in shock. Before she can recover enough to reply, I lean in and whisper, "Be careful that you don't fall off that pedestal, Millicent. A tumble like that could break bones."

I straighten, shoot her another syrupy smile, and then promptly turn my back on her.

My brief moment of triumph over my former self is quickly dashed when my eyes collide with my father's. He's standing on the other side of the room, watching me, quiet fury on his face.

Impulsively, I raise my chin, a statement in and of itself. And Daddy will know exactly what it means.

Slowly, he shakes his head. One sharp gesture that speaks as loudly as mine did. And I feel it like tremors of an earthquake all the way down to my soul.

For a few terrifying seconds, I feel like crumbling. Crumbling under the pressure of who I was, of what's expected of me and what I've done tonight. But before I can, Nash steps in to save me from myself.

Fingers touch my elbow.

"How 'bout a drink to wash down all that bitterness?" he asks.

I have to make an effort to swallow my huge sigh of relief. When I look up at him to accept his kind offer, I see the faint light of respect in his eyes. Or do I? Could it be that I'm imagining it? Maybe because I want so badly to see it? I can't be sure. Either way, it feels good. It feels good to finally have the respect, no matter how minute, of someone who thought so little of me. Of someone who knew what kind of person I was.

Was.

Maybe that's why he's saving me. Because that's what he's doing by offering me this escape route. He's saving me. Even though it seems he's not the saving type, he stepped up to do it. Twice now.

The first, of course, was when he showed up with Cash to rescue me. I can still remember hearing his voice, so distinguishable from Cash's. So stern yet so safe. Familiar, but not in the way I would've expected. I felt protected all the way home, even though he hardly spoke. And now, here he is doing it again, tonight. .

But why? Why now?

The answer comes as quickly as the question.

Maybe it's because now he thinks I'm worth saving.

Pushing the troubling thoughts aside, I opt for a bright smile. "Thank you. I'd love one."

As he leads me away, I glance back over my shoulder to see Millicent flounce off to rejoin her fiancé, Richardson "Rick" Pyle, whom she'd left behind when she spotted me. I'm sure she'll give him an earful as soon as it's acceptable to do so. It won't be long before, one by one, everyone I know is given a perverted version of what just happened. And guess who the bad guy will be? Nash's voice penetrates the chaos in my mind. "Not the cakewalk you thought it'd be, huh?" he asks quietly. I glance up at him again. He's facing forward, but I imagine his expression is one of smugness. It's upsetting when I realize that, despite what just happened, Nash doubts that I'm strong enough to change. That I *have* changed.

The realization is a devastating blow to my fragile confidence. I say nothing to him because, on some level, I'm wondering the same thing. Can I really change? Should it be this much of a struggle? Or am I just as irrevocably damaged as these people?

We stop in front of the elegantly appointed bar. Without asking what I'd like, Nash orders—a vodka martini, dirty, for me and a Heineken for him. I wait until the bartender is busy fixing my drink before I say anything.

"Are you just that good? Or am I just that easy to read?"

Nash shrugs. "You seem like a martini girl." He glances at me from the corner of his eye, his expression dark and steamy. "And, when you're not kissing ass, I'd say you're a dirty one."

I brush off the first part of his comment and focus on the latter half. I feel my face flush. It spreads all the way down my chest, making me feel hot and damp. I resist the urge to fan.

I don't know how to respond to his suggestive assessment, so I simply don't. "You don't seem like a beer guy. I would've thought something harder."

The words are out before I realize my response is every bit as suggestive as his was.

Ohmigod!

"I can get a lot harder," he says in his low, velvety voice. "But tonight, I think drinking a beer will cement their trashy impression of me."

"So you *want* them to think you're less than them?"

"No, they can think whatever the hell they want. I'm *definitely* not less than them, regardless of my hair or my drink. I ordered a beer because, not only do I happen to like it, I also get a kick out of knowing that it bugs the shit out of these judgmental assholes having someone like me, someone with long hair and tattoos, walking around at their fancy party."

I can see by the twist at the corner of his mouth that he's pleased with himself and his rebellion. I wish I could be so blasé about what they think and how they judge. But right now, I can't. I have to fight it every step of the way. Every *baby* step of the way.

Maybe one day I'll get there. Maybe.

So many *maybe*s lately, and I keep piling them on. The disequilibrium of it, the uncertainty of it suddenly feels like a suffocating hand over my mouth, much like the one that I felt just before I passed out and woke up in captivity a few days ago.

Panic sets in and a cold sweat pops out on my forehead. All I can think of is the need for air. And wide open spaces.

Freedom.

Frantic, I search for a way out. I spot the balcony doors directly across the room, behind Nash. The never-ending expanse of black night just beyond them looks like heaven.

"I think I need some air," I say before I set off in that direction, not waiting for Nash's response.

Thankfully, the balcony is empty when I step out onto it. I go straight to the railing and lean my hip against it. Reaching out, I lay one palm along the cool wrought iron, letting the refreshing temperature of the metal permeate the rest of my body like a soothing summer breeze.

I remind myself I'm safe, that I'm here in this moment, not back in the most terrifying one of my life.

I'm safe. I'm safe. I'm safe.

"Are you okay?"

Nash's voice is a barely discernible rumble in the moonlight.

"I'll be fine."

"Something happened. Tell me what it was."

He's about as sensitive and tactful as a bull in a china shop, stating the obvious and then demanding answers. But I know that's just the way he is. I'm not sure he's capable of more. Or ever will be. Nash is hard, rougher around the edges than probably anyone I know. And profoundly broken, I think.

But then again, so am I.

I turn around, putting the rail at my back, ready to give him some semblance of an answer, but the words die on my tongue. He's standing in front of me, taking a sip of his beer, watching me with his raven eyes. Something about the scene—the balcony, the balmy air, the beer, Nash, me—seems so familiar. It's almost like déjà vu.

A gush of warmth sweeps through me, stealing my breath. I have no idea where it came from or why, but I'm so aroused I feel hot all over. And moist.

"What is it?" he asks, his eyebrows knit together in a frown.

"I don't know. Something about you and . . . and this balcony and you drinking beer . . . I don't know. It's just . . . I don't know. *Familiar* almost. Weird," I say casually, trying to blow if off, but feeling anything but nonchalant.

Don't tear his clothes off! Don't tear his clothes off!

My palm is sweaty beneath the bowl of my glass. The fingers of my other hand curl around the wrought iron at my back when he takes a step closer to me.

He stops only inches from me. He stares down into my face for a moment, thoughtfully, before he raises his beer bottle to my mouth and rolls it across my bottom lip. "Yeah. Weird."

We stay like this for a couple of torturous minutes. All I can think about is how much I want him to kiss me, to touch me, to take me in his arms and drown out every*thing* and every*one* else.

But he doesn't. Without a word, he steps back, turns slightly to the side, and takes another swig of his beer.

Almost like he didn't feel a thing.

THIRTEEN

Nash

"So, why have you never asked questions about me and Cash? Why weren't you surprised, or at least confused, when I drove you to your father's house after the kidnapping? You can't tell me you didn't at least wonder who I was." I stare out into the night, careful to keep my eyes off her.

I hope Marissa doesn't think my abrupt change of subject is suspicious. I didn't want her to keep thinking about the balcony. She's getting too close. Too close to a memory I don't want her to find. Too close to something I want to forget. But something I *can't* forget.

I force it from my mind, determined not to think on it. I see now that it was a mistake to follow her out here.

I can't help but be curious what she knows, though. If that's why I catch her staring at me so often. What will she think of me if she ever puts two and two together?

"I'll admit it was shocking to see you, but more shocking than confusing because I already knew what was going on."

I turn my head slightly, just enough to see her. I arch my brow. "And you expect me to believe that? That you just figured it out?"

She frowns. "Oh. No. That's not how it happened. I found out while I was being held captive. I overheard two men talking."

"Ahhh," I say. That makes much more sense. Marissa is astute enough to catch on, but I'm sure Cash limited the amount of time he let anyone who knew him see him as both Cash and Nash. He wouldn't take a reckless risk like that. It would have been difficult for Marissa to realize the truth—especially when she had no reason to suspect he was playing both brothers. When I think of her answer, though, it still doesn't make sense. No one should've known until *after* we had possession of Marissa. "Exactly what did they say?"

"Just that one of their plants had called in the night before and said that one of you had been pretending to be both twins, but that the other one—the real one—was back."

"A 'plant'?"

She nods again. "That's what he said. Or at least that's what it sounded like he said. He had a very thick accent."

"Russian?"

"Yes, it sounded like it."

I feel my frown deepen right along with my concern. "And this guy said the plant called in the night before? When was it that you overheard this?"

"Um, the day you brought me home, I think. They kept me bound and gagged and blindfolded almost the entire time, so my sense of time is skewed. When I think back to those hours, I can't . . . seem . . . to . . ."

A shiver passes through her and she closes her eyes for a second.

It's plain to see she's still shaken by the whole thing. I'm sure most people in her position would be. She just puts on such a good front that it's easy to forget she's been through a traumatic experience. And very recently, too. I guess with everything that's going on, the movement of time seems, by turns, inordinately fast or inordinately slow.

I suppose all of our lives are in a kind of holding pattern until we get this over and done with, and behind us. And, like it or not, we're all in this together. These bastards have adversely affected and touched each of our lives.

I think over the timeline. If she's remembering correctly, that means someone tipped off the Russians on Sunday. Presumably after I arrived in town. That means they have eyes on the club most likely, which doesn't surprise me. But was it merely someone in the club, a patron? Or was it someone . . . closer? Closer to Cash? Someone on the *inside*?

He's been pretty cautious, so I'm inclined to think it was some-one watching him and watching his life from the perspective of a clubber.

I growl through my gritted teeth.

"What is it?" she asks.

"Cash is a godda—" I catch myself before I finish the phrase. I guess some parts of the old me never died, like the ingrained urge to watch my language around a lady. "He's a damned idiot for trusting any of you people."

"Any of 'you people,' " she says, clearly taking exception. "I know you can't possibly mean me."

"And why the hell not? You might be the worst one of them all."

"How could you even say that? I've done nothing to deserve your distrust."

I scoff. "Maybe not, but you've done nothing to earn my trust, either."

"So not telling anyone who you *really* are isn't enough to rate a little trust?"

"Hell no! It serves your purposes just as much as mine. I can just imagine the kind of social shitstorm you'd stir up if you told anybody about the man you *thought* was Nash." My laugh is bitter. "No, don't act like you're doing me some big favor. Your motives are selfish, just like the rest of us."

"You can't go through life not trusting anyone."

"Watch me," I snap.

She looks wounded, no doubt some kind of feminine ploy practiced specifically to manipulate. Well, it won't work on me. She's not getting under my skin. I want her; that's no secret. But that's the only thing I'm interested in—sex. Nothing more. I even did the right thing and warned her about me. If she chooses to ignore that warning, that's on her.

"I think this was a mistake," she says, her voice small in the heavy air.

"Let me give you a valuable tip about people and life. Everybody wants something. Everybody. As soon as you can get that through your head, the better off you'll be."

She looks down at her hands as she toys with the stem of her martini glass. "And what is it that you want?"

"Revenge," I bite out. "Justice." She nods slowly but doesn't look back up at me. Again, I think of my goal to have those long, long legs wrapped around me. I should hide it from her. Woo her instead. No doubt it's what the high-society types expect. But that's exactly why I won't do either. I want to shock her. I want her to know that I change for no one. I yield to no one. "And a few hours alone with you."

I want her to be clear about my intentions. Because we will be sleeping together. And sooner rather than later. I'm the kind to take what I want. She needs to know that.

It won't change anything. I know when a woman is already mine. And this one is.

Much to her detriment, probably. But again, that's on her. She can't say I didn't warn her.

On our way out, Marissa does her best to stick to the wall and dodge virtually everyone in the room. Again, I think to myself that this isn't easy for her, letting this life go, letting this person go. And this is just the first night. What does she think will happen after word gets out? Or when she goes back to work? When she's shunned? I should probably warn her that she doesn't have it in her, that she's nowhere near strong enough. But then again, it's not my place, so I'll just keep my mouth shut.

An attractively curvaceous girl stops Marissa just as she's trying to dart toward the exit, the home stretch. She has chin-length blond hair, a nice rack, and hips to hang on to. I'm sure most of Marissa's friends call her fat, but I'm also sure most of Marissa's friends are anorexic bitches, so . . .

"Marissa! Wait!"

There's no polite way to pretend she didn't hear, so Marissa turns toward the girl and smiles.

"Heather, how are you?" Marissa turns on her overly happy, public face.

"I heard you had to pull out early from your trip to the Caymans."

Although I'm sure she doesn't appreciate the reference to her cutting short the trip for personal reasons, Marissa's smile is unwavering. She's good under pressure. "And where did you hear that?"

"Tim mentioned something about it."

"A gossipy *man*? That's not very common."

The girl, Heather, looks stung, but she recovers quickly. "I don't think of it as gossip. It's just that you're so . . . dedicated, he thought something was wrong. I just wanted to catch you before you left tonight to make sure you're okay."

I feel a pang of sympathy for this girl. She seems like she's genuinely concerned, like she'd like to be a friend to Marissa. Little does she know, she's better off not.

If I had to guess, I'd say this girl, Heather, is a lot less jaded than most of the icy bitches in this room. And it's probably *because* she's a nice person that she never ranked very high on Marissa's list of important people. She hardly rates a short conversation. That much is obvious.

I can see by Marissa's expression that she's relieved "Nash" wasn't mentioned. "Well, I'm fine. And you can pass that along to Tim as well."

"I'm glad to hear that," she says pleasantly, but she doesn't leave well enough alone. She's obviously a glutton for punishment. "You know if you ever need to talk, you can always call me. I'm always home. All alone in that big ol' house." She laughs uncomfortably, like she divulged too much or she's embarrassed not to have more on her social calendar. I imagine that's something shameful in these circles.

Damn pit vipers!

"I'll keep that in mind," Marissa says politely before she starts to turn away. My guess is that she's not used to such a genuine expression of kindness. But then, as if that very thing suddenly occurs to her, her expression softens and she reaches out and puts a hand on Heather's arm. "And I appreciate the offer, Heather. Really. Thank you."

I watch Heather's eyes go round and sort of glaze over. If I blew in her face, she'd fall right over. She's that shocked. I'm pretty surprised myself, and that's not an easy thing to accomplish. But Marissa has done it. And she's risen a notch in my opinion, too. Maybe I underestimated her character. Maybe, just maybe, there is something more than a snobby, calculated, privileged brat beneath that beautiful skin.

Obviously, she's a little more complex than I'd originally thought. I can't decide if her default mode is vicious bitch and she's trying to fight it, or if the vicious bitch part is more like a hard candy shell, protecting the softer center. I guess only time will tell.

"Have a good night," Heather says simply before she steps back, allowing Marissa to leave.

"You, too, Heather. Tell Tim . . . tell him hello for me, okay?"

The girl smiles broadly and nods. For a second I think she might get all giddy and start crying for Marissa's autograph, but she pulls it together and walks back the way she came.

I wait until we're out in the anteroom, away from the crowd, before I speak. "Bravo," I say sarcastically. "I didn't think you had it in you."

She whirls on me, her eyes flashing in a bit of temper I didn't realize she had. "You're just not going to cut me any slack, are you?" she snaps.

"People overlooking your flaws for your whole life is what got you in the position in the first place. What you need is someone who's honest with you. And someone to spank that ass every now and then. Do you some good."

"And you're just the man for the job," she says before turning to walk away.

"There's only one need I'm interested in filling," I admit, but I don't think she hears me.

I follow her out. She stops at the curb and waits for the valet to scurry off after the car. When she responds, I know she actually *did* hear me. "I don't need anything thing from you. Not one single thing."

"Maybe not, but you *want* something from me. You can deny it all you like, but we both know it's true."

Her eyes dart over my face and she stammers like she's flustered. "You're . . . you're just as delusional as you are twisted," she replies. I've got her off balance. She's not used to people treating her this way. Or being honest with her, I suspect.

"We'll see."

The valet pulls up in front of us with the car he parked only a short while ago. I tip him and open the door for the very stiff Marissa. I have the urge to laugh over her petulance. That's another unusual occurrence tonight. Laughing isn't something I do very often.

I climb behind the wheel and shut the door. Marissa must've been holding her rebuttal until we were in private.

"If you think I'm sleeping with you, you can think again. I'd rather be kidnapped again."

This time, I do laugh at her melodramatic response. "We'll see," I repeat, shifting into gear and speeding off down the road.

We've been on the road for at least five minutes before she stops pouting long enough to realize we're not heading toward her condo.

"Where are you going?"

"I need a drink. And so do you."

FOURTEEN

Marissa

Even though I want to argue with Nash, just to ease my frustration, I don't. He's right. I need a drink. I might even need two.

I lean my head back against the headrest and close my eyes, trying to forget about the last hour or so. And the disappointment of it. I don't look up again until I hear Nash shift into park and cut the engine. When I open my eyes and turn my head toward him, he's watching me, his expression blank. I'd love to know what he's thinking.

Or would I?

I decide I probably don't. I'd say he thinks I'm a monster. And, at the moment, I feel an awful lot like he might be right.

Feeling ashamed of myself, I look away, through the windshield, to see where we are. I half expected to see Dual in front of me. I don't really know why. That makes no sense. I'd say that's the last place Nash would want to go to relax. But of all the other places

I might've imagined him picking, this place is possibly even more surprising.

We're parked in the lot of a piano bar. Before I can ask any questions, Nash speaks as if he'd read my thoughts. "My mother used to play the piano. It always relaxes me to hear it." He gets out and comes around to my side to open the door. I'm surprised when he takes my hand. It's such a gentlemanly gesture. And he's no gentleman. But he sure does have a way of keeping me off balance. I'll give him that. "Plus our fancy clothes won't be *that* big of a deal here." I wouldn't have even thought of that, but I'm glad he did.

"Why the calm courtesy tonight? This isn't like you?"

He looks at me and arches one brow. "Maybe I don't mind pretending to be something that I'm not, either."

"Is that what you're doing? Pretending?"

"You're complaining?"

"No. I'm just . . ."

"Just what? Suspicious?"

I smile. "Maybe."

"Good."

Nash releases my hand more quickly than I would've liked. I remind myself that it's for the best. The more distance I can keep from him emotionally, the better off I'll be.

But already a part of me is arguing that I don't *want* to keep distance. I want to get closer, close enough to feel the heat. The problem is, close enough to feel the heat usually means close enough to get burned.

His hand at the base of my spine causes chills to erupt down my arms. Self-conscious, I want to cross my arms over my chest;

I know my nipples are hard. But I resist the urge. Rather, I put my focus on enjoying the touch of his hand.

The bar is dimly lit but for the circle that spotlights the piano. The smell of expensive cigars permeates the air and creates a haze that further obscures the half-moon-shaped booths that line the walls. Nash guides me to an empty one, pushed deep into a corner.

I slide in behind the table. Rather than sitting across from me, Nash scoots in beside me, forcing me to move around to the back of the booth, almost entirely hidden from the room, but with a great view of the piano.

When I stop, so does Nash. He doesn't look at me as he slings his arm over the back of the booth; he's already watching the pianist work magic with his long fingers. But that's not the case with me. I can't concentrate on anything except Nash.

His body is plastered to mine from my knee to my shoulder, which is tucked snugly under his arm. Even above the smoke, I smell his clean, manly scent. It envelops me.

I let my eyes slide to my left. Nash fills my vision. If I were to tilt my head and lean in, I could press my lips to the pulse I see beating in his neck, just above his collar.

As if he feels my eyes on him, he reaches up with his free hand and loosens his bow tie, expertly unbuttoning the top button of his shirt. The tie lists to one side, dangling at a sexy angle. Thoughts of undressing him run through my head, making my mouth dry.

With perfect timing, the waitress comes to take our order. "Vodka rocks and a Grey Goose martini, dirty." Again, I'm fine with what he orders. Not that it would matter. He'd probably order whatever he wanted, anyway.

I wonder to myself if he does things like that because he's *that* thoughtless, or if it's because he likes total control. Maybe it's a bit of both. One thing is for sure—the thought of giving him total control, of letting him take the reins, of letting him take *me*, gives me a thrill like no other.

Nash keeps his silence and basically ignores me until the drinks come. He downs his in two large gulps and signals the waitress for another before she can even step away from the table. Reaching forward, he slides my drink closer to me and shifts in the booth until he's slightly tilted in my direction. His body creates a barrier against the rest of the room, like I'm shielded by him.

Or being overtaken by him. Overwhelmed. Slowly consumed.

"Drink," he says softly, drawing my eyes to his. They're deep pools that look like the perfect place to get lost, to hide out from the rest of the world. "Tell me about it. Tell me what happened."

I don't need him to clarify; I know exactly what he means. He's referring to the days I was held captive. A shiver works its way through me, as it always does when I think of it, which I try purposely *not* to do.

"Let's talk about you first. I'm happy to give, but I want something in return."

"If I answer your questions *first*, that's not 'something in return.' That's bribery. What is it, Marissa?" he asks softly, his dark eyes taunting me. "Don't you trust me to satisfy you?"

"No, I don't."

He reaches forward to push my hair back over my shoulder, his fingertips grazing my neck. "Well, I can promise you I won't leave you anything *but* satisfied."

I struggle to think past his smooth words and magnetic gaze. "You know what I mean, Nash," I say as sternly as I can manage.

I can't *hear* so much as *feel* his sigh. He's so close to me, his chest brushes my arm when he inhales. "What do you want to know? That I haven't already told you, that is."

You've got to be kidding! You've barely told me anything!

I want to know everything, everything that has led to this moment, everything that has made him the man he is today. Everything that turned a promising young boy into this hardened, bitter person. It would be cruel to dredge up memories of the day his mother was killed, though, so I spare him that in hopes that maybe one day he'll tell me voluntarily. "Tell me about your years at sea. You did say you worked on a smuggling ship, right?"

"That's right. What else is there? I was involved in a lot of highly illegal, extremely unethical shit. You don't need to know anything more than that."

I feel the sudden chill in his attitude. This is obviously a sensitive subject and he very definitely has no interest in telling me all about it. But I'm a lawyer; it's not in me to back down from a line of questioning just because someone doesn't want to give me answers.

"Surely there had to be some good days. Tell me about one of them."

I don't know why I'm so desperate to know him, to know some part of him he doesn't want anyone to see. But I am. I know it's dangerous, but it's beyond me to stop.

Nash sighs again, looking toward the ceiling. He's quiet and appears frustrated, and it seems as though he's not going to answer me.

But he does.

Maybe eventually, too, I will learn to expect the unexpected with him.

"My first year on the ship was pure hell. I was homesick, I was heartbroken, and I despised the idea of being involved in anything criminal. But I knew I had to survive. For Dad. For Cash. I knew one day I might be able to save us all with what I'd seen. And that boat was the only way. At least for a while. Dad promised he'd send for me, and I held on to that hope for a long time. Until I learned that hate could keep me alive, too. That it could save my life." He falls quiet for a few seconds, lost in some kind of hell I can only fathom. But then he clears his throat and visibly shakes off the darkness in favor of something pleasant. "Anyway, a few months in, they brought on a Somalian. He wanted safe passage for him and his family to America, and the Russians had agreed to sneak them onto U.S. soil in exchange for his help for two years.

"His name was Yusuf and he reminded me a lot of Dad. He was younger, but it was easy to see he'd do anything for his family, to get them to safety, even if it meant being away from them for two years. He took up with me right off the bat. He spoke pretty good English and Russian, so he taught me quite a bit of both his native Arabic and some Russian while he was with us." Nash smiles as he remembers and talks of this Yusuf. "We played cards a lot at night. He had the shittiest poker face in the world." His lips curve up into the closest thing I've seen to a genuinely tender smile. But then it's gone. "Anyway, on one of our runs to Bajuni, the island where we made port when we had an . . . exchange, I caught him sneaking into one of the smaller boats one night. At first, he didn't want to tell me what he was doing, but when I threatened to sound the alarm, he changed his mind.

"See, when Yusuf agreed to help the Russians, Alexandroff, our . . . captain, had promised him he could send money to his wife and see her occasionally when we were back in the area. Only they never allowed it. So he was sneaking off to see her, to take her some money so she and his daughter wouldn't starve. I wouldn't let him go without me, of course, so we paddled across to the Somali coast and put in at a little bay to travel to his village of Beernassi. We only got to spend a couple of hours there, but I got to meet his wife and his little girl. They got up like it wasn't the middle of the night. His wife, Sharifa, made us something to eat, and his daughter wouldn't let us out of her sight." His smile is sad as he speaks of her. "Her name was Jamilla. It means 'beautiful.' And she was."

He gets quiet again, so I prompt him, wanting to hear more of his story. "What happened next?"

Nash looks up at me. His eyes have gone cold, his voice even colder. "Alexandroff found us. He walked right in, put a gun to Yusuf's head, and pulled the trigger. Killed him right in front of his family. Two of his men, two guys I hated from the second I got on board, held me, made me watch, and then beat me in the head with the butts of their guns until I passed out. I woke up on the ship two days later, stuck to my pillow in a pool of my own blood. I was gagged and tied to the bed."

I'm speechless. And I'm heartbroken. I ache for what Nash must have felt, what he *still* must feel. And this was one of his happy memories, for God's sake! My throat is thick with emotion and my eyes burn with unshed tears.

"Oh God, Nash. I'm so sorry."

Why did you have to know, Marissa? Why? Why put him through this?

"Nothing good happened on that boat. Nothing. Ever. I learned a hard lesson that night. One I've never forgotten."

I'm almost afraid to ask. "What's that?"

"I learned to hate. To really hate."

"I understand it, and I'm sure it's natural to feel that way—for a while. But it's not healthy to hang on to an emotion like that for long."

"It is when the alternative is even more self-destructive. Then it's healthy. It's healthy to hang on to hate when letting it go could kill you."

For one fraction of a second, the perpetually angry mask Nash wears lifts and I see the wounds behind the tough scar tissue. I see a small glimpse of the person he used to be, maybe could be again.

Without thinking, I reach up to touch his cheek with the tips of my fingers. "Maybe one day you can find something other than anger and hatred to live for," I say softly, almost absently.

As if my touch woke him from a stupor, as if he knows he's letting me in deeper than he'd like, Nash looks away. He reaches for his vodka, takes a long, slow sip, then sets the glass gently back onto the table. When his eyes return to mine, they're curiously blank. There's no hurt, no anger, no . . . nothing in them. Just a wall, an impenetrable barrier that's been years in the making.

"You got your warm, fuzzy story. My turn. Tell me about Saturday night."

My stomach curls up into a tight ball and my pulse picks up speed as I remember what happened after I parked the car. I was preoccupied, stewing about the breakup with "Nash." Of course, I had no idea who I'd been dating. Or who was breaking up with me. That still blows my mind. And infuriates me sometimes. It makes me feel like an idiot if I think about it too long.

I push those thoughts aside and let my mind go forward, through the chain of events that still terrify me when I let them out of the lockbox where I've been keeping them.

"My mind was on the breakup. At first, it was a pretty big smack to the ego. All Na—*Cash* told me was that he was interested in someone else and that it wasn't fair to keep seeing me. He was very vague and secretive about it, and he refused to answer any of my questions. So, I was preoccupied and wasn't really paying attention to much of anything else when I unlocked the door.

"I set my purse on the table and went back to my bedroom to change clothes and then have a glass of wine. After I put on my pajamas, I realized I'd left my phone in the car, so I went back out to get it. It was when I came back in that I sort of snapped out of it and realized that the television was on and turned up really loud. I thought that was odd because Olivia had obviously worked a shift. I mean, she was at Dual closing up when I was there. And she never leaves the television on. She's much too responsible to do something like that.

"Anyway, I was standing there in front of the door, wondering over that, when I saw him move toward the living room. It was like he stepped out of the shadows and was just . . . there. A silhouette. A black presence against the white, flickering light of the television. I knew instinctively that it belonged to no one who was familiar to me.

"All this happened in probably twenty or thirty seconds. It's like he appeared right as my brain was starting to work, but that delay . . . that short delay was enough. It cost me what little advantage I might've had. Could've cost me my life, I guess.

"Just as it was all coming together in my mind, that there was a strange man in my living room in the middle of the night, I opened my mouth to scream. That's when he lunged at me. I tried to dodge him. And I almost did. It was just his arm that caught me. Knocked me back into the table where I'd put my purse. I remember hearing the crashing of the lamp when it hit the floor. He knocked me off balance and I hit the wall and then stumbled into the living room, still trying to stay out of his reach. I couldn't think of anything more than the need to get away from him, to make sure he didn't catch me. He grabbed my leg and I fell. I kicked at him so he couldn't get my ankle, but he yanked me back toward him and straddled my legs. I was on my belly, so it was hard to do much of anything. I did manage to dig my keys into the back of his hand when he pulled my head back by my hair. I was still holding them from going outside to get my phone. But then he put something over my mouth and I could barely breathe. I remember smelling something harsh, like a chemical, and then there was nothing. Until I woke up wherever they kept me, blindfolded, bound, and gagged.

"I've never been more scared in all my life. They must've had me in a basement somewhere," I tell Nash, my mind going back to the horrifying sensations—smells, sounds, the feel of cool, smooth stone beneath my cheek and hip. I feel small and alone and still afraid when I remember it. "The floor felt like the coldest concrete in the world. And it smelled like must and something metallic, something coppery. Like blood. And when it was quiet, I could hear water dripping. And someone breathing." I stop and look up at Nash, who's watching me intently. "I still don't know who was down there with me. Or what happened to them. Eventually the breathing just . . . stopped."

Another shiver runs through my body like aftershocks of an earthquake. During the hours I was curled up on that floor, I imagined that the person lying near me was another woman, scared and alone. Unable to move or see or speak, like me. Only she was wounded. Badly wounded. Maybe beaten unconscious.

She never made any sounds; her breathing never changed when I moaned and struggled to talk to her behind my gag. Until her breathing stopped, until it ceased to sweep through the quiet of the room. After that, the silence was deafening.

I lay on my side, my arm, shoulder, hip, and thigh having long since gone numb, and I cried. I cried for whoever had lain on the floor of the same room and passed away without a sound, without a loved one. Without a prayer of being discovered. Surely somewhere someone is mourning her loss, maybe even looking for her. Unless they know what she was mixed up in. And who she was mixed up *with*.

Then again, maybe it wasn't even a woman. Maybe it's best that I never know.

I'm not even aware of the tears coursing down my cheeks until the feel of Nash's fingers brings me back to the present, back to the land of the living.

"I shouldn't have asked."

I smile a watery smile. "I guess we're even, then."

He gazes down into my eyes, neither of us saying a word, his fingers still pressed to my damp cheek. The sound of the piano fades into the background, as does the world and all the pain I've found in it so recently.

Instantly, I'm absorbed, consumed. Just like I want to be. For whatever reason, when I'm with Nash, I'm free of my life and the worry of it. I'm free of the past and the terror of it. I'm free of everything but him. He's overwhelming and I need to be overwhelmed. He's uncontrollable and I need to be out of control. He's the promise of something . . . else and I need something else.

"I think there are times in life when you need something to lose yourself in, something to take away the pain, take away the *feeling* of everything else. Something to numb it. Just for a while." As quietly as the beat of my heart, Nash articulates exactly what I've been thinking and feeling. And then he makes me an offer I can't refuse, one that I don't even *want to* refuse. He leans in closer, his lips brushing the shell of my ear as he speaks. "I can be that for you. We can be that for each other." Chills race down my arm.

Nash's hand moves into the hair at the nape of my neck. He cups the back of my head and angles his face until he can draw the lobe of my ear into his mouth. I feel the brush of his hot tongue and my eyes drift closed. "I could make you forget everything else. I can make sure that you feel nothing but pleasure, that you can't think past what I'm doing to your body, what I'm making you feel. With my hands," he says, pulling his fingers from my hair and trailing them down my arm to my hip. "With my lips," he continues, moving his mouth across my cheek. "With my tongue," he whispers as he spreads wet heat across my bottom lip with the tip of the very tongue of which he speaks. "And I promise, you'll love every second of it." As if to punctuate his statement, he bites down ever so lightly, sinking his teeth into my flesh.

My breath catches in my throat just as his mouth fully covers mine. I part my lips, eager to taste him, to feel a part of him inside me.

The lingering hint of mint is mixed with the vodka on his tongue. He tastes like a cocktail. And he's every bit as intoxicating as the alcohol he's drinking.

With a will of its own, my hand moves up to the back of Nash's neck, my fingers threading into the silky strands of his loose hair. He tilts his head and deepens the kiss. He teases my tongue with his own, drawing it out until he can suck it into his mouth to tangle with his own.

Beneath the table, I feel his palm move from my hip to my thigh, then inward until skin meets skin. The dramatic slit of my dress allows him nearly full access to me. And I want him to take it. I part my legs the tiniest bit, an invitation. I don't care that we're in public. I don't care that my father would disown me for the scandal. I don't care about anything but this man and what he makes me feel. I only want him to touch me. I *need* him to touch me. And for this moment, the crowded piano bar is nothing more than a backdrop for the electricity that sings between us.

His hand moves to within inches of the apex of my thighs and stops. It's perfectly still but for the movement of his thumb. It makes an arc over the sensitive skin of my inner thigh. Back and forth, so close to where I want most to feel it.

I'm panting into his mouth when Nash's lips disappear. I open my eyes, confused. His face is a mere inch away, his eyes burning holes into mine. They're on fire and I feel the heat all the way to my core. "I bet your panties are wet right now," he murmurs, his hand inching up a fraction, then stopping again. My heart is racing and I wiggle a little in my seat. An impossible ache radiates from between my legs. "And I bet your nipples are hard," he says quietly, leaning forward to nuzzle my neck. "Hard and throbbing, Begging, like the rest of your body. To be licked. And sucked. And fuc—" he groans, catching himself.

And he's right. It does. My whole being wants it. I feel like nothing will be right with the world until I'm filled with Nash, until my body is stretched tight around his, pinned beneath his weight.

With his scent all around me, his firm length pressed warmly to mine, his breath fanning my skin, his hands tormenting me, something begins to niggle at the back of my mind. Something seems so . . . familiar.

The house lights come on and applause breaks out all around us. With a frustrated sigh, Nash leans back, removing his hand from my leg, removing his heat from me. The performance was so amazing, the crowd is on their feet. A standing ovation. I think to myself that I had a private performance that was definitely worthy of such praise.

And I can only imagine how much better it gets.

The lowest part of my belly squeezes at the thought of what might be to come, what I feel is inevitable between us. What I *want* to be inevitable between us.

"Come on," Nash says, sliding from the booth and offering me his hand. "I think that's our cue to leave." His smile is a wry twist of his lips that makes him even more handsome, even *sexier* than he usually is.

Personally, I didn't think that was possible.

FIFTEEN

Nash

I don't know what Marissa's thinking and I'm not the kind of man who really cares or feels it's overly important to find out. She's quiet, but I figure if she's uncomfortable or she's got something to say, she'll say it. She's an adult. She doesn't need me to pry it out of her. And if she does, tough shit.

Surely she knows where this is going. I think I've made it pretty plain that I have every intention of sleeping in her bed tonight. Not that either of us will be getting much sleep. The one thing I'm certain of is the only thing that matters. She's game. I know she is. She wants me every bit as much as I want her. That's the only thing that would stop me tonight—if she said no. I'm no rapist. But that won't be a problem. She won't say no. I'd bet my life on it.

I press a little harder on the accelerator. It's been a few weeks since I've been with a woman, so my need is at fever pitch. Add to that Marissa's response to me and I'm fighting not to find an empty parking lot. I'd pull her into my lap, rip her damp panties off her, and watch her ride me until she comes so hard she can't breathe. I'm throbbing just thinking about it.

I resituate in my seat, trying to ease some of the pressure off my stiff dick. I can't help but wonder what Marissa would do if I were to suggest that. Or, better yet, just do it. I know she's never had a man like me, and I know I intrigue her. I'm sure there's some part of her that knows about us, that remembers. Maybe that's a factor. Either way, she's willing to go with it, to go with *me*. Knowing that it goes against the grain for her, that she's feeling wild and reckless, is a very potent cocktail. Makes me want to show her things she's never seen. Or done. Or felt.

Yeah, Marissa's unique. I've never met a woman with her particular . . . blend before—classy, reserved, but willing to let the tiger off the leash when I'm around—and I'm anxious to savor this time with her. I'm sure it won't last long, which is perfect for me. We can just tear into each other and slake this hunger until it's gone. We'll both be satisfied and then it'll be over. We'll move on, go our separate ways. Clean and neat, cut and dried. No fuss, no muss. Just the way I like it.

I park the car at the curb and cut off the engine. I glance over at Marissa. She's watching me with those sultry blue eyes. For a few seconds, I say nothing. Neither does she.

"I'll be sleeping in your bed tonight," I finally say, matter-of-fact.

"Yes," she answers simply, confirming what I already knew.

Without another word, I slide out from behind the wheel and walk around the hood to her side. I help her out and put my hand at the small of her back to guide her up the sidewalk. My fingers itch to sink into that round, perfect ass of hers.

When we get to the door, she takes out her keys. I grab them from her fingers and unlock the door. She precedes me and stops just inside the entry. I shut and lock the door behind us, then turn to her. Without a word, I take her purse from her hand and lay it on the table by the door. It holds nothing now, not until she gets a new lamp.

Bending, I sweep her into my arms and carry her back to her bedroom. I set her on her feet at the end of the bed. She watches me as I lower myself onto the mattress and lie back, propping myself on my elbow.

In silence, I stare at her. She stands perfectly still as I let my eyes roam her from the top of her platinum head to the tips of the toes I can see poking out of her sexy, strappy shoes.

I'm gonna enjoy bringing the hellcat out in this one. She wants to be free of her past, free of who she was, but she has to be free of control first. So I'm going to take it from her.

SIXTEEN

Marissa

"I'm gonna give you something you've never had before. And you're gonna give me what I want," he states. It's as though I have no choice in the matter.

A little thrill races through me. I've always been in control. And before, I would never have let a man talk to me that way. But with Nash it's different. He's different. He's wild. He's dangerous. And I'm ready for that. All that. I need it, crave it. I know it can never be anything more than this, but for one small space in time, he's mine. And I'm his.

"Take your hair down," he orders. Reaching for the pins that hold my hair in place over one shoulder, I remove them, without question doing as he asks. There's something exciting and a little naughty about being subservient to him in this sexual way. Warmth gathers in the lowest part of my belly.

Part of my hair cascades down my back. I shake my head so the rest of it follows.

"Unzip your dress."

I've never done a striptease before. I wouldn't even know how to do a sexy one, so I don't even try.

For a moment I feel lost. Maybe even a little shy, which is new for me.

I turn to the side, in profile to him, and I reach behind me to unzip my dress. The strap on my shoulder slips off and I hold the bodice in place, hugging it to me in modesty.

I glance over at Nash where he's reclining on the bed, watching me. His eyes are throwing flames so hot, I feel my skin flush. And I like it.

"Let it fall."

I let my shaking arms fall away from my body, and the dress slips to my hips and stops, revealing my entire torso, covered in nothing but a lacy strapless bra.

"Now the bra."

I unhook my bra, taking a deep breath as the air hits the sensitive skin of my erect nipples. Nash's eyes are on them. I can feel it as though it's a physical touch.

"Now the rest."

I run my palms down my hips, dragging the dress with them until it falls into a heap on the floor, pooling around my ankles. From beneath my lashes, I glance at Nash again. His eyes are on my butt.

"And the panties."

My heart is slamming against my ribs as I hook my thumbs under the lace band of my panties and pull them down my legs. I don't stop until they're lying at my feet with my dress. I stay bent over, ready to work open the strap of my shoe, when Nash stops me.

"No. Leave them on." I straighten, but remain turned, still in profile to Nash. "Now face me," he murmurs, his voice low and deep. I take a breath and hold it as I pivot toward him, clad in nothing but a blush and my five-hundred-dollar stilettos.

His eyes burn fiery holes into mine before they drop and travel the length of my body. Slowly, they make their way back up again. I've never been more self-conscious of my thin frame or my small breasts. Nevertheless, I stand confidently and let him look his fill, even though I'm quaking inside.

When his gaze locks onto mine again, it's even hotter than before.

"You're perfect," he says simply. Relief floods me, followed quickly by a rush of blood, pouring hotly into all the right places at once. "Pink nipples that beg to be sucked," he whispers, "a tight stomach that begs to be kissed, and long legs that beg to be spread."

His words are delicious fingers that tickle my skin. Chills spread across my chest and down my abdomen. I feel my nipples tingle as if he were actually doing what he said. Hot, sticky honey gushes to the apex of my thighs.

"I want to know what you like, how you like to be touched. And you're going to show me. Bring your hands to your breasts. And touch them."

I'm long past being embarrassed. It's either go big or go home. And I'm already here. So I'm going big.

Raising my hands, I cup my breasts. His eyes follow my movements.

"Squeeze them," he commands, so I do, massaging them in a slow, gentle knead. "Now the nipples," he says. "Pinch them, make them hard." Taking the pebbles between my thumb and forefinger, I roll them until they are like firm buttons. "That's right, baby. Now put one hand between your legs."

My face burns, but I'm only vaguely aware of it. I'm transfixed by Nash's hot gaze. His eyes are black as sin and heavy lidded as he watches me. They follow one of my hands as it travels down my stomach to the achy spot between my thighs. When I move my palm over my damp flesh, his tongue sneaks out to wet his lips. My pulse speeds up in direct correlation. "Mmm, I love watching you make yourself feel good."

It's incredibly erotic, listening to his words, touching myself with him watching, knowing he's enjoying it.

"Come lie down on the bed with me."

I'm so ready to feel his hands on me, I don't even ask any questions. I simply walk to the bed and sit beside him.

"Lie back," he commands softly, his eyes never leaving mine. They're dark and forbidden. Just like Nash himself. He's inaccessible, unattainable. He's everything that I shouldn't want, yet I do. So I'll take what he's willing to give me.

I lie back and I wait while his eyes rove over me again. "Bend your knees and put your feet on the bed."

I do.

My skin is damp and dewy with desire, with the need for him to take me places I've never been before. I would almost beg for him to touch me as he watches. But he doesn't. Instead, he gets to his feet and moves to stand at the foot of the bed, his eyes meeting mine from over my knees.

"Spread your legs," he whispers. I move my feet apart. "More." I let my knees fall open a little more. "Mmm, perfect. Now show me where you want me to touch you."

A small part of me feels flustered and self-conscious, but if it will bring him to me, bring him *into* me faster, I'm willing to give him what he wants.

I close my eyes and imagine that Nash is touching me. I slide one hand down my stomach and over the short hair between my legs. I pause there, a moment of insecurity overwhelming me. My eyes pop open and I see Nash watching my hand. In my stillness, his gaze rises to meet mine. It's flashing and fiery and, without a word, it urges me on.

Slowly, I move one finger down and push it inside me. Nash's eyes drop to my hand again. I pull my finger out and massage my clitoris with it. I jerk against the contact. I'm so ready for him, if he doesn't hurry, I'll finish before we even get started.

Desperation spurs me on. My fingers move in a mindless rhythm that pleases my body as my other hand finds my tight nipple again. The stimulation coupled with his eyes on me is sensory overload. I moan, unable to help myself. I see the muscle in his jaw tic as he grits his teeth. That's when I realize that, in playing his little game, the victor has become the victim. He's torturing himself.

I grow bolder. I let my legs fall farther apart and I rub myself, my body writhing under my touch and his watchful stare. I slip another finger in alongside the first and I move them together, in and out.

Nash's lips part the tiniest bit and I hear his breath huffing between them. He's just as excited as I am. That knowledge sends an electric pang of desire zipping through my body to land right beneath my moving fingers.

With lightning speed, Nash moves forward and grabs my wrist, his fingers winding around it like bands of steel, stopping my movement. His eyes never leave mine as he tugs my fingers out of my body and raises my hand to his mouth. He rubs my fingertips back and forth across his bottom lip, leaving a streak of moisture there. I catch my breath when his tongue sneaks out to taste it. "God, you taste good," he groans before he sucks my fingers into his mouth.

I feel the slick heat of his tongue rasping along my sensitive fingertips as he licks them. I feel the sensation all the way down to my core. I gasp in delicious surprise when I feel his teeth nip my fingertip. The muscles between my legs clench in wanton anticipation.

"That just makes me want more," he whispers. "And something tells me you want me to take more." As he speaks, he moves to put one knee on the bed, insinuating his hips between my legs. Still holding my wrist, I feel his free hand work its way down the inside of my thigh to the unbearable heat at my center.

He pushes one long finger inside me, stealing my breath. He moves it farther into me as he thrusts his hips forward. "Unzip my pants," he commands gruffly, finally releasing my wrist. He moves another finger inside me, crooking them both as he pulls them out. "Right now." My comprehension is slow, his words barely penetrating the sensual web that his fingers are weaving over me.

Bending slightly at my waist, I reach for his zipper. The button is already undone and I can feel his hardness straining against the backs of my fingers as I pull the little gold tongue down.

The material parts to reveal his long, thick shaft. Without even thinking, I reach inside and wrap my fingers around it—soft skin over warm steel. I hear the hiss of air through his teeth just before he pushes a third finger inside me. Hard and deep, he penetrates me as I squeeze his length.

"I don't have a condom, but I'm clean. I assume you're . . . protected?"

I can only manage a nod as my thumb slides over the moistened tip of him and he arches into my hand.

He groans. "You're gonna come for me, come like you've never come before. Then I'm gonna lick you until you come again. With my tongue inside you."

Removing his fingers from me, he widens his stance as he slides both hands under my hips and lifts them off the bed. Guiding his thick head to my entrance, he looks up to meet my eyes just before he pulls me roughly toward him, my body sliding wetly over his. With my legs wrapped around his waist and my back arched sharply off the bed, he plunges into me over and over again until I feel the dam break.

I cry out, the pleasure more intense than anything I could ever have imagined. It completely overwhelms me, captivates me, transports me. I'm in a world where only Nash and I exist, only what lies between us. Only the passion that we share.

Nash slows his rhythm to a deep grinding, the friction accentuating each wave of my orgasm. Before the spasms of my pleasure subside, he moves me back up onto the bed until my hips are once more supported by the mattress. He eases out of me and drops to his knees, hooking my legs over his shoulders and burying his face in the warm, pulsing flesh there.

My body jerks at the first touch of his hot tongue. Gently, he licks at my swollen flesh until my orgasm has nearly died, and then he becomes more aggressive.

Reaching around my leg, resting his arm on my stomach, he parts my folds with his fingers and draws the rigid nub at the top of my crease into his mouth, sucking on it and flicking it with the tip of his tongue. Once more, I feel the tension escalate. I fist one hand in the duvet and curl the fingers of my other hand in his long hair, holding hold him to me.

"Ohmigod, Nash. That feels so good."

"Let me have it, baby. One more time. Let me taste it all."

The vibrations of his words stimulate me even further as he moves the fingers of his other hand to my core, thrusting one into me, pushing me closer to the edge.

Putting his hands behind my knees, Nash rolls my hips up, toward my head, pushing my legs as far apart as they'll go, opening me completely to him and his wicked mouth. In and out he moves his fingers as he licks and flicks with his tongue, faster and faster.

I melt into my second orgasm in slow, breathtaking waves. I feel my body squeeze his fingers. "Oh yeah, that's it. Come for me." Spreading me wide, Nash rubs my clitoris with his thumb as he thrusts his tongue inside me, lapping up every drop of moisture my body spills for him, for his touch. Just the thought of what he's doing, of him wanting to taste me like this, is enough to renew the spasms of my climax.

When my body is limp and nearly numb from pleasure, Nash crawls up onto the bed, between my legs. From between the slits of my eyelids, I see him guide his engorged head to my entrance. And then he's inside me and I can't breathe again.

He stretches me so tight, he pauses to let me adjust before he withdraws and plunges into me. Wetly, he pulls out and thrusts again.

His lips find mine and he groans into my mouth. I swallow it along with my own sounds of abandon. I taste the salty sweetness of my body on his tongue. It sends a thrill through me that this was what he so wanted from me—my essence, the evidence of my pleasure.

His lips are rough on mine. Hungry. His hands are callused on my breasts. Urgent. His body drives deep inside me. Desperate.

My entire world is on fire. I can't tell if I'm nearing my third orgasm or if he's just managed to rekindle the embers of the last one, but I feel my body clutching at his, milking it, begging for its release.

He tears his mouth away from mine long enough to whisper into my ear. "Tell me I can come inside you. I want you to feel it."

His words strengthen the contractions of my body around his. More than anything, I want to feel him come inside me. "Yes," I pant shallowly.

With a growl, I feel him stiffen as the first hot spurt of his orgasm fills me. Two more thrusts and then Nash slows his rhythm, grinding his hips into mine, rubbing me both inside and out, liquid heat spilling into me and out of me at the same time. The sensation is violent in its intensity. I dig my nails into his back to keep from falling off the edge of the world.

"Mmm, that's right, baby. Feel it."

His words are like gasoline on an already raging fire. They're a physical touch that keeps me on the crest of swell after swell of my climax.

SEVENTEEN

Nash

I knew sex with this woman would be satisfying. The depth of satisfaction I feel right now—lying on top of her, still inside her, our damp chests clinging together—is just a testament to how much I needed this.

Badly.

Very badly.

I fully expect my desire for her to start tailing off. It always does. No woman holds my attention for very long, and it's always strictly sexual while it lasts. Besides, I still have a feeling Marissa will remember one of these days. And when she does, when she realizes what happened, she'll hate me. As well she should. It was a pretty shitty thing to do.

I guess it's a good sign that I'm starting to feel bad about it. Guilt is a nuisance, but maybe the presence of it means I'm starting to remember what humanity feels like. It's been lost to me for a long time, living among the animals. The criminals. The lowest of the low.

But I could do without the return of guilt. It figures that it would be the first sentiment to pierce my thick scar tissue, the only one sharp enough to penetrate my years of emotional exile.

Marissa wiggles beneath me, situating, settling in for a long snuggle. My immediate inclination happens inside her. Blood rushes to my soft head, turning it semihard. I'm ready to go again, which is not unusual for me at all. I have a very healthy sexual appetite and short recovery time.

No, it's my second reaction that I find strange and bothersome. The muscles in my arms actually twitch and I nearly pull her in closer to me. *That* is very unusual.

Maybe it's just the fact that I haven't had any in a few weeks. Yeah, that's gotta be it. I've just missed women close. Any woman.

That rationale doesn't make me feel any better. It doesn't make me any more comfortable with it. And still, I don't like it.

Extricating myself from the tangle of our arms and legs, I roll to the end of the bed and get to my feet, zipping my pants. "I'm thirsty," I say casually. "You want something?"

Marissa is sitting up in bed now, her arms curled around her torso, covering herself. Her expression isn't as much wounded as it seems to be puzzled. I'm okay with puzzled. It's the wounded part that bugs the shit out of me. I hate it when women get all pissy and hurt because I'm not the warm and fuzzy type. You'd think they'd figure that out within ten minutes of talking to me, but they don't. That or they all think they can be the one to change me. But that's just not gonna happen.

"Um, no. I'll, uh, I'll use the bathroom and get ready for bed, I think."

I nod and make my way to the kitchen, leaving her to all her girly rituals.

I grab a beer from the fridge and take it to the sofa, intent on doing some brainstorming, going over my plans in case the Dmitry situation doesn't work like I hope. Of course, even if it does, all the other pieces would have to fall together perfectly, too. And that doesn't happen very often. So it behooves me to have as many other options as I can think of.

My mind is whirling away on the different pieces and players in the grand scheme of this tangle when an image of Marissa moaning beneath me rises up to distract me. I push the thought aside in favor of the faces of the Russian mafia members that I've seen. Within two minutes, I'm thinking of her again, of how soft her skin is and what her neck smells like.

I take another long pull from my beer bottle, examining it closely and feeling guilty all over again. Over what I did so long ago.

Damn, she's gonna be pissed.

Maybe she won't ever remember. Maybe she'll never find out. I don't know why I even care, but I kinda hope she doesn't. It's not like I set out to make her hate me, like I *want* for that to happen.

The swelling of my dick behind my zipper is making it impossible for me to think, so I drain my beer, put the bottle in the trash, and head back toward the bedroom.

Let's see how willing she is to play along now.

When I get to the door, she's just pulling back the covers to get into bed. She stops and looks at me. We stare at each other for at least two full minutes before she drops the covers and turns to fully face me.

I cross the room slowly and stop in front of her, giving her one last opportunity to change her mind. I thread my fingers into the hair at her temples, gazing into her beautiful blue eyes. When she shows no hesitation, no sign of resistance, I take her lips in a kiss that's meant to consume. The problem is, within seconds, I'm not sure who is consuming whom.

I rub the thick, soft towel across my chest and down my arms, drying water droplets and thinking about how rested I feel. I don't think I've slept that good in months. Maybe years.

Good sex'll do that to a man.

I dry my abdomen, making note of the red line where I was stabbed. It doesn't bother me at all this morning and looks to be healing perfectly. I continue drying.

The muscles in my arm flex, drawing my attention to the winding, scroll-like tattooing that covers my right arm from elbow to deltoid. I think of the significance of each band of swirling art and I hope that maybe, just maybe the days of not knowing if I'll live to see my next sunrise are over. Maybe I'll never add another layer of tats to my arm.

For some reason Marissa pops into my head. She's so different from anyone I've had in my life for the last seven years. She's like a reminder of what life could've been, what it should've been for me. And it's nice to experience a little bit of that, even if it is too late and only an illusion. My life can never be what it was meant to be. My future is set to some extent. Inevitable. Unavoidable. Unchangeable.

I growl at my thoughts, at the trapped feeling I'm getting. I don't like inevitable. I don't like anything I can't control.

I'm partly relieved when I hear voices. On the one hand, they're a welcome distraction. But on the other hand, I feel uneasy when I hear a man's voice, one I don't readily recognize.

I dress quickly and make my way out to the living room. I'm not at all pleased to see Cash's friend Gavin sitting on the couch across from Marissa, relaxed and chatting away like he belongs there.

When I stop at the coffee table, arms crossed over my chest, Marissa glances up at me, causing Gavin to look up, too.

"Good morning, mate. Looks like Doc got you all squared away," Gavin says. I couldn't hear the hint of his accent from the bathroom, but now I can. It's not thick, but it's there.

His demeanor is friendly. But I still don't like him.

I grunt in response. "What the hell are you doing here so early?"

"I was on my way to the club. Thought I'd stop by and check on Marissa."

It aggravates the hell out of me that he's not intimidated by me. He's nearly as big as I am, so I wouldn't expect my size to make an impression, but I'm a lot rougher than Cash, and I would think a guy like this might sense danger. And steer clear of it. He's treading on thin ice right now. I'm not sure why his presence here irritates me, but it does and he ought to be smart enough to sense it and get his ass out of here.

"Well, you have. And as you can see, she's fine. I've been with her. I'll keep her safe. No reason for you to be concerned about her anymore."

Gavin's sharp blue eyes narrow on me. He makes no response, nor does he make any move to leave, which only further aggravates me.

Marissa clears her throat, drawing our attention to her. She smiles brightly. "Who wants breakfast?" she asks as she rises.

"We don't want you to go to any trouble. I think I'll just grab something later. I'll follow Gavin over to the club. I need to talk to Cash, anyway."

Gavin's grin is playful, like he finds it amusing that I just cock-blocked him. I don't find it amusing at all.

Asshole.

Marissa just looks from me to Gavin and back again. No one says anything until Gavin gets up.

"You don't have to leave, Gavin. And it's no trouble to fix something, Nash," Marissa says pleasantly.

"You don't need any more trouble, Marissa. And I can tell you that this guy's trouble. If he gives a damn about you, he'll keep his distance." I turn to Gavin, daring him to argue. "Right, Gavin?"

I've never been one to beat around the bush.

Gavin smiles again. "It's funny, I was thinking the same thing about you."

"I'm here to keep her safe, not to bring more shit into her life."

"You're saying that your mere presence doesn't put her in more danger?"

"I'm saying I can keep her safe."

If I'm being honest, I can't say that I don't bring danger to her door, because I probably do. But that's different.

"I can, too. Probably even better than you can. Maybe we should just leave it up to Marissa."

I grit my teeth. This guy needs his ass kicked. "That's a good idea, especially for me. She's already said she wants me to stay with her."

Even though that's not exactly what happened, I doubt Marissa will refute it.

Gavin looks to Marissa. "Is that true?"

"Yes, I told him he could stay here."

Gavin laughs and nods in my direction. "Not quite how he made it sound, but I understand your predicament. A nice sheila like you will always do the polite thing. Just know that if you need anything at all, you've got my number. I'm only a phone call away."

He already gave her his number? What the f—

He turns to me, all smug and arrogant. "I guess we'd better be on our way then, right, mate?"

He gives my shoulder a friendly slap as he passes. The thing is, it's a little on the firm side. Makes me want to rip his arm off and beat the shit out of him with it.

I clench my jaw against the urge. Instead of acknowledging Gavin, however, I walk to Marissa. Looking down into her face, I raise my hands to cup her cheeks and bend toward her.

I didn't intend for the kiss to be a chaste, standard good-bye kiss, but I didn't intend for it to be so . . . stimulating, either. It's like we're combustible, like we have one default setting between us—fire.

Her lips are enough to make me ache in all the right places. The pain in the ass, however, is that I can't do anything about it. Instead of carrying Marissa back to her bedroom and doing depraved things to her, I've gotta escort this ballsy bastard back to Dual.

When I lift my head, I'm surprised to see that Marissa looks angry rather than turned on like I am. Her eyes fume for a few seconds before she puts her hands on my shoulders and rises to her tiptoes to whisper in my ear. Her words leave me in no doubt as to why she's mad.

"If you ever kiss me like that again just to make a point, I'll slap the taste right out of your mouth. I don't care who's watching."

When she leans away, she's smiling politely, but her eyes are like sparkling firecrackers. If anything, I'm even more turned on.

I can't help but grin.

I'll be damned. She can be feisty.

"Fair enough," I say before turning back to Gavin. I give him a broad, cold smile.

I hope that smug prick is squirming on the inside.

EIGHTEEN

Marissa

I've cleaned the kitchen, polished the floors, scrubbed my bathroom, had a shower, and given myself a pedicure. As I sit on the edge of my bed, surveying my bedroom, I realize there's absolutely nothing I can do to keep my mind off Nash. I knew he would get under my skin; it happened almost immediately. There's something about him that's so familiar, beyond his being the twin of a guy I used to date. It pulls me in like a physical tie.

It helps that I was primed to latch onto someone like him. I wanted to get lost in something far from the normal, far from what's expected in my life. I needed it, needed *him*. Still do. But I didn't expect it to be this . . . intense.

Every few minutes, my mind will stray back to last night, to his hands and his lips, to his body and his words. I get all hot and bothered within seconds. And that's aside from the sweat I broke while cleaning.

It's not such a bad thing, my attraction to him. It's the emotional distance I feel from him that's bugging me. I suspected he'd be in and out of my life like a flash of lightning—bright and electric and then gone without a trace—but on some level I must've expected him to be a little more open with me, a little more . . . feeling. But it's like the only thing he feels is my physical presence, my *body*. And, of course, anger. Lots and lots of anger. It's always there, hovering just beneath the surface. It's like nothing is stronger than that, no feeling or person or emotion.

I think he loses himself in me much the same way I lose myself in him, only his is much more temporary and transient. As soon as his mind strays from our physical connection, from desire, he's right back in his miserable past and his equally miserable present.

What bothers me most is that I'm starting to suspect there's nothing I can do about it. No way I can change it, no way to make a dent in his life and his heart the way I think he'll be making one in mine.

Hearts don't often break even. One person is usually more hurt while the other is more relieved. But in this instance, there is likely to be devastation on one side. And it's likely to be me. Yet here I am, thinking about him, anxiously anticipating the next time I'll see him or hear from him.

You're like a schoolgirl with one horrific crush.

Or maybe a glutton for punishment.

There are a thousand reasons I should stay away from him and only one that I shouldn't. But that one reason is powerful enough to keep me right here, in the thick of things.

He's the forbidden fruit. And I'm tempted beyond what I can resist.

With a growl of frustration, I walk to my closet to put on some presentable work clothes. I've got to get out of the house. But I don't want to go to work. I figure a trip to the library will be both distracting *and* productive. At least I can continue trying to build a case, a case I know little about against people I know nearly nothing about.

Three and a half frustrating hours later, I'm driving home, considering calling one of my law professors for some guidance. What gives me pause is that it would be utterly humiliating to admit that I knew where my career was going because I was a spoiled little rich girl with a future set in stone, one that had nothing to do with criminal law. I felt zero need to retain what I'd learned in several of my classes.

Only now I need it. And so do the people I care about. I want justice not only for myself, but for Nash and Olivia. And a tiny bit for Cash, I guess. He *did* play a big part in rescuing me.

I still have mixed feelings about him for the most part. What I like least about him is that he reminds me of someone I no longer want to be, of someone I'd rather not ever think about again. But when I see him, that's what I'm reminded of—the old me. And I don't like it.

Every thought in my head is banished to a back corner as I approach the condo door. I haven't walked through the front door by myself since the night someone was waiting on the other side of it. And even though my brain tells me I'm being ridiculous, that I wasn't even the one they wanted that time and that there's no reason for them to grab me again after they let me go, my muscles freeze. I'm stuck in a terrified stare, on the sidewalk, facing my front door, with no one around to help me.

The muted *bleep* from my phone sounds from deep inside my

purse. I force my muscles into action, reaching with one shaking hand into my bag to retrieve my phone. I slide a trembling finger over the button at the bottom of the rectangle to light up the screen.

It's a text. Three letters. Two words. One sentiment. Something so simple. Yet it changes everything.

U ok?

It's Nash.

There's nothing in the message to identify who it is. But I know. Deep down in my soul, I know who it is. And he might as well be behind me, standing with me, an ever-protective shadow. The effect is that profound.

Maybe it's knowing that I'm not really alone, no matter how often I feel that way. Maybe it's knowing that there's someone out there who cares about what happens to me. Maybe it's just the fact that it's from Nash. Maybe it's that he was thinking of me, that he took the time to text me. Maybe it's that he wanted to check on me, that he even *thought* to check on me. Maybe it's that he seems always to be there for me when I need him, even though he doesn't necessarily set out to be.

Whatever the real reason, whether one of those, none of those or a combination of them all, it breaks the firm grip of fear, not completely but enough to let rational thought in.

I type out my short reply.

Yes.

I slide my phone back into my purse. I know I won't get a response from him, but that doesn't matter. Even though I know it's a mistake, that it's probably leading me nowhere good, I walk toward the door with a smile on my face and hope in my heart.

I feel much more at ease once I'm safely inside with the door locked behind me. I won't lie. I checked every closet and under both beds, but that's just being responsible. Right? Right.

I peel off my suit jacket and hang it in the closet. I grab a hair band as I pass through the bathroom, pulling my hair into a messy bun as I set about changing the rest of my clothes.

I'm attempting to stuff wayward strands of blond hair into a fairly neat pile atop my head when the doorbell rings. My hands pause in midair. Reflexively, my pulse speeds up. My mind rushes through names and faces of people who might be visiting me at such an odd time.

I know it can't be Nash; he's not that polite. He'd try the door-knob first, and then when he figured out it was locked, he'd knock. Loudly, I'm sure. Unless he knows which key on Cash's BMW key ring belongs to my door. I didn't tell him. I mean, he's staying with me, but I didn't give him *that much* freedom. That would've required too much trust.

I make a mental note to get that key back from Cash.

I return to puzzling over my visitor. It shouldn't be my father. Or anyone else from the office. Daddy's working and anyone else would call first.

Who else could it be?

I reason with myself that it's broad daylight, and that the like-lihood that it's someone with nefarious plans is slim to none. Still, I look out the peephole before I slide the deadbolt open.

I'm puzzled by what I see. Shoulder-length blond hair, pretty face, skintight miniskirt and snug T-shirt, all on a Christina Apple-gate look-alike. It's Olivia's friend, Ginger. And she looks irritated. The question is: Why is she *here*?

Probably looking for Olivia.

I flip the lock and twist the knob, opening the door.

"Hi," I say stiltedly. I'm uneasy. I realize my instincts are spot on once Ginger speaks. The conversation does *not* start off well.

"I think we can both agree that you've treated Olivia like shit most of her life, but," she says emphatically, "I'll give you one last chance to make it up to her before I'm forced to kick your ass and steal your man."

I'm essentially dumbstruck by her speech, so it's no surprise that I find a response to only one small portion of it. "I don't have a man."

"Sure you do," she says with a grin. "I've seen you watching that other brother. I don't know how in the *hell* one uterus can spit out three boys that look like that, but I thank God every day for just such a phenomenon."

I learn a couple of things during this very short introduction to Ginger. Number one, she has no idea about what's going on with Cash and Nash. Obviously, she assumes Nash is actually a third brother.

The second thing I learn is that I like Ginger. I can totally see why Olivia enjoys her company so much.

"Well, you can't very well steal what I don't have."

"Please," she says with a roll of her eyes and a dismissive swipe of her hand. "Even if he *was* yours, if I wanted some o' that, I could get it. Men are helpless to resist me when I turn on the charm." The grin she gives me is devilish and teasing. Evidently she's joking.

I think.

"The point is, you're a beautiful girl and you can have him if you set your mind to it. But"—her look turns warning—"if you hurt Olivia, I'll destroy you. Plain and simple. Fair enough?"

I feel the urge to laugh, but I don't. I have a feeling Ginger could be quite feisty if she thought I wasn't taking her seriously. "Fair enough," I agree mildly. "So, what brings you here? Other than threats of bodily harm."

Her eyes light up. "A surprise party. You interested?"

Despite the life of privilege I've enjoyed, I've never participated in a surprise party. I've never really wanted to. Until now. It sounds like lighthearted fun. And I need some lighthearted fun. Heck, I just need some lighthearted *anything*. Although I'm making some major changes that should have the opposite effect, it seems my life has gotten *even more* intense and complicated than it was before. Still yet, I'd take it over the blind, thinly disguised misery I was previously trapped within. Any day of the week.

Any.

Day.

"I'm sure I should ask more questions before I agree to anything, but I'm gonna throw caution to the wind and say yes right away. What did you have in mind?"

"Can I come in? Or are you gonna make me stand outside all day?"

"Oh. Sorry," I say, stepping aside so she can come inside. Ginger walks into the living room as I shut the door. She stops right in front of the coffee table and turns toward me. Her eyes are narrowed like she's assessing me. I stop and look left and right. "What?"

"You know, I think you really have changed. You don't strike me as a wicked bitch-on-two-sticks at all."

I grin, not sure how to take that. "Um, thank you?"

Ginger smiles and drops down onto one end of the sofa. "You're welcome. But your legs are pretty skinny."

Ahhh, so that's what the "two sticks" meant.

I look down at my legs, poking out from beneath my skirt, and then I look at Ginger's as she crosses them toward me. "They're not much thinner than yours."

"I didn't say it was a bad thing. They're better to wrap around prey, don't you think?"

I grin again. Yes, this woman is a character. "I've never really thought about it like that, but I guess you're right."

"Of course I'm right. That's something you should get used to. There's no sense in arguing. Just ask Olivia. She'll tell you. I'm full of raging hormones and wisdom. And, on the weekends, vodka," she adds with a wink.

"Don't you work on the weekends?"

I thought Olivia had told me she was a bartender where she used to work.

Ginger looks at me with a blank expression. "What's your point?" As I stammer for something to say, she starts laughing. "I'm kidding. What kind of an employee would I be if I turned up pickled every weekend?"

"A bad one?"

"Damn straight. And I'm a great employee. And you can pass that along to Cash, since I'm seriously thinking about moving to the city and I'll be needing a job. And, you know, any job where there's a chance I'll run into one or a dozen hot young men is the job for me."

"I'll be sure to mention it."

"Great. Now, down to business. Olivia's birthday is tomorrow and I'd like to throw her a little surprise party."

"Olivia's birthday is tomorrow?" I think to myself that I really am a terrible person. Not only is she related to me, but we live together and I had no idea. And of course she'd never mention it. Because she's decent. And that's what decent people do. "Ohmigod, I really am a wicked bitch-on-two-sticks, aren't I?"

"Let's call you an *ex* wicked bitch-on-two-sticks. And 'ex' doesn't mean shit, right? Like ex-boyfriends. Who gives a damn about them? The past is the past. Let it go and move on. The point is to learn from our mistakes and do better the next go-round. And now's your chance. You in?"

I feel Ginger rubbing off on me already. "Hell yeah, I'm in!" I agree enthusiastically, laughing as I say words that sound so out of character for me.

"That's more like it," she says excitedly, leaning in toward me conspiratorially. "Okay, so I got Tad to agree to it, so we can have the party there. Olivia's dad's in and I've already told all of her old friends, so that takes care of my end. The problem is, I didn't have any of you Atlanta people's phone numbers, which is why I had to drive my ass all the way up here to get in touch with you." Ginger reaches into her bright red purse and pulls out her cell phone. "I'm taking care of that right now, though. Here," she says handing me her iPhone. "Put your number in there. And Cash's, if you know it. We're all one big, happy family," she says with a smile. Her expression sobers a bit. "I just wish we shared everything. Damn, those twins are hot! And that third brother, too. And even the foreigner. Good gawd!" She fans her face and crosses her legs in the other direction. "I love a man with an accent."

"You must mean Gavin. I don't think he's seeing anyone. At least not that I know of."

"Realllly," she says, arching a brow with increased interest. "I've always thought it's only polite to make sure your best friends get laid on your birthday, too. Maybe it's a Southern thang and Olivia was raised the same way."

I laugh outright. "Or maybe it's a Ginger thang."

"Even better," she says, wiggling her eyebrows. "Ginger thangs are *always* a good idea."

"I'm beginning to see how you'd think so."

She nods and winks at me. "I like you. And you're smart, too. Two things I require in a friend. You and I are gonna get along just fine."

"Glad to hear it."

Ginger leans across the couch like she's going to tell me a big secret. "I don't know if Olivia told you, but I give great advice about sex, so if you get hold of that hot piece of ass and don't quite know what to do with it, don't be afraid to call. I've always got some ideas." She nods as though she's done her good deed for the day.

Ginger's public service message.

"If he gives me any trouble, I'll be sure to call."

"Girl, if he *doesn't* give you trouble, he's not half the man he looks to be. That one, the rough one, looks like he could tear a woman to shreds with just one look. I'd be highly disappointed if he didn't turn your panties inside out and your world upside down."

I wonder for a second if I should tell her that he's already done both of those things, but then I decide against it. No matter how funny I think she is or how much I think I'll like her, Ginger is a stranger to me. And I've still got enough discretion bred into me to be inclined to keep my mouth shut. So I do.

"I'll keep you posted. How's that?"

"Fair enough, but be warned that I like details, so if you call me, be prepared to tell me everything. Besides, I work better if I have the full picture of what's going on. And I'm a huge pervert. We can't forget that." She winks at me again.

"I doubt I'll be forgetting that any time soon."

"Good girl," she says, patting me on the knee.

Yep, I like this woman. How could I not?

NINETEEN

Nash

After a frustrating morning, I'd hoped my day would get better. Only it hasn't. I'm just as frustrated now, driving back to Marissa's, as I was when I left this morning.

I followed Gavin to the club, mostly just to make sure he didn't decide to pay a return visit to Marissa. It's not like I'm jealous. I'm not that guy. I don't get jealous over women. I can take them or leave them. There's always another one just around the corner. No reason to get too attached to any particular one. So I know it's not that. I think it's primarily that he messed up my morning. And I just don't like the thought of that Australian asshole hitting on Marissa. It pisses me off. I don't like him and I don't want him around. Period.

Cash had been taking Olivia to school, so once he returned, he and Gavin got down to taking care of some club business. Nothing I had any interest in. Once I was sure Gavin was thoroughly occupied, I took off.

My inclination was to go back to Marissa's. And that's exactly why I didn't. It's too soon. I shouldn't want to go back to her yet. Not even for sex. So I didn't.

But that hasn't stopped me from thinking about her every few minutes all day.

For the same reason, I purposely stayed away all evening, too. I texted her a few times, just to make sure she's okay. I used the same two words each time.

U ok?

And her response was the same single word each time.

Yes.

It's the responsible thing to do, especially considering that she's only in this mess because of my family. The least I can do is make sure she doesn't get herself killed.

But that doesn't mean I have to stay with her every minute of every day. And it's the fact that I sort of *wanted* to go back that kept me from doing exactly that.

I don't like feeling weak, and there's something about her that's starting to make me feel weak. I think about her too often, even when I try not to. It's like I might not be in complete control of the situation. And that's unacceptable. So I avoided her.

I spent most of the afternoon and evening in Cash's "Nash" condo looking through law books. No, I haven't been to law school, but I have enough gray matter to be able to read law and interpret it, especially when I have an Internet connection and access to all the reference materials I might need for clarification purposes.

What I've managed to discern is probably pretty much what both Cash and Marissa already knew—there are a lot of pieces to a RICO case. While it's definitely doable, in our case, it would require the cooperation of more than one person. And what I know from extensive past experience is that you can rarely count on other people to do the right thing.

Which is why I wanted a plan B. And C. And D. As many as I can get, in fact.

My plan A is and will always be to put a bullet in Duffy and any of the other involved parties I can identify and get my hands on. It's not like I've never had blood on my hands or dead men on my conscience. But, considering the consequences should I get caught doing it on American soil . . . I wouldn't mind if we could get them the legal way, either. It's not exactly my dream to spend my last days in prison.

My anger returns, anger that I'm even in this position to start with. And with it, frustration. And the desire to stop thinking for just a little while.

I press harder on the accelerator. I remind myself that I'm not speeding toward Marissa per se; I'm speeding toward a much-needed distraction. Nothing more.

Anticipation curls in my stomach and I feel blood rush south as I think about sinking into her soft, warm body. I mean, sex is sex, but I have to admit we have damn good sex. Damn good!

I feel a frown pull my eyebrows together when I pull up out front and have to park behind a Mercedes. It could belong to any-body, but I don't like that it's here, whoever the owner is. Most likely it's someone from Marissa's old life, the one she hates and wants to escape, so I automatically dislike this person.

It's an E-Class, sleek and black with tinted windows. I have no trouble imagining that it belongs to some polished douchenozzle of a lawyer.

I'm instantly grouchy. Well, grouch*ier*.

I cut the engine and look at the clock in the dashboard.

And what the hell is someone doing visiting so late, anyway? It's nearly nine.

I walk quickly up the sidewalk to the front door. I don't knock; I simply twist the knob and walk in, unannounced. If Marissa doesn't like it, she can kiss my ass. And if whoever is visiting her doesn't like it, they can kiss my ass, too. Unless they'd prefer to make it physical, which I'd be more than happy to do. Breaking some bones might make me feel a whole lot better about the situation. About life in general.

My irritation spikes to anger when I see the lawyer from the library sitting on the couch across from Marissa—Jensen something or other. It only makes it worse that Marissa looks the way she does. She's wearing some sort of sexy lace top that cups her breasts perfectly, and a skirt that makes her legs look long and slender. Her hair is up with a few strands dangling down over her shoulders. She looks like she just climbed out from under some lucky man. And that she's ready for more.

Who the hell does she think she's trying to impress?

She smiles when I stop at the edge of the living room. "Cash," she says with emphasis, "you remember Jensen from the library, right?"

My only response is a grunt of agreement.

"I came across some case information I thought Marissa might find helpful," he says politely by way of explanation.

"I bet you did," I say snidely. "And you felt like it couldn't wait until morning, right?"

Jensen laughs uncomfortably and glances at Marissa. "Uh, well, I have court early, so I'll be at work well before dawn, and this is a big case, so I wasn't sure when I'd have a chance to get it to her otherwise."

"How thoughtful of you," I say sarcastically. "Well, now that you've dropped it off, I guess you'll need to be on your way. Get rested up before the big day, right?"

Jensen clears his throat and rises to his feet. "Actually," he says, looking down at Marissa, "I do need to be going. I appreciate the coffee and I hope what I brought helps."

Marissa rises, too. "Thank you so much, Jensen. It's very helpful information and I really appreciate you going to all the trouble of looking this up and then bringing it over."

"It's my pleasure. Really."

I watch as Marissa smiles up at this poser. For some reason I want to snap his scrawny neck.

"If there's ever anything I can help you with on the corporate side of things, let me know. I owe you."

"I might just take you up on that," he says with a predatory smile.

My blood is boiling.

He turns to walk past me to the door. Marissa follows him, shooting me a stern look of disapproval as she passes.

Before he can make it out the door, my phone buzzes from my pocket. I pull it out and look at the lighted screen. My pulse picks up when I recognize the number. I dialed it very recently.

Dmitry.

The timing couldn't be worse. I can't talk in front of this guy— or Marissa for that matter—but I'm not leaving until he's gone. Like, I-see-his-taillights-at-the-stop-sign gone.

I slip my phone back in my pocket and follow Pompous Ass to the door. "I'll walk out with you. I need to make a phone call and I don't want to disturb Marissa while she's getting ready for bed."

I know my comment sounds very familiar, intimate. Maybe even a little suggestive. But not enough for Marissa to take exception to it. It could be a perfectly innocent comment. It's not, but it could be. It's not my fault if Pompous Ass deduces that Marissa and I are sleeping together. But that would go a long way toward keeping his face from coming to blows with my fist in the near future.

"Fine," he says sharply. "Marissa, call if you need anything. My secretary can get hold of me, even if I'm in court, and I can call you back."

How very thoughtful of you, I think wryly.

"I'll try not to bother you," she says kindly.

"You're never a bother," he responds smoothly. After a few seconds of undressing her with his eyes, Pompous Ass looks back to me. There's a challenge in his expression that sets my teeth on edge. "Ready whenever you are." I'm not sure if he means it like I take it, but it sure as hell sounds like he does, like he's ready to throw down over Marissa. Not that it matters. He'll lose. I play to win. Always.

"After you," I say, nodding toward the door.

Jensen opens it and walks through. I give him a good lead and turn to look at Marissa. She says nothing, and neither do I. Her eyes aren't flashing in anger, but there's something in them. I just don't know what it is.

Without a word, I walk out the door and close it behind me. I wait until Pompous Ass is in his car and heading down the street before I slide behind the wheel of the BMW and start the engine.

I pause only long enough to hit the redial button before I slam the car into gear and speed off down the road, away from Marissa's. Dmitry doesn't answer; I get only an automated voice mail greeting. I dial again. Same thing. I stop at the stop sign and check my phone. Sure enough, he left me a message.

"Nikolai," he says in his gruff, strongly accented voice. "You will not be able to contact me at this number. It's no longer safe. I'll be in touch with you soon. Expect my call."

A loud click signals the end of the message. I hit replay and listen again. *It's no longer safe.* Something has happened, but what? And why? Why now? Does it have anything to do with his association with me? Could they have found out that he harbored me, the other son of a traitor?

A surge of fury rises up inside me. Impotent rage. I want blood. Their blood. On my hands, quenching my thirst for revenge. But it seems every step of forward progress I make, they're there, countering it. Tying my hands.

My frustration is at peak level and I need to vent, to release some angst. One face comes to mind. I'm too angry to think of why it does or the wisdom of going to her. I simply act.

I yank the steering wheel, whipping the car around. With a squeal of the tires, I race back down the street. Back to the condo. Back to her.

The brakes scream as I screech to a stop along the curb. I climb out of the car, slamming the door behind me. When I reach her door, again I don't bother to knock. I twist the knob and walk right in, thankful it's still unbolted. The fact that it was, which is incredibly stupid on her part, only adds fuel to the fire of my anger.

I stomp down the hall toward Marissa's bedroom. Her bathroom door is partially open and I can see her reflection in the mirror. She's standing in front of the sink with a tube of toothpaste in one hand and her toothbrush in the other.

She has already changed clothes. She's wearing a tiny little nightie thing. It's not trashy or blatantly seductive, but it's sexy as hell nonetheless.

It looks more like something a girl might dress her baby doll in. It's girly and pink and hangs in a straight line to the tops of her thighs. Thin satin straps hold it in place over her shoulders, like a sundress. Where it departs from anything a child or baby doll might wear is in the material. It's nearly transparent. I can see the shadow of her nipples through it, as well as her navel and the outline of her panties. It's both innocent and provocative, and I want to rip it off her.

I push the door open and it bangs against the stopper on the wall behind it. Her hands pause in midair. Her eyes meet mine in the mirror. They're wide as she watches me. She says nothing.

I walk over to stand behind her. With my eyes on hers, I reach around her and grab her breast. I squeeze it, maybe a little more firmly than I intended, and she flinches. But I don't care. Right now I need to be rough. And right now I need her to take it.

As if in answer to me, I feel her nipple tighten beneath my palm. Maybe I wasn't too rough. Or maybe she likes it rough.

I feel myself straining against my jeans. With my free hand, I reach for her toothbrush and toothpaste, jerking them from her fingers and flinging them into the sink.

I lower my hands to her hips and curl my fingers in the material of her nightie. I raise it. When she doesn't resist, I pull it over her head and toss it onto the floor behind me.

Her nipples are puckered and ready for my touch. Her chest rises and falls with her accelerated breathing. Her bottom lip trembles in anticipation. Yes, she likes it like this, whether she'd ever admit to it or not.

I palm both breasts and pull her back against me, flush against my chest. She lets her head fall back, but she watches me from beneath her lashes. "You're so fu—damn sexy," I groan, catching myself.

I roll the tight nipples between my fingertips, lightly pinching them. Her lips part and I hear a tiny gasp escape them. I press my lower body toward her, grinding my hard-on against her. She arches her back and pushes that firm, round ass out, rubbing it back and forth over me. I grit my teeth so hard I could bite nails.

I move my hands down to her hips, holding them still while I move against her. I bend my head to her neck and gently sink my teeth into her scented skin. Her eyelids flutter shut.

Sliding one hand around to her stomach, I push my fingers under the edge of her panties, then down to cup her warm flesh.

Her lips part further and she widens her stance. Just a little, just enough that I have better access.

Yeah, she likes this. She wants it. But I want to see the desperation in her eyes.

She moves against my hand. I know what she needs, where she wants me to put my fingers. But I want her to wait a little longer for it.

Without parting her folds, I move my hand over her, teasing her. I can feel the moisture against my palm. It makes me throb with the need to be inside her.

But at the moment, I want to look in her eyes more than anything. I move my free hand to her hip. With one quick jerk, I tear her panties. The thin band breaks easily under the force. She gasps in surprise, but she doesn't open her eyes. They're still closed. But

I don't want them to be. I want them open. I want to see her reaction. I want her to know that I'm angry and that I'm taking what I want, not asking for it. And that she's giving it to me.

I want to see that she accepts me this way.

I slap her on the ass and growl, "Watch." Her eyes pop open and focus on mine. They're dark with passion. And acceptance. And excitement. "Good girl," I say, rewarding her by sliding one finger of my other hand between her swollen lips. She's slick with desire. I rub my fingertip over the firm nub at the top of her lips and her eyelids drift shut again. I give it a little pinch and she moans. "Watch," I demand again.

Obediently, she opens her eyes to meet mine. They're slow to focus. She's under my spell. I reach up to tease her nipple with my free hand and I put my lips against her ear. "You want to know what's inside my head? This is inside my head. Anger," I say gruffly as I push two fingers down between her folds and into the slippery heat of her body. I pull them out a couple of inches and then drive them back into her, deep and hard. Rough. I feel her knees buckle, but I hold her against me and make her ride my fingers.

"But you like it, don't you? You like me like this. You want me to take what I need. You want to be free with me, don't you?"

Faster and harder, I jam my fingers into her. Faster and shallower her breathing becomes. When I feel her muscles tighten around my fingers, squeezing them, I move my thumb to the firm button of her clitoris and I make small circles over her, faster and faster. I see her body tense and I don't relent until she's standing, breathless and waiting, on the edge of her orgasm.

And then I stop.

I move my hand from her breast to my jeans, unzipping them, then placing my palm in the center of her back to push her forward.

She braces herself on the granite countertop as I move one knee between her legs, urging them farther apart.

"I want you to beg me," I hiss through gritted teeth. "Beg me to put my cock in you and come inside your wet body. Beg me or I'll walk right out that door."

I'm holding nothing back now. This is the real me. This is all there is now. Fury. Rage. And blistering heat.

"Please. I want you inside me. Please," she breathes.

"Tell me to put my cock in you."

"Please, put your cock in me."

Moving both hands to her hips, I thrust into her, deep and rough. She's so wet, I'm exploding within three strokes. I hear a loud, angry roar. It's me, the sound ripped from my body as I pump forcefully into her.

As I spill hot fluid into her body, I feel the spasms of her muscles get tighter and tighter. Her breath comes in deep, heavy moans as the waves of her orgasm flood her body. "You like that, don't you? You like the feel of me coming inside you, don't you, baby?"

I pull her tight against me, grinding into her. I look down and see my thumbs biting into the perfect round globes of her ass. Saliva gushes into my mouth. I want to sink my teeth into it. I want to see the red mark that I make on her and then I want to soothe that ass with my lips and my tongue.

The desire to lose myself in her is stronger than ever. Lose myself in her body, in her taste, in her scent. Impulsively, I withdraw from her and drop to my knees, giving in to the urge to bite her ass cheek. I hear her yelp, so I lick the spot, caressing the other cheek with my hand.

I move my hands to her hips and turn her around, facing me. With my palms against her skin, I move up the inside of her thighs and part her legs. I run my tongue between the crease of her lips, sucking her clit into my mouth while I delve into her wet body with one finger. The tunnel is slippery with our combined fluids and still spasming gently, her orgasm beginning to ebb.

Straightening, I bring my wet finger to her shocked and parted lips and I slip it into her mouth.

"This is us together. Taste it."

Obediently, she takes my finger into her mouth and closes her lips around it, sucking, her smoldering eyes locked on mine.

When my finger is clean, I reach behind her and grab her toothbrush and toothpaste, handing them to her. Automatically, she takes them from my grasp.

Without a word, I zip my pants, turn around, and walk back out the way I came.

I rub my stinging eyes, the interstate in front of my headlights blurring for an instant before my focus comes back. I glance down at the dashboard clock. It's nearly two a.m. I don't know exactly what time it was when I left Marissa's, but I know I've been driving for hours. I knew it was time to turn around when I crossed over into Tennessee.

After I left her standing in her bathroom, I went out to the car. As soon as I started it up, I wanted to shut it off again and go back inside. That's the only reason I didn't—because I wanted to. And wanting to is not a good sign.

I was already feeling guilty about taking her in such anger, and that didn't leave a good taste in my mouth. Guilt and I don't get along, much less guilt over a woman. That's exactly why I avoid emotional entanglements with the opposite sex. In the last few years, I haven't been in one spot long enough for it to be an issue, but I remember all too clearly from life before exile what it feels like to get involved with a girl. Thanks, but no thanks.

It irks me that I'm anxious to get back to her condo. I keep telling myself it's because I'm tired. But it's not the bed I keep picturing. Well, at least not an *empty* bed.

I texted her a few minutes after eleven, just to make sure she was okay. I don't think she's in any danger, but I'd be an idiot not to at least be cautious. My question was the same simple question I've asked before.

U ok?

And her answer was the same simple word it's been each time I've asked.

Yes.

But that was a while ago. Surely she'll be asleep when I get back. That ought to make things a little less . . . messy.

I'm relieved when I see the familiar curb come into sight, and even more so when I see that all the windows are dark. I make my way to the door and slip the key Cash told me belonged to her door into the lock. I guess they haven't really had time to sort out all that his-shit, her-shit stuff. Quietly, I creep through to her bedroom door. It's open and I can see her form beneath the covers. It's illuminated by a shaft of moonlight peeking between the curtains.

I realize the considerate thing to do would be to crash on the couch. Luckily, I'm not the considerate type, so she would expect nothing less than for me to come to bed. To her bed. At least she *should* expect that from me.

Silently kicking off my boots and stripping out of my clothes, I ease onto the bed and slide under the sheet. She's rolled up in a ball on her side, facing me. I watch for her eyes to open and listen for her to speak or stir, but she doesn't, so I close my eyes and relax into the pillow.

A couple of minutes later, just before I drift off to sleep, I hear her voice. It's quiet in the darkness, but still it startles me. And the touch of her soft fingers gives me chills.

"What does this mean?" she asks, tracing part of the tattoo on my arm.

"You scared the piss out of me. I thought you were asleep."

"I couldn't sleep until I knew you were back."

I don't know if that means she was afraid of being alone or she was worried about me. I like the thought of her worrying about me, but at the same time it irritates me *because* I like it.

"Well, I'm back, so go to sleep."

"I can't yet. I'm too keyed up. Talk to me. Tell me about your tattoo."

"I don't talk about it. Ever."

"But you can tonight, can't you? Please."

Something in her voice, in the vague glint from her eyes that I can see in the darkness, pricks me, pricks my thick scar tissue.

I sigh and close my eyes again, going back in time to places and people and events I'd rather forget. Only I can't. I'll never be able to.

"When I first started on the boat, I had no idea what kind of business those guys were into. I thought it was just a cargo ship. I figured we'd haul merchandise from point A to point B and then go back for more. It wasn't big enough to haul very many containers, and all the ones I got to see the inside of were full of tires. There was no reason for me to think there was anything foul going on." I pause as I remember the day I first witnessed a deal for something other than tires. "Until we made our first trip into the Indian Ocean and the Arabian Sea."

Marissa moves in closer to snuggle against my side and lay her head on my shoulder, her fingers continually tracing the swirling patterns on my bicep.

"The first time, I was more an observer than anything. I stayed on the ship while some of the crew loaded crates that were buried behind the tires onto a smaller boat and took them to shore. It was broad daylight and we could see everything that happened on the beach. I thought it was strange that we were meeting on a near-deserted island, anyway. When I heard the gunshots and saw two of the guys from our ship fall, I knew why. I knew something illegal was going on.

"That night, Dmitry, the one my father put me in contact with, came to my room and told me that if I didn't keep my mouth shut, he couldn't protect me and there was nowhere on earth I could hide. He was very matter-of-fact about it, but I knew he was serious. I didn't ask questions, but I tried to stay out of anyone's notice as much as I could. It was one day a couple months later that I heard Dmitry arguing with Alexandroff, the ship's captain I was telling you about.

"As I mentioned, Yusuf had taught me some Russian, so I knew enough to piece together the conversation, especially when I kept hearing *Nikolai* come up. That was what Dmitry called me, and I was the only one on the ship that went by that name.

"I asked Dmitry about it later. He told me that Alexandroff had become suspicious of me and that I needed to take part in the next deal or he'd put me off the ship, which was code for shoot me in the head and dump my body in the sea."

Marissa's gasp is soft. I keep my eyes closed, but I imagine the look of horror on her pretty face. I don't want to see it because it will change if I tell her the whole story. But it might be best. Maybe she'll realize I'm a terrible person to get mixed up with. Maybe she'll demand that I stay the hell away from her.

I don't know if I would, or if I even could. But she could try.

"What did you do?" she asks softly.

"I had no choice but to agree, so Dmitry made arrangements for me to accompany him on the next exchange. He said he'd do everything he could to protect me, to keep me out of it as much as possible. I just had to go, just to show I wasn't some kind of rat.

"It was with a different group of bastards, some Dmitry knew to be a little more reasonable, and he thought it might be a safe way to prove myself to Alexandroff. So he gave me a gun, showed me how to shoot it two days before the trade, and then I went ashore with him to sell guns to terrorists."

Marissa says nothing for a few minutes. I wonder if she's planning an exit strategy even as she lies next to me with her body pressed against mine.

Her question surprises me. She's pretty intuitive, it seems.

"Did you have to use your gun?"

I know my answer will likely cement the decision she's already toying with, but she needs to know. She needs to know I'm toxic. It's better for both of us this way.

"Yes."

"Is . . . is that what the tattoos are for? For people you've . . . for every time you've had to use your gun?"

"No," I reply. "There's one band for every trade I lived through.

Sometimes my gun wasn't necessary." I pause before I add, "But a lot of times it was."

I feel her shift beside me. Her warmth disappears. Her reaction, her decision stings more than I thought it would, more than I'd like to admit. I figure it's better now than later, though. I can't afford to get attached. And it's better for her if she doesn't get attached, either.

I keep my eyes closed, ready to give her the cold, silent indifference that comes second nature to me. If she's gonna leave, she won't know that I give a shit. I won't let her see.

But then she surprises me. I first feel the tickle of her hair as it dangles over my chest. Then the light touch of her lips on my cheek as she bends to kiss it.

"I'm so sorry for the life you had to lead. You were so young," she says, her voice thick with emotion. "You didn't deserve that."

Her hand splays across my chest as she scatters kisses all over my face and neck. I feel drops of warm wetness every so often. I don't realize they're tears until one hits my lips and I taste the salt.

She makes her way to my stomach, then down my right leg and back up again, dragging her lips and tongue along the inside of my thigh.

It's not often I see the goodness in people. Or that they surprise me with compassion. Yet Marissa has. I just told her I'm a criminal and a killer, and rather than running the other direction, she cried for me.

Something burns deep inside my chest. I don't have time to think about it or deny it, or devise a plan to rid myself of it. Marissa sees to that when her lips close over my engorged head. She makes it so that she's all I can think about. She erases all other thoughts with the first swipe of her tongue. And I'm happy to let them go.

TWENTY

Marissa

I could watch Nash sleep for hours. In rest, the stern set of his mouth is more relaxed and the anger that seems to burn perpetually in the dark pits of his eyes is absent, leaving him just incredibly handsome. Not complicated.

There's no denying he's a twin. He looks nearly identical to his brother, so his features aren't *un*familiar to me. But in a way they are. There are subtle things that I see right away that set him apart from his brother, things like a small scar that disrupts the smooth line of his right eyebrow, the lighter streaks in his hair from time spent under the sun at sea, and the bronze sheen to his skin. In my opinion, he's ten times more handsome, more rugged than Cash. And certainly far more dangerous.

I realize what I'm doing as I stare at him.

Stop staring! You're like the creepy watch-him-while-he-sleeps, obsessed girlfriend.

I make myself roll away from him and get out of bed. I'm as quiet as I can be. Nash is such a strong force, it's easy to forget that he was stabbed not so long ago. No doubt his body needs the rest.

I head for the bathroom and a much-needed shower. As I lather and rinse my hair, I let my mind wander back to the conversation Nash and I had last night, to the things he told me. My heart aches at the thought of what he's had to endure, at the thought of what he's probably seen and done as a result of someone else's mistakes. It's no wonder he's angry and bitter. And the loss of his mother—essentially his entire family—on top of that is horrific. I decide it's a testament to his strength of character that he survived as well as he did.

But I think parts of him might be forever damaged, if they, in fact, survived at all.

I shake off the depressing thoughts. I don't like to think about the very real possibility that he'll never feel anything more for me than what he does right now, that he'll never be capable of a more meaningful relationship.

But I knew that going in. He himself told me that he would hurt me. I guess I was either stupid enough or arrogant enough to think that I might be different, that he might change for me.

As water sluices down my body, I come to the harsh and disturbing realization that if anyone can help Nash feel again, it's likely going to be someone a lot nicer than me. Someone more like Olivia. Someone with less baggage, someone who isn't just as broken as he is. Together, our pieces might make one whole person. But I doubt it.

My morose thoughts only worsen when I get out of the bathroom to find not only an empty bed, but an empty condo. There's no note, no indication of where he went or when he might be back. No nothing. Just an echo of my earlier worries, an echo that says Nash is inconsiderate because he just doesn't care. And that he never will.

I feel a twinge of pain somewhere in the vicinity of my heart. For once in my life, my feelings for a man have nothing to do with my ego. I *wish* that were the case. Wounded pride is much easier to deal with than this increasing feeling of hopelessness.

As I walk back to the bedroom, I hear the *bleep* of an incoming text. I detour to the table by the door where my purse, and, therefore, my phone rests. I plugged it in last night to charge it and never went back to get it. Nash distracted me.

I'll say.

A warm flutter dances in my belly just thinking about him standing behind me in the mirror last night. I'm sure I shouldn't have liked him being so rough and angry. I'm sure I should've objected, both as a woman with some self-respect and as a human being. But I don't regret that I let it go on. For some reason, it felt like one of the most honest exchanges we've had thus far. He wasn't holding anything back. He wasn't pretending to be anyone or anything. He was just Nash. Raw, angry, sexual Nash, taking what he wanted and needed. And he took it from me.

I know I shouldn't read so much into him coming to me for it, but I can't seem to help it. Just as quickly as the hopelessness set in, a tiny seed of hope grows to overwhelm it.

I'm sure it will be the reverse in a few minutes or a few hours. I seem to have become emotionally bipolar since meeting Nash.

As I reach for my phone, I chastise myself for seeing and feeling things that aren't there and setting myself up for a devastating letdown. What I find only gives my foolish heart more reason to hope.

> I'm with Cash. Call if you need me. I can be home in
> a few minutes.

I text my short reply and try not to smile too broadly.

> Okay.

Home?

My optimism returns tenfold. For a moment, I don't think about anything but the fact that he's being considerate of me, caring. Feeling. And that he referred to this as home.

But at the same time all this hope is filling me, rational thought is arguing with it from somewhere far in the back of my mind. It's warning me that I've fallen for Nash, that I've fallen hard. And the thing is, I'm smart enough to know that a fall like this could break me.

Permanently.

The caller ID makes me sigh. It reads *Deliane Pruitt*. My secretary. And the fourth person from work to call me in the last two hours.

What happened this morning? Did the floodgates of gossip open up?

"Good morning, Del. How are you?" I greet her pleasantly.

"Good morning. Am I interrupting?"

"Not at all."

"Okay. Good. The word is out about your return, and I'm getting calls from people wanting to set up lunches and meetings and fund-raisers. Are you coming in today?"

Her question irritates me, as does everyone's assumption that I'm working, just because I'm back in the country. Of course, I know they're just doing what they've always done. I'm always available for those things. Lunches and fund-raisers have always been more play than anything, and a "meeting" is just another name for a social gathering for drinks at a posh restaurant.

A thought occurs to me, striking me momentarily speechless.

"Marissa?" Del's voice brings me back to the conversation.

"What? Oh, sorry. Um, no, don't put anything on my schedule yet. I'm not sure when I'll be back in the office. Or back to work, for that matter. I've got some things I need to tend to first." I pause before I ask Del a question, a question related to the thought I had. A question I'm not entirely certain I want the answer to. "Um, Del, has anyone called about the Peachburg accounts? It's about time for them to follow up."

The Peachburg accounts are the ones that Daddy and I went to the Caymans to look at. At the time I thought nothing of him bringing along a "team" to help and to familiarize themselves with the accounts, but now it seems like much more. Now, it makes sense.

"No, ma'am. I think Garrett Dickinson is handling most of that now."

The blow is crushing. The disappointment of reality sits on my chest like a five-hundred-pound gorilla. My suspicion was correct.

"Okay, thank you. I'll be in touch with a date when you can open up my schedule."

"Yes, ma'am." I'm ready to hang up when Del stops me. "Marissa?"

"Yes?"

"Is everything okay? I mean, you can talk to me if you need to."

I can tell her offer is genuine. If anything, I think her kindness actually hurts. It's not that I've ever been mean to Deliane, but I've never treated her as anything more than an employee. A lowly one. I've never given her more thought than a go-between for all the people I know and the activities we're involved in. She could've been automated for all the credit I gave her.

But now I see very clearly that she's a real person, one much better than me. She's extending an offer of help and comfort to someone who's never given her more than the most basic of polite gestures. She's rushing to the aid of someone who doesn't merit her consideration.

"Thank you, Del. I might take you up on that," I say, even though I know I won't. She doesn't deserve me unloading on her.

"You've got my cell. Call me anytime."

"I appreciate that, Del. I'll be in touch."

After we disconnect, I let my phone drop to the carpet between my feet. I think back over the years since I graduated law school and passed the bar exam. I think of all the accounts my father has "brought me in on" or told me he's "grooming me to take over." Each one, for one reason or another, ended up being someone else's baby while he moved me on to something else. Every meeting he ever asked me to attend was more an informal kind of meet-and-greet than anything with teeth, anything where we actually reviewed numbers or talked real business. What my father has been grooming me for is to be the wife of an important person. He's taught me how to conduct myself in the company of some of the richest, most powerful people in the world. He's taught me how to raise tons of money for causes that make us look like decent people, and he's taught me how to throw a party with the best of them. But not once has he ever trusted me with something that's actually important, that requires the knowledge I went to school for years to obtain.

Not. Once.

All along, he's seen me as the wife of a politician, one he can carry in his hip pocket to use for favors and influence when he needs it. He's raised and groomed a pawn, nothing more. And the realization is devastating.

All sorts of random memories come crashing down around me—my father asking me to sing for an Asian diplomat when I was a child; my father refusing to let me date any boys other than the sons of his influential friends; my father getting me into law school when I was still undecided on my major; my father introducing me to all the "right friends" in law school; my father asking me to wear a nearly transparent dress and "forget" my underwear when I went with him to dinner on an oil tycoon's yacht. I was seventeen at the time. I didn't object because I was always so happy when Daddy gave me attention, I didn't care what it was he was asking me to do. It's been that way all my life, anything to win Daddy's approval, anything for a smile or a pat on the head. As far back as I can remember, I've been vying for his attention, begging for his love and doing anything to get the tiniest drop of it. I didn't even realize how twisted it was or what a monster I was becoming. Like my father, I gave no thought to anyone but myself and saw everything and everyone as a means to an end. My end. My father's end.

I've been the ultimate party favor since I was able to "perform." A whore. Not always for money and not always using sex, but a whore nonetheless.

Like living a lifetime in a daze, I feel shell-shocked and bruised, bruised by the harsh light of reality.

Since the kidnapping, I've felt like a stranger in the world around me. Now I know why. It was a lie. All of it. One big lie.

Feeling claustrophobic, I slip on some slacks and heels and grab my purse. I need to focus on something real, something genuine. If not, I might shatter like a crystal goblet, explode into a shower of diamond-bright drops that hit the ground and disappear into nothingness.

Tears are streaming down my face as I climb into my car and race down the street, away from the familiar. My phone signals that another text has come in. I glance at it and my heart squeezes even tighter inside my chest.

Two words. From someone I'll never be good enough for.

U ok?

I ignore it as my sobs fill the quiet interior of the car. Purposely, I think of Olivia. I owe her what little bit of goodness I might have inside me. I owe it to her to get the dangerous associations of her boyfriend's family off the streets, to get her out of harm's way if I can.

I guide the car to the jeweler that my family and most of the partners at the firm have always used to buy gems and settings that dazzle. I laugh bitterly as I pull into a spot outside the small, unassuming shop.

I'd always thought we were in the business of justice, albeit the corporate, financial kind. But that was never the case, I feel sure. I think on some level, I always suspected my father used influential people to get certain things, but I never wanted to see it. I never really wanted to see past the beautiful lie of the outside. I went along with it all. I let him use me in some of his manipulations. Because I was weak.

Like the jewelry my father purchased here, I was nothing more than a shiny bauble to dangle in front of just the right people. Without even realizing it, I was in the business of bedazzling people. And I learned from the best how to use something bright and shiny to distract others from what lies beneath. I'm nothing more than a diamond-encrusted space. I'm hollow on the inside. Full of nothingness. Empty.

Wiping my eyes, I drag myself from behind the wheel. A delicate bell signals my entrance to the store. An attendant greets me in the foyer. She calls me by name.

"Ms. Townsend, so nice to see you again. What can we help you find today?"

"Something emerald. For a friend."

The shop is set up so that there are different foci in different areas. You can walk from room to room via adjoining doors, but if you know what you want, an attendant will simply take you to the room with the type of jewelry or stone you're looking for. I know from past experiences that emeralds, rubies, and pearls are in the third room on the left, so I follow the girl down the long, wide hallway, glancing in at each luxuriously appointed room as we pass.

A familiar profile catches my eye and my step falters. I'd probably recognize it anywhere, especially in a place like this where his ponytail and goatee are particularly out of place.

It's Nash. But what in the world is he doing here? He'd said he was with Cash, which means he lied.

He's alone in the room, with only one male attendant. He's

looking at bracelets, likely diamond ones considering which area he's in. But why? And for whom?

He had to have asked Cash where he could go for jewelry. This place isn't exactly on the beaten path. But why would he lie? Unless he didn't want me to know, didn't want me to ask questions.

I feel betrayed and near tears, and I jump when the attendant speaks to me. "Would you like to look at the diamond bracelets instead?"

"Uh, no. No, I'm only interested in emeralds."

I hurry to move away from the doorway, unwilling to get caught in such a humiliating situation. My feet feel leaden as I follow the girl farther into the back of the store. I'm having trouble focusing on why I even came to the jewelry store in the first place. My enthusiasm for picking out a wonderful present for Olivia is even more dampened now.

It only takes me a few minutes to find the perfect gift for her, but I browse a lot longer. I don't want to risk running into Nash.

Nearly forty-five minutes later, I make the purchase so I can leave. On my way out, I look cautiously into each room as I head down the hall toward the exit. I'm relieved that there seems to be no sign of Nash.

As I'm getting into the car, my phone sounds again. It's a text. And it makes my heart hurt. Again.

U ok?

Again, I ignore it. Nash is playing games that are far beyond my ability to withstand. I thought I could take the heat, but I think I gave myself way too much credit.

I refuse to shed any of the tears that threaten the backs of my eyes. I give myself a quiet talking-to, something to help me keep my focus where it needs to be.

I'm going home to pack a small bag and then I'm heading to Salt Springs. I'll see if Ginger needs any help getting things ready for Olivia's party. I gave Ginger Cash's number. If she didn't tell him to invite Nash or if Cash didn't think to, it's not my fault. He can just stay in Atlanta and wonder where everyone went.

That thought gives me some small amount of satisfaction. I like the idea that he will realize he doesn't have me under his thumb. Everything that has happened so far, I've *let* happen. I've been a willing participant. But the instant I decide it has to stop, it will. The end.

A tiny, irritating voice speaks up from the back of my mind. It's laughing at me, asking if I really think it will be that easy to just walk away from Nash.

Much as I did Nash's text, I ignore it.

My jaw aches from clenching my teeth in determination, but I feel somewhat accomplished an hour later when I zip my small overnight bag closed. The prospect of getting out of this condo, out of Atlanta is incredibly appealing at the moment.

I hear the front door slam and my heart stutters in my chest. I wonder if I'll always have that reaction now, whether rational or not. Once my brain kicks in, it reminds me that it's got to be either Olivia or Nash. Or Cash, although unlikely. They're the only ones who could even possibly have keys and I locked the door.

I wait a little breathlessly for the footsteps to make their way to my bedroom. When Nash's big body fills the doorway, my heart skips another beat. He's so incredibly handsome. And so incredibly angry.

"Why the fu—hell haven't you answered my texts?"

"I wasn't aware that I was required to."

His teeth are gritted. I can practically hear them grinding. He hisses through them. "You're not *required* to. It's just common courtesy. I thought you rich, snobby bitches were all about pretending you have manners and putting on a good show."

Although I know he's probably using it as a generality, it still stings to hear him lump me in with bitches. "Maybe we rich, snobby *bitches* don't always follow the rules."

I see the anger in his eyes dim. "I didn't mean it like that."

I suspect that he didn't, but I refuse to ease his conscience by saying so.

"Maybe you should learn to watch your tongue."

"Believe me, I don't say half of what I'm thinking when I'm around you."

"Well, then maybe you should say what you mean."

Nash stomps across the room and stops with less than an inch between us. At nearly five nine, I'm tall for a girl, but he still towers over me. I resist the urge to back up. Rather, I raise my chin and meet his eyes in defiance.

"Trust me, you don't want to hear that."

"Maybe not, but maybe I *need* to hear it."

His fingers wind around my upper arms like bands of carbon steel and he pulls me tight against his chest. I get the feeling he'd like to shake me. "I haven't given you enough reason to hate me? To stay the hell away from me?"

"Maybe now you *finally* have," I spit through the tight line of my lips. He's not the only one who can get angry.

"What is wrong with you?"

"Nothing for *you* to concern yourself with."

We stare at each other, both unwilling to give an inch, but both unwilling to walk away. For the first time, I can see past his carefully crafted façade. He doesn't want to want me, he doesn't want to feel anything for me, but I think he's beginning to, despite all the warnings and reasons that he shouldn't.

After what feels like an eternity, Nash releases my arms and takes a step back. He reaches up to smooth hair that isn't mussed back into his ponytail. His eyes flicker to the bed and stop.

"Going somewhere?"

"As a matter of fact I am. Not that it's any of your business."

His eyes slide back to mine and narrow. "Were you even going to bother telling me?"

I narrow my eyes right back at him. "I figured I'd text you later."

Since you're so fond of that method of delivering your lies.

"Later, huh?"

I can see the sparks in his eyes again.

"You don't check in to tell me every detail of *your* life and *your* day."

It feels good to get a little dig in, especially considering his recent trip to the jewelry store, a trip that he lied about. But when I see his lips twitch, I realize my barbs aren't even making a dent. He finds it amusing.

Of all the times to get a sense of humor . . .

It's infuriating. *He's* infuriating!

"Somebody's got a temper," he says playfully.

I feel like stomping my foot. But I don't want to give him the satisfaction.

When Nash takes the step to bring him back closer to me, it's not in anger this time. There's something else in his eyes. And it makes my knees weak.

He reaches out and twirls a lock of my hair around his finger, tugging until my nose is nearly touching his. His voice is little more than a whisper when he speaks. "I can be very . . . therapeutic if you need to get some of that anger out. Want me to show you?"

Looking into his eyes, listening to the velvet of his voice, I feel dazed. Mesmerized. Hypnotized. If not for his secret trip to the jewelry store, I'd press my lips to his and sink into the distraction of him like a stone in water.

But I can't get past the lie so easily. Of all the things I can tolerate from him, that I can overlook and deal with, dishonesty isn't one. When most of my life is built on lies, I need something that's real and honest. And I thought that was Nash.

But I was wrong.

Holding his gaze, I take a purposeful step backward. I let a chill drip into my voice. "I'll keep that in mind."

One dark brow rises. I don't know if it's in surprise or in challenge, but it causes a little shiver to skitter down my spine.

"Fair enough." Slowly, he turns and walks back to the door. He looks back at the last minute, his lips still curved. "I'll leave you to your packing, then."

I don't move until I hear the front door open and close. As I carry my bag into the living room, I can't help but feel like I just lost some sort of battle.

TWENTY-ONE

Nash

Cash mentioned Olivia's birthday in passing. Her present was one of the things I went with him to pick out today. What he really wanted me along for, though, was to ask me if I'd be his best man. He's planning to propose to Olivia.

"I know it seems like it's too soon, which is why I'm not doing it now. And definitely not around her birthday. But I want to go ahead and get the ring, so that when the time is right, I'll have it," Cash said this morning on the way to the jewelry store.

"What the hell do you need me for, then? I'm no diamond expert."

Cash shrugged. "Mainly because I wanted to ask if you'd be my best man."

I'm sure my shock resonated in the car like the thud of a bass drum.

"No offense, man, but why?"

"There's no doubt I know Gavin better. He'd be the logical choice. And I happen to like him a lot better, too." He glanced over at me and grinned. I know he was probably telling the truth—no doubt he *does* like Gavin better—but what he was saying is that I'm his brother. I'm his blood. And it's the one thing that can't be erased, the one bond that can't be broken, no matter how estranged we are.

And I understand what he feels. I feel the same way.

"But I'm your brother. I get it."

He looked away from the road long enough to glance at me again, then nodded. That's how I knew we were on the same page.

"So, you in?"

I took a minute or two to consider what he was asking, as well as my willingness to make such a commitment. I wouldn't tell him yes if I wasn't sure I could hold up my end of the bargain.

"Yeah, I'm in."

Cash nodded again. He knew what I meant was that, come hell or high water, if I'm alive when his wedding rolls around, I'll be there. I'll be his best man.

After that, we fell into a fairly comfortable silence. I went with him into the most unconventional jewelry store I've ever seen. It was more like an old house converted into a posh store. It had different rooms for different types of jewelry. I'd never seen anything like it. Cash said it was one his law firm favored. He'd probably bought something for Marissa from there, although I didn't bring that up. Not really out of deference to him; more because I didn't really want to know.

He picked out a nice bracelet for Olivia for her birthday, then went off by himself with some woman into a room where they keep loose diamonds. Evidently he's going all-out and having something unique crafted for her.

Poor pussy-whipped bastard.

Looking at all the jewelry and thinking of the girlfriend I might have had, the one I might've been able to buy things like that for, just put me in a bad mood. And then when Marissa didn't respond to my texts . . . Well, I was pretty pissed off by the time I got to her condo.

But to find her there in a fit of her own . . . Damn! That was kinda hot. I wish she'd been a little more agreeable to working off some of that steam.

I can't help but frown as I think about the way she was acting, like I'd done something wrong. I *have* done something wrong, something terribly wrong, but I don't think she knows what it is. If she did, she'd have probably thrown me out on my ass and sworn never to talk to me again. But she didn't. So I doubt she knows about *that*. But what else is there? I all but told her I'm a lowlife. She knows I'm not the kind of guy she needs to be involved with. For God's sake, I told her I'm a killer and she gave me a blowjob.

Maybe she's had a crisis of conscience since then. Maybe. But it doesn't seem likely.

Women!

This is exactly why I avoid getting too close to them. Most of them are batshit crazy and more trouble than they're worth.

I should just walk away from this one. Only . . .

I thump my fist on the steering wheel in frustration. I don't know what comes after the *only*.

I take the turns as Cash directed. I don't know if he intended to invite me to Olivia's birthday party, but after talking to Marissa,

I invited myself. I figure that's where she'll be. Cash was just nice enough to give me directions.

I see the bar up ahead and make the left into the parking lot. In a shitty podunk town like Salt Springs seems to be, my guess is that this is the only spot for miles to get a drink. That or Olivia has an ass-ton of friends. Either way, the lot is packed with cars and pickup trucks.

I'm no stranger to walking into a bar like this one. I know just what to expect, and I'm never disappointed. People give me a wide berth. The men eye me like I'm competition; the women eye me like I'm dessert. I don't really give a shit what they think. I usually have one thing in mind. Either getting laid or getting drunk.

That's the only way this night and this bar differ from all the others. Tonight, I'm not here to get laid or get drunk, although if both happen I won't complain. Actually, I'm not really sure why I *am* here, but I know it has something to do with Marissa. I've given her the impression that I'll look out for her, that I'll protect her. I can't very well manage that when I'm hours away. It also has a little something to do with whatever bug found its way up her ass. I'm curious about that. And I wouldn't mind exploring that little temper of hers. Other than that, I have no interest in what her deal is. I've got nothing to apologize for. At least not that she knows of.

My gaze is drawn to her right away. It's not that she's necessarily easy to spot in the crowd. This place is so full of blondes I might get high from the fumes. But Marissa's hair is a natural blond, pretty easy to pick out of the yellowed bottle-blondes all around her. Plus, there's just something about her that draws my eye, no matter how crowded the room.

Besides that, she's sitting by herself. She's probably never been to a bar like this one. Dual is probably the closest thing, which isn't really very similar at all, since it's more of a club.

She looks like an elegant fish out of water, even though she tried to dress the part. Her denim short-shorts are a little too new-looking and her T-shirt is probably designer. My guess is that it cost more than some of these people make in a month. And her smile is stiff, like she's uncomfortable. I gotta give her some credit for trying, though. She came because she's trying to do right by her cousin, because she's trying to prove herself. Even if it means doing so in the enemy camp.

The girl's got some balls.

When her eyes light on me, I see them freeze into icy blue points in the perfect oval of her face. She looks away, out toward the dance floor and the crowd moving clumsily there.

I don't approach her. Instead, I go to the bar and order a beer. When the bartender slides me the green-tinted glass bottle, I immediately regret my choice. My dick twitches in response.

You meant to torture her and Cash, but the only person eating a shit sandwich is you! I think to myself as I try to put that night out of my mind.

I force my thoughts to something else before my body gets out of hand. New Orleans is one of those things that's better off dead. If only I were as fortunate as Marissa and didn't remember it at all . . .

A nice, soft breast rubs up against my arm. I look to my left to see a busty blonde lean in next to me. The chair on the other side is empty, so she's got plenty of room. She just doesn't want to take it. She'd rather have my attention instead.

She orders a margarita, then turns her heavily made-up eyes to me. "Don't think I've seen you 'round here before."

"That's because you haven't," I respond.

"Didn't think so. I'd remember a man like you."

I smile at her overt tactics. "Yes, you certainly would." I bring the cool beer bottle to my lips and take a sip. Instantly, I think of Marissa. The beer and the thought leave me thirsty, but not for anything in front of me.

I frown as I swallow my mouthful of brew. Normally, ass is ass. As long as it looks clean and willing and smells nice, I'll tap it. That's what condoms are for.

But not tonight. For the first time in . . . well, *years*, my appetite is very specific. There's one thing I want, one person. And it's not the blonde at my side. It's the one sitting coolly by herself on the other side of the room.

Following my thoughts, my eyes flicker to where Marissa is seated and collide with hers. Before she glances guiltily away, I see fury. Jealous fury.

Normally, I don't put up with that kind of thing, but in this case, I find it intriguing. It seems out of character for her, like a hidden flaw that's coming to light. Makes me want to explore it. Just like her anger from earlier.

Whatever the cause, anger is something I can relate to, identify with. But it makes me feel drawn to her, connected to her in a way that I don't want to feel. I'm a loner. I don't need roots or ties or involvements. Marissa's the exact opposite. She's the type that needs all that.

I'm the leaving kind. And she needs the staying kind.

Maybe we both need reminding of that.

With that in mind, I grab the hand of the blonde who's busting out of her top and take her with me to the dance floor.

TWENTY-TWO

Marissa

My heart splinters right inside my chest as Nash leads the girl through the crowd. I should stop watching him. But I can't. I can't stop watching him any more than I could stay away from him when I could've avoided all this.

I knew what kind of guy he was, what kind of guy he *is*. One look at him will tell any girl with half a brain what kind of guy he is. He's the kind that will break your heart. Without a thought or a backward glance, right before he walks out of your life.

It's not like he didn't warn you.

That only makes me feel worse. It makes me feel stupid on top of everything else.

As I watch him dance with the slutty blonde—which he does amazingly well, I might add—I can't help but feel a devastating sense of letdown. It sounds crazy, no doubt, but I think some part of the new me hoped that I'd find love in an unexpected place, in an unexpected way. Nash is both.

Having him fall for me, being the one who could heal him and make him love again, would've been a wonderful way to start my new life. But maybe it's not meant to be. Maybe I'm supposed to cut all ties and find my way on my own. *Completely* on my own. I've never been on my own like that before. Maybe it's time I am.

In my head, that sounds all Antigone-esque, but in my heart it just feels lonely. And empty.

Suddenly the room and all its happy celebration feels suffocating. I slide from my bar stool to flee the weight that's pressing in on my chest, but a firm grip on my shoulder stops me. I turn to see Ginger. She shakes her head, as if telling me not to leave, gives me a wink, and then turns to speak into the crowd.

"Who'd like to see the birthday girl open her presents?" Even with the loud music, Ginger's voice can be heard easily. No doubt that's a pretty handy talent for a bartender to have. As if on cue, someone lowers the music and the sea of faces turn toward Ginger.

I sit back down. I'm stuck. There's no way to exit now without appearing rude and inconsiderate. Plastering a smile on my face, I look around to find Olivia, purposely avoiding looking at Nash and that . . . that . . . woman.

I see Cash first. His head is visible above practically every other one in the room. He's smiling, his chin resting atop a shiny, black head. I lean a little to my left and see Olivia wrapped in his arms, hugged against his chest, facing her crowd of friends. She's smiling like the happiest girl alive.

My chest aches and my eyes burn. I envy her. Not that I begrudge Olivia happiness. I don't. I just wish I were more like her. In every way.

My chin trembles and I force back tears. I was never this girl before—emotional, wistful, possessive, particularly caring, out of control—but I guess being a better person, being considerate and sympathetic, can't come without some pain. I just didn't realize it would be so much.

I look at Olivia and see the payoff, though. She's in a room full of genuine friends who love her for who she is, not what kind of stock she came from or how she can help them rise to a higher place in the world. She's met the love of her life and wound him around her little finger. And she can lay her head down every night knowing she's truly loved and that she was a bright spot in a dark world that day. She doesn't need riches or material possessions. She doesn't need a powerful father or a great family name. She didn't need a fancy (and useless) degree. She's just decent. Soul-deep decent.

"Mine first, mine first!" Cash says, waving his hand toward someone in the crowd. I look back through the faces until I see Nash step forward to hand Cash a long, narrow box wrapped in simple yet luxurious red velvet. I know instantly where the package came from. And my heart hits the floor. I have a sinking suspicion I misjudged Nash.

I watch Cash take the box he probably hid from Olivia with Nash and hand it to her. Her smile still in place, she loosens the matching velvet bow and pulls the material away from the rectangle. Cash reaches around her to lift the lid away and Olivia's eyes get round.

"Oh, Cash! It's beautiful!"

She pulls out a bracelet. Even from my distance and vantage point, I can see that it's got three rows of jewels—an emerald one with diamond rows on either side. It's stunning and will go perfectly with the emerald earrings I bought her.

"It is, but it doesn't hold a candle to you," he says, smiling down into her face when she turns in his arms. She hands him the bracelet, then her wrist. He fastens the glistening band around it, then raises her fingers to his lips. His words aren't loud. They're meant only for Olivia, but everyone is so quiet, so respectful and reverent of what's going on between them, it's easy to hear him. "I love you, birthday girl." Olivia throws her arms around his neck and whispers something in his ear. He chuckles and then kisses her when she leans back. "I'll hold you to that."

"It'd be a shame if you didn't," she says, making all her onlookers snicker.

One by one, her friends and loved ones step up to hand her their gift. Some are nice gifts, some are comical, some are purely meaningful, but all are very thoughtful and meant to show Olivia that she's loved. That's the one overarching, undeniable theme—she's adored. Deeply. For nothing more than the person she is. And that's the way it should be. It just took me a lifetime to realize it.

When there's no one else stepping up to give her something, I reach inside my purse and pull out a small square box, also wrapped in red velvet. I feel guilty just looking at it. Not for what's inside, but for assuming the worst about Nash, assuming that he lied to me about where he was. I was judging him as though he were one of the people I'm most accustomed to in life—people who lie and betray and mislead without a second thought. I'm not used to people like these, people who are honest and caring.

And Nash is one of them.

I don't know if he cares about me, but he cared very deeply for his mother and, evidently, still cares for his father and brother, whether he'd admit it or not. And I'd say he's pretty honest, too. Nash is the kind of guy who would just tell you the truth, regardless of how much it hurts. In fact, he's already shown that he will. He warned me off getting involved with him, only I wouldn't listen. He was honest from the beginning. And he was honest about where he was today. He *was* with Cash. At the jewelry store. But I didn't give him the benefit of the doubt. And that's on me.

I slip off the bar stool to walk my gift to Olivia. She's smiling when I reach for her hand. I take it in mine, placing the box in the center of her palm. I wait for her gaze to meet mine before I speak. I want her to know I'm sincere. I want her to see it on my face, in my eyes.

"If I could choose to be like anyone in life, I'd choose you." I bend slightly to press my lips to her cheek. "Happy birthday. You deserve all the happiness in the world."

Her eyes are brimming with tears when I lean back. She hooks one arm around my neck and pulls me in close for a hug.

"Love you, cuz," she whispers. And the thing is, I really think she means it.

"Love you, too."

When I turn around to find my way back to my seat, it's to see another tall head making its way through the crowd. This time Nash is heading for the exit. And in front of him, tugging on his hand, is the blonde from earlier. I watch until he's out of sight and the door is closed. Not once did he look back.

Not.

Once.

I can hardly wait for Olivia to open my present and things to get back to the party portion of the night. Then I can escape unnoticed. And I need that. Desperately. I feel like I can't breathe, like someone stole the air from the room. From my lungs. From my soul.

When the music is blaring once more and the celebration is in full swing, I cling to the outskirts of the room and make my way to the door.

The cool, quiet night slaps me in the face the instant I step outside. I welcome the shock. It makes me feel alive when so much of me feels dead and hopeless. I'm preoccupied with thoughts of getting to the car and letting loose the ocean of tears that are threatening, so I jump when I hear a voice right behind me.

"Care to give an old man a ride?"

I turn, one hand still clamped over my racing heart, to see my uncle Darrin, Olivia's father, smiling at me from his wheelchair, his casted leg sticking straight out. Ginger brought him to the bar; I assumed he'd be leaving when she did.

"Sorry. You scared me."

"Didn't mean to. I saw you creeping out and I followed. I was just waiting for Liv to finish with her presents so I could ask Ginger to run me home. I'm old and it's way past my bedtime," Uncle Darrin says charmingly.

"Of course. I'm parked right over there," I say, pointing to my car.

I walk more slowly so Darrin can keep up. Thankfully the lot is paved or he'd have trouble navigating it in his wheelchair.

"I would open your door, but this thing gets in the way." He glances down at the offending limb. I think it's sweet that he'd even think about it. I'd forgotten what a nice, genuine country guy he is. I'd be willing to bet there's not an ounce of guile in him. I don't know too many people like that. I'm related to even fewer.

"How 'bout I open it for you, just this once?"

He sighs loudly. "If you insist," he says playfully. I hit the button on my fob, listening for the click of the locks before I open the passenger-side door and hold it for Uncle Darrin. I watch as he comes to a stand on his good leg, then expertly pivots, moving from the wheelchair to the car seat.

"Like a pro, right?" he says as he folds up his wheelchair. "Doc won't clear me for crutches yet." I nod, having wondered about that. "Think you can slide this into the backseat? Or the trunk? It's not heavy."

"Of course."

Once I get the chair into the backseat, I get in on the driver's side and start the car.

He's quiet for the first half of the short drive to his house. When he finally speaks, it's not the small talk I would've expected.

"There's something different about you. You're not the spoiled little rich girl you used to be."

I could probably take offense at that, but I don't. I take it as a compliment.

"I'm not. And I don't ever want to be again."

I glance over at Darrin and he's nodding, taking it in.

"I didn't think you'd stand a chance against that damn brother of mine. I'm glad to see you're stronger than he is, stronger than his influence."

I look at him again. He's watching me, like he's seeing me for the first time. And like he approves of what he's seeing.

I say what I truly feel. "Thank you."

"It hasn't always been easy for Olivia, either, what with her mother giving her such a hard time about who she is and the kinds of choices she makes. I'll tell you what I've always told her. Blaze your own trail in life. Make your own choices and make your own mistakes. It's the only way you'll find your own happiness, not someone else's."

I say nothing to him, only nod. His words are so profound,

they resonate so deeply, that I don't know what I could possibly say in response. I feel like I've waited my whole life for someone to tell me those things, to tell me that it's okay to make mistakes, that it's okay to be me, to be my own person. But in my whole life, no one has ever allowed it. And they never will. If I'm to be the Marissa I want to be, it will be away from my family, my friends, from the life I've always known. Blazing my own trail means burning bridges with the flame.

And I just don't know if I'm strong enough to do that.

But I know I have to try.

When we reach the house, I put the car in park, but I don't cut off the engine. I get out and walk around to get his wheelchair out. I pry it open before pushing it to the now-open passenger door. Like the pro he teased about being, Darrin reverses his earlier movements and stands on his good leg, pivoting and then plopping down in his wheelchair.

I move to the back of the chair, grabbing the handles to push him up the driveway.

"You gonna leave your car running all night?"

"I'm not staying. I think I'm going to head back home tonight. I've got some . . . trailblazing to start tomorrow."

I see him nod. He gets my meaning. He doesn't speak until we're at the front door. He wheels his chair around to face me. His smile is pleased.

"Good for you," he says, a twinkle of pride lighting his eyes. It's something I've never seen before, not even from my father when I graduated law school. It makes me feel like I can leap tall buildings in a single bound.

He digs his keys out of his pocket and unlocks the door. Before I can ask him if he needs help with anything, he cuts me off. "Drive safe," he says warmly. "And don't be a stranger. You're always welcome here. You're family."

I nod and smile before I turn to walk back to my car. My throat is so tight with a lump of emotion I doubt I could squeak out a single syllable. When I reach the idling car and slide behind the wheel, I look up to see Uncle Darrin sitting in his wheelchair in the doorway. He waves to me once more. I wave back and put the car in reverse. I pull out of the driveway and into the road. As I'm driving away, I glance into my rearview mirror. Uncle Darrin is still sitting in the doorway, watching me go.

TWENTY-THREE

Nash

My mouth is so dry I could spit cotton balls. I need something to drink, but the blonde from the bar is lying on my arm, pinning it to the black sheets.

Like a magician pulling the tablecloth out from under the dishes, I jerk my arm out fast and roll to the edge of the bed. I don't bother to look back at her. If she wakes up, she wakes up. If she's stupid enough to open her mouth, she'll deserve the cold shoulder she gets.

I left with her last night to make a point. To myself and to Marissa. The only thing I managed to prove is that Marissa is under my skin.

The blonde, Brittni with an *i*, didn't seem to notice that I was distracted, nor did she seem to care that I wanted to get some liquor in me before I did more than kiss her. But even then, with a head all fuzzy from a mixture of vodka and tequila, all I could think about was a different taste, a different smell. A different girl.

No matter how much I drank, I couldn't seem to forget she

wasn't Marissa. Luckily, Brittni drank too much, too. Passed out before I had to tell her I wasn't interested in doing anything with her but drinking her liquor.

I'll be gone before she wakes up. After I get a drink of water, that is.

I grab my shirt and pull it over my head as I stumble from the bedroom. I find the kitchen with relative ease. Her condo is about the size of a cracker box.

I open the fridge, hoping for bottled water. But there's none. Only Diet Coke and beer. Without shutting the refrigerator door, I get a glass from the dish drain and hold it in front of the light. Thank God it looks clean. I run some cold tap water into it and gulp it down. Then I do it again. Water is the best thing for a hangover.

My head is still swimming a little, so I flop down on the sofa until it clears enough to drive. Heaven forbid I get pulled over. I avoid the law like the criminal that I am. *Decent people* worry about tickets on their record. *I* worry about someone finding out who I am and what I've done and throwing me in prison with no possibility of parole.

I slump down in my seat and lean my head back against the cushion, letting my mind wander for a while. It travels back in time to a night that I'm living to regret, one that haunts me. It's the night I became a victim of my own game, a victim of my own need to make my brother suffer.

I was in New Orleans a year or two ago. Even now, I can remember the smell of the air with perfect clarity. I breathe it in, just like I did that night, and I remember . . .

The air is balmy and laced with the scent of salt water. I let the loud music and wild celebration flood my mind, rid it of all other thought. For just a little while, I need to forget who I am, what I've done and the road ahead. I need to get lost in the moment, and there's no better place than Mardi Gras.

I'm anonymous. In the French Quarter during this time of year, everyone is. I'm not wearing a mask or costume like most people, but I'm just as masked in every other way. No one knows me here. And that's just the way I like it.

Girls flash their tits from balconies all along the street, collecting strings of beads for their efforts. The people are drunk, the music is loud, and hedonism is the theme of the night. The same holds true for the luxurious private homes I pass.

This one is no different.

All the French doors are open. Music and light are spilling out into the street, and laughter can be heard as it mingles with the other elements of the party.

Something breaks the monotony of the night. It reaches out to grab my attention and pull me back to the present, to my troubles, like nothing else can.

It's someone calling my name. It's a woman's voice.

But who the hell would know me here?

I look around and see no familiar faces. I hear my name again. This time, I use the sound to triangulate where the voice is coming from.

Then I see her.

She's standing on the balcony of the house, leaning over the intricate scroll of the wrought-iron railing.

My eyes meet hers and I know she's talking to me.

"Nash! Ohmigod, what are you doing here? Come on up!"

She's smiling down at me. Widely. Almost too widely. I think she's drunk. I've seen her only a few times, but I've seen enough to know she's pretty much a cold bitch. But not tonight. Tonight, Marissa, my brother's girlfriend, is feeling warm. And I'm feeling the warmth of taking a little revenge.

Before I can contemplate the wisdom of it, I turn onto the well-lit sidewalk of the home and make my way to the front door. The knob isn't locked, so I enter.

In the foyer, a few people glance in my direction, but no one calls me out or tries to stop me when I head for the stairs to my right. I wonder if it's because some of them think they recognize me, if it's because they think I'm my brother, Cash. My brother, the imposter. My brother who's pretending to be me.

The familiar bitterness stings the back of my throat like acid. I revel in the burn. I let it feed the anticipation coiling in my stomach, the anticipation of a little payback.

As I climb the steps, it heats my blood. I know it's probably not smart to risk giving myself away like this. I just hope everyone's too drunk to remember seeing me here. Or at least too drunk to question it if the topic should ever come up in conversation later. It should be easy enough to blow off. Especially for Cash. He thinks I'm dead. No doubt he'll assume everyone was too shitfaced to know what they saw.

When I reach the second story, there's a hall that extends left and right. It's a crossroads, much like the one I find myself at. I could leave right now—no harm, no foul. Yes, I would feel cheated out of an opportunity to take a little vengeance, but I wouldn't be jeopardizing my deceased status.

Or I could go ahead. I could seize this night, this chance, and, for just a few minutes, feel the satisfaction of having a laugh at my brother's expense.

My choice is a no-brainer. I brush aside the voice that's telling me this is stupid and I proceed to the right. From the street position, I figure Marissa must be on a balcony in that direction, so I head that way.

There are three doors on the street side of the house. The first is closed, so I don't open it. The second one is open and filled with people. It's some sort of upstairs parlor and I can see through it to the other side of the room where narrow doors open onto a balcony. This has to be the one.

I make my way through the tight crush of bodies toward the doors. I hear a couple of people speak as if they know me. I smile politely but don't respond. I don't want to draw anyone into conversation. My goal is singular. I can see it standing on the balcony. I can see her standing on the balcony.

She's wearing a shiny, royal-blue dress that fits her like a second skin. The top pushes her tits up into a luscious heap beneath her chin and the bottom of the dress is split dead center all the way to mid-thigh. It separates into two distinct pieces, giving the appearance of a tail as it flows to the ground. Her long blond hair hangs over her shoulders in thick waves, some pieces braided, with seashells dangling from the ends. It doesn't take a genius to figure out she's a mermaid.

I stop to watch her, letting the anger brew. My brother is one lucky bastard. He gets to live a great life, my life. He graduated from law school and got a job at a prestigious Atlanta law firm. He's got a good name and he's screwing the boss's daughter (no doubt with his consent). And the kicker? She just happens to be gorgeous. Cold as ice, but gorgeous.

She's gonna get a little warming up tonight, though. Then she's gonna get some humiliation to cool her back down. I'll piss her off real good, all while wearing my brother's face, and leave him to clean up the mess and explain how he can be such an insensitive asshole. In the meantime, I get to get a little taste of the good life. Sounds like a win-win to me.

I continue across the room and step out onto the balcony, right in the middle of something funny evidently. Marissa is laughing her ass off, hanging all over some tiny brunette as if she's the only thing holding her up. And she probably is. Marissa's plastered.

As the tuxedo-clad servant passes to exit the balcony, I grab a beer from his silver tray. The top is already off. How convenient.

I stand just outside the French doors, taking a long swig from the bottle as I wait for Marissa to notice me. When she does, she squeals in delight and launches herself at me, throwing her arms around my neck and smashing her body to mine.

She leans back to look at me, her face close to mine, her arms still draped loosely around my shoulders. "I had no idea. Seriously. This is the best surprise ever. I thought you meant it when you said you were busy."

I shrug, turning my head to take another long pull from my bottle. My dick twitches when I feel her tongue on my throat. Apparently she warms up quite nicely when she's drinking.

"I'm so glad you changed your mind," she purrs, rubbing her chest against mine. "And I love the wig. Longer hair suits you."

My hair is loose, my bangs hanging on either side of my face, all the way to my chin. It's a wonder she recognized me at all. Or thinks she did, anyway.

Impulsively, I wrap my free arm around her waist and lift until her feet are off the floor. Slowly, I back her up until I feel the resistance of the railing behind her. Then I set her down again.

"Why so glad?" I ask, keeping talk to a minimum so there's a lesser chance of her discovering who I really am.

"Because I need someone to kiss right now. And it's only us girls out here." She pauses to look around. I do the same. But for us, the balcony is empty now. "Well, was," she giggles. It appears everyone has left and wandered back inside. It's just me and Marissa and the half million people milling around on the streets below us, some of them no doubt watching.

"Well, I'm here now," I say, staring down into her almond-shaped eyes. She might be a frigid bitch most of the time, but she's got some spice in her. I can see it in the smoky invitation of her gaze, in the sexy curve of her mouth.

"Yes, you are." She leans into me, pressing her lips to mine. While the kiss is warm, like she's familiar with whom she's kissing, it lacks real . . . heat. I wonder if this is all that she and Cash share. This superficial, perfunctory kind of chemistry.

I remind myself that I don't give a shit about them or their relationship. I came up here for one reason. It's just a bonus that I get to slake my lust for revenge with lips like this, with a woman like this. She's a far cry from the kind of females I usually visit when I'm on shore.

Moving my hand up her spine, I wind my fingers into her hair and tug her head back and to the side, deepening the kiss. I slide my tongue against hers and I feel the vibrations of her moan. She seems a bit unsure of herself at first, but it doesn't take her long to respond to me.

She threads her fingers into my hair and holds me to her. She's liking this, which will just make it that much sweeter for me.

I slide my hand from her hair and drag it down the smooth skin of her bare back. I reach between her and the railing and give her ass a squeeze. I press her hips into mine and give her a little feel of what's between my legs. I'm gratified when her fingers curl into a fist and tug at my hair.

"You like that?" I whisper against her mouth.

I can feel her shallow breath fanning my face. "Yes."

"How 'bout this?" I ask, grinding my rigid body into hers.

She does this breathy gasp-moan kind of thing and leans back to look at me. There's a question in her eyes. For a second I think I'm busted, that she knows I'm not Cash. Or, to her, not Nash.

But she doesn't ask the question. Whether it's because she doubts herself or because she doesn't really want to know, I don't know. But she keeps quiet and just goes with it. "I like that even more."

She pulls my head back down to hers and lifts her leg, running her calf along the outside of my thigh, opening herself up to me a little more.

I slide my hand over her hip until I feel the skin of her bare leg. I run my palm up under her dress to the edge of her panties. With one quick jerk, I tear the wispy material. I feel her nails dig into my scalp. It just prods me to continue.

My clear intentions of humiliating her and, therefore, my brother become diluted in the burning lust for the hot little minx in my arms. But the thirst for revenge is too strong. It doesn't disappear completely. Still, I want to push her to a place she would never go, to a place she's not entirely comfortable with. Even if she doesn't remember it and Cash never finds out, I'll know. And that's what matters. I'll know.

I turn my body slightly to the side and move my hand between her legs. I slide a finger inside her. She's so wet it drips down to my knuckle. Blood rushes to my dick and I groan into her mouth as she moves her hips against my hand.

I pull my slick finger out of her and move my head back just enough that I can see her face. Her eyes are wide, her pupils round with excitement.

"Open," I say simply, my eyes dropping to her mouth.

Her lips fall open and I slide my finger between them. My stomach clenches into a tight ball when she closes them on my finger and sucks. I'd be willing to bet she's never done that before. But I could be wrong. So I push her further.

Reclaiming my finger, I reach around behind her and I take the beer bottle into my right hand. Moving it between our bodies, I touch the cool glass to the inside of her leg. Her shiny lips part on a gasp. It fuels me like gasoline.

She's excited. But how much further will she go?

I drag the bottle up her leg to the heat I can feel coming from between her thighs. I touch the cool rim to her and she shudders visibly. But she doesn't stop me. She just watches me, panting, her fingers still tightly wound in my hair, her face an inch from mine.

"Do you think I can make you come in front of an audience?"

I hear her breath hitch. She holds it as she listens, her eyes flickering beyond me as though confirming that we aren't, in fact, alone. My guess is she's so involved in the moment, she's forgotten we're practically in public.

She doesn't answer. But she doesn't move, either. So I slide the tip of the bottle inside her. I feel her knees buckle and I wind my other arm around her, holding her up as I move the bottle neck farther into her. Very, very slowly, I pull it out. Her lips tremble.

She closes her eyes and her breathing comes in deep, fast gulps. She's close. I can almost feel it.

"Look at me. I want to watch you."

When she opens her eyes, I push the bottle back into her, farther this time. She bites her lip to keep from crying out. I slide it out and back in, rotating my wrist, moving the bottle inside her, bringing her more pleasure with every tiny movement. I pull it out and push it into her again, and again, and again in quick succession. In my hair, I feel her fingers fist and relax, fist and relax until her eyes closed again. I see her mouth fall open and I feel the gush of her breath hit my face. I know she's coming. Coming for me, the guy she thinks she's dating. Coming for me, with thousands of strange eyes on us. I press my lips to hers, licking her tongue with mine as she rides the wave, rides the bottle I have shoved between her legs.

When her breathing slows, I sink my teeth into her bottom lip just before I pull back to look at her. Her sleepy eyes open a crack to stare at me. She's not smiling, she's not frowning; she's just watching me. Curious. Maybe a little confused.

I pull the bottle from inside her and take a step back. With my eyes on hers, I bring it to my lips. Purposely, I tip the bottle back, inch by inch until cool liquid hits my tongue. The flavor of Marissa mingles sweetly with the cold beverage. I swallow.

"Best beer I've ever had," I say.

I release her and, without another word, I turn around and walk back the way I came. I don't glance back until I reach the bottom of the steps.

When I turn, I see Marissa standing at the top of the stairs, watching me. We stare at each other for a few seconds. With a smug smile, I turn and walk out the door. Without another glance at the house or Marissa inside it, I disappear into the crowd.

I make my way along the street, trying to leave behind what just happened. But the lights, the music, the people, the hype of the night—nothing can get Marissa out of my mind. The farther I walk, the more I think of her. The look on her face, the feel of her lips, the passion that rests just beneath the surface. My body throbs with it. The worst part is, I know it won't do any good to look for someone else. She's the only one who will satisfy me tonight. And I can't have her.

She may never know it, but she won the night. Tonight, Marissa made me a victim of my own game.

"What are you doing?"

Brittni's unwelcome voice stirs me, bringing me back to cold reality with a thud.

"I'm leaving," I say, deadpan. "Thanks for the drinks."

Even in the dark, I can see her open mouth and offended expression. More than ever, I don't give a shit. There's only one person's opinion that I'm really starting to care about. I just don't know what to do about it.

TWENTY-FOUR

Marissa

The click of the deadbolt opening wakes me. I listen closely, trying to determine if I was dreaming the sound or if it was real. The closing of the door assures me it was real. Very real.

My heart starts to race inside my chest as my mind flits through my options. I'm just getting ready to ease out of bed and head for the bathroom to lock myself in when I hear the light metallic clink of keys hitting the table in the foyer. It's where I always put my keys. For some reason that makes me feel less threatened. Anyone breaking in with an ill intent wouldn't likely be dropping off his keys on the table.

One thought runs through my head, one face.

Nash.

When he appears in the bedroom doorway, I recognize him instantly. Something about the way he moves is familiar to me, like I'd be able to pick it out anywhere, as long as I could see a silhouette.

He doesn't say anything as he makes his way to the bed. I'm both excited and a little aggravated, considering that he left the bar last night with a trashy blonde. Thinking of her, of how it felt when he left with her, rises to the surface first.

"Where's your friend?" I ask tightly.

At first he doesn't say anything. I can see his movements and hear the shift of his clothing as he undresses. Despite my irritation, desire sweeps through me, making me breathless and achy.

He walks to the side of the bed, staring down at me in the dark. I can see just enough of his face to discern his expression. It's serious. Determined. Heated.

"I realized something tonight."

The mattress depresses where he sets his knee on it. I feel the brush of his fingers against my skin as he curls them into the covers at my shoulder. He pauses, as if waiting for me to respond.

"What's that?"

My stomach is full of lava. It pours through my core and down my legs when he slowly pulls back the covers.

"I realized that no matter how tightly I closed my eyes, no matter how much I tried to ignore it, no matter how much I wanted her to be . . ." His voice is so quiet, I have to strain to hear him, even in the silence. "She just wasn't you."

My racing heart flips over in my chest.

Nash's hand stills, hovering at my hip. He's waiting for my permission, for my acceptance. For my participation.

I reach down and cover it with mine. Now we both wait—motionless, speechless, breathless. It's as if something important is being decided. Or declared.

Then, purposefully, I roll onto my back and bring his hand to my breast. I hear him suck in a breath.

"Show me," I demand simply. I know what I want him to show me. I know what I hope he meant by wishing she had been me. What I don't know is if he'll do as I ask, if he'll show me that he's in this, too. Just like me.

He makes no verbal response, but his answer is as clear as if he had. He slides onto the bed, stretching out beside me. He stares down into my face, his eyes sparkling black diamonds in the sliver of the moonlight pouring through the crack in the curtains. He watches me, his thumb absently moving back and forth over my nipple.

Finally, he lowers his head to mine, his lips brushing softly, sweetly over mine. "I don't know what to do with you," he whispers.

"Love me," I answer, reaching behind his head to pull his mouth more firmly against mine. I don't want him to comment and ruin the moment. I just want him to love me, like we aren't two broken people with an impossible future. At least we can have this—this moment, this feeling, this one perfect night.

My heart and my soul and my body thrill at his touch. Nash's hands and fingers, his lips and tongue move over me like they were made to do nothing else in life. Expertly, he brings my aching body to a fever pitch before he slips between my legs and positions himself at my entrance.

It feels as though the entire world is on pause, waiting in breathless anticipation for him to thrust into me and ease the ache that only Nash can give me.

My eyes are closed and every nerve in my body is focused on the place where our bodies are touching most intimately. His voice surprises me when he speaks.

"Look at me."

I open my eyes and they meet his. He stares at me for several long, puzzling seconds before he flexes his hips and moves into me, inch by excruciating inch. And when he's deep inside me, filling me up in so much more than just a physical way, he presses his lips to mine in a kiss that reaches the most sacred, terrified part of me.

When I feel the brush of his tongue, tender turns to passionate and my body clamps down around his. He begins to move within me, pushing me relentlessly toward a pleasure I've only ever experienced in his arms, at his touch.

My orgasm is unlike any other. It washes over me like warm honey, slow and sweet.

"I love to feel you, so tight and wet all around me," he groans, slowing his delicious torture to prolong my pleasure.

He doesn't stop until the earth is firm beneath me once more. Then, with a gentleness I haven't seen in him thus far, he slips out of me and rolls me onto my stomach.

I'm boneless, with neither the will nor the desire to resist him as he stuffs a pillow beneath my hips. I feel like I have nothing left to give when his lips touch me.

"I love this ass," he says softly, kissing my cheek then nipping it lightly with his teeth. His hands caress my butt, then travel down my thighs to tenderly spread my legs. He slides a finger inside me and, much to my surprise, I feel a gush of heat flood my stomach. Again. "There's at least one more in you," he says. I feel his weight against my butt when he leans over me and whispers in my ear, "Can you do that for me? Can you come for me one more time?"

I don't know the answer to that, so I say nothing. But when his finger moves down to rub back and forth over my clitoris, I feel like there's a distinct possibility.

His legs between mine force them farther apart and I feel his thick head probe my entrance just before he pushes into me. That full feeling, that glorious full feeling, makes me groan and my body comes immediately back to life.

He moans as he pulls out and thrusts back in. "That's what I thought."

I push up onto my elbows and arch my back, giving him deeper penetration. "Oh yeah," he whispers, his hands grabbing my hips and pulling me harder against him.

Moving the fingers of one hand around, I feel his fingertip at my clitoris again, rubbing rhythmic circles that keep perfect time with the thrusts of his body. It isn't long before I feel the familiar ache of tension building.

I rock against Nash. His breath starts to come in pants and I know he's getting close, which excites me that much more. When he suddenly stills behind me, I feel the pulse of his own explosion and it triggers mine. Together, we climax, my body squeezing his, his throbbing inside mine.

Almost absently, he rubs his palms over my lower back and butt, over and over in soft, wide circles. Just before he pulls out and collapses onto me, I feel his lips between my shoulder blades. It sounds like he whispers something, but the darkness swallows it up, never to be heard again.

TWENTY-FIVE

Nash

The ring of my phone wakes me. I roll over in bed, still groggy. Sleepily, I reach for the noisy square and glance at the display. I shoot straight up in bed, coming fully awake. There's no name associated with the number, but I know who it belongs to regardless.

Dmitry.

"Hello?"

"Nikolai, meet me in two hours," he says in his thick accent. He proceeds to give me the address of a motel in a town about an hour's drive from Atlanta. "Room eleven. Come alone. We'll talk more when you get here."

I hear the click of the broken connection. I lower the phone and stare at it for a few minutes, marveling at the reality of my life.

Shit like this is only supposed to happen in the movies.

As quietly as I can, trying not to wake Marissa, I get up and shower. With Dmitry, there is no hesitation. He's one of the few people that I *nearly* trust. Even with such an ambiguous, ominous message, I'll still do as he asks. Oh, I'll be cautious, of course. And I'll be armed. But I'll still go. He knows my ultimate goal better than almost anyone. And I get the feeling what he has for me is pertinent to it.

It's barely nine, but I can tell the day is going to be hot and humid. My shirt is already sticking to my back after five minutes in Cash's car.

By leaving now, I should arrive about half an hour early, which is far better than arriving late. I can sit at a reasonable distance and watch the place for a few minutes before showing myself.

My thoughts on the trip are a bizarre splicing of Marissa and all the unwanted emotions she inspires in me with the rage and bitterness that has gnawed at my gut for what seems like an eternity. What could be the strangest thing of all, however, is that, more often than not, I find that my mind strays from revenge and death and loss to Marissa. Again and again and again.

Could I be wrong about everything? Could there be a future for us? Could I finally have the life I was supposed to live all along? Is it too late for a guy like me? And could it ever work with a woman like Marissa? Do I ever stand a chance of being good enough for her?

You're a fu—damn idiot for even thinking *stupid shit like this!*

But even as I chastise myself, I shake my head at the change in my thoughts. Even when she's not around, when she can't hear me, I'm censoring myself. For her. Out of respect for her.

I'm no clearer on what the hell I'm thinking or doing when I arrive at the intersection across from the motel. It looks like a serial killer's wet dream, what with its peeling paint, rusty doors, and erratically blinking neon sign. It might as well read "Bates Motel."

Slowly, I guide the car to the right rather than going through the intersection to the motel. I pull into a defunct gas station and head for a small crop of trees at the back of the lot. I think I can see room number eleven from there.

And I can. I put the car in park and I watch. And I wait.

A couple of times, I see the curtains that cover the big picture window part. Dmitry isn't close enough to the glass that I can see him. I only see a shadow move against the dim light in the interior of the room.

Time crawls by until I finally decide to make my appearance. I drive back the way I came and, this time, make another right at the intersection, bringing me alongside the entrance to the motel.

I bypass the office and the greasy bifocaled man I see sitting behind the counter watching television. Instead, I head around the side to the row of parking spaces in front of the motel room doors. I drive all the way to the end and park in front of number twenty.

From the corner of my eye, I closely examine every vehicle I pass and every window of every room I pass, cataloging them in intimate detail. Nothing looks amiss. But that doesn't mean it's not.

I knock on the door to number eleven. The third time I rap my knuckles on the cold metal, one of the ones in "11" comes loose at the top and swings down, dangling by its bottom edge.

Nice.

The curtain over the window parts again. This time I can identify Dmitry. My muscles ease the smallest amount.

The door opens just enough for me to step through. Dmitry is behind it, so I have a clear view into the empty room. My tension eases even more.

He closes the door and moves to hug me. He gives me a hardy slap on the back and grabs my face in his hands, as many Russians do, and kisses both cheeks, then gives them a slap as well.

"You look good, Nikolai," Dmitry says, walking to the dresser that he's using as a minibar. He pours two snifters of vodka and hands one to me. I down it in one gulp.

"Why are you holed up here, Dmitry? What happened?"

Dmitry sighs into his glass, staring into the bottom like he might find answers, before he takes a sip. Before he responds, he walks to the bed and perches on the edge of the mattress. In the sliver of light coming through the small gap in the curtains, I can see him better. And I can see that he doesn't look good.

Dmitry is tall for a Russian, but not nearly as tall as me. I'd call him stocky. Paired with the tenacious set of his square jaw and his steely blue eyes, he tends to intimidate most people. But I doubt he would today. His shaggy dark-blond-and-gray hair looks like it hasn't seen a shower in days, and his cheeks have at least three days' growth on them. But it's the set of his mouth that tells the tale. It's grim. And tired.

"Good God, you look like you haven't slept since I saw you last. What the hell is the matter with you?"

"I know who killed your mother, Nikolai."

I frown. "So do I. Is that why you brought me here? To tell me who the triggerman was?"

"No. Not only that." He pauses. It's dramatic, whether he intends it to be or not. My teeth are on edge until he continues. "I brought you here because I have him. Here. Tied up. Waiting for you."

My heart thunders against my ribs. Everything in the world disappears but me and the man across from me. And the possibility that seven years' worth of yearning might culminate right here.

Dmitry has delivered to me the only gift men like us can give each other—the satisfaction of revenge. Retribution.

My ears are ringing so loudly I can barely hear my own voice when I ask. "Where?"

"In the next room," he says, tipping his head to a door on one wall, a door that adjoins the room next door.

I feel like I'm in a daze when I walk to it and push it open. It's surreal, almost more than my mind can process, when I step through to find Duffy tied to a chair in the center of the room, a gag stuffed in his mouth and a trail of dried blood leading down from his nose.

His eyes meet mine. One is nearly swollen shut. But the other is clear. And in it is resignation. I don't doubt for a second that a man like him knows that the likelihood of his meeting a bad and untimely end is extremely great. Few men get to see death coming. But this one does. The second I stepped through the door, he had to know that his life is over. Without Cash here to stop me, I can take the revenge I've waited seven long years to take.

Cold metal touches the skin of my right palm. I glance back to see Dmitry standing behind me. He's pressing a silencer into my hand. After all this time, he knows what kind of gun I carry and what kind of suppressor will fit it.

I take it from him and toss it on the floor.

"No. I'm doing this my way." I bend just enough to reach into my boot and bring out the long, wickedly curved knife that I always keep stashed there. I hold it up and turn the handle just enough that the razor-sharp edge of the blade glints in the low light. "I'm going to slip this between his ribs and push it into his traitor's heart so I can watch him bleed until there's no life left in him. I want him to know a small part of the pain I felt when he blew my mother to bits in the marina that day."

I walk slowly toward him, taking in every detail, savoring every sweet second that leads up to the only thing I've thought about for all these years. I had begun to think I'd never have my revenge. But today, I'll get it. Today, I get to be free of the hatred.

I stop in front of Duffy, my fingers squeezing the knife hilt so tightly my knuckles ache. I look down into his one good eye and I'm confused by what I see there.

It's peace. This is a man who has come to terms with his life. And with his death. He's ready for it. Possibly even eager for it.

And that's when I see her.

Marissa.

She's not in the room, but she might as well be. Her presence is that tangible. I feel her as though she's standing right in front of me, touching my face. I can picture her beautiful blue eyes. And the tears that are spilling from them.

I feel the warmth of her fingers grow cold just as the image fades. And just like that, it's gone. She's gone.

I find myself at another crossroads, much like the one I felt in New Orleans. On the one side is Marissa. On the other side is . . . everything else.

If I go through with this, there will be no coming back from it. Every man I've killed in the last seven years has been out of self-defense. I've never taken someone's life in cold blood.

I'm smart enough to know that this will change me. This will be me turning a corner I can never come back from, making a choice I may or may not be able to live with. It will cement my future in ways that I won't be able to change, like the fact that I'll have to leave this country. I'll be a hunted man for the rest of my days. And I could never invite Marissa into a mess like that.

The Nash who's standing here right this minute has a few possibilities in front of him. The Nash who puts a knife in the man who murdered his mother won't. I'll have one option. To run.

"Nikolai?"

It's Dmitry, wondering what I'm waiting for. He's handed me all I've ever wanted on a silver platter. And I'm hesitating.

With a pounding pulse, I realize it's not all I want anymore. I want a life. A real one. With some of the normalcy I haven't had the luxury of enjoying for the last near-decade. Maybe even a life I can share with someone. Maybe . . .

I don't want to get ahead of myself. And I don't want to make any rash decisions. In need of some clarity, I turn away from Duffy and walk back into the other room.

"What's the matter with you? Isn't this what you want? Since I've known you, it's all I've ever heard you talk about."

I look at Dmitry, at his troubled blue eyes. Is this what's bothering him? Was he afraid I'd chicken out? Or was he afraid I wouldn't?

For the last many years, he's been like a father to me. He's protected me as much as he could in the life I was forced to lead and, in some ways, I think I was the family he never got to have. He's me in another twenty years if I go down this road. But do I want that? Do I want that life? Is the satisfaction of taking the life of the murderer in the next room worth it? Worth becoming a murderer myself?

Adrenaline focuses my mind. It's sharp and quick, and the idea swoops in like an eagle, its deadly talons sinking into my brain and holding on tight.

"I'll spare his life on one condition," I tell Dmitry.

"What's that?"

"That he testify against the man who put him up to it. I have to get justice for my mother, even if it's not the kind that I would like most."

"That will only fix one problem. And that's if he even agrees to it."

"Yes, his testimony alone will only fix one problem. But what if I could get more? My father would testify if I could assure him it would work out and make us all safe."

The idea grows in my mind. Its roots go deeper, its foundation becomes more solid. I feel an optimism I haven't felt in a long, long time.

"You would need to have enough to get Slava and his councilor, Anatoli, at the very least. But I don't think any of us would really be safe unless you could get Ivan. They are the only two truly loyal to Slava. In fact, I believe that Konstantin, an old acquaintance and the fourth in command, might look favorably on the opportunity to move up. He was always an ambitious bastard. He might be a friend in the organization, if there is such a thing. Maybe we could reach a truce of sorts."

Like a veil, I see the exhaustion and hopelessness lift from Dmitry's features. He sees a better way, better than murder.

He would never have tried to take my revenge from me, but it's obvious now that he wished he could. He loves me too much. The son he never had.

"With Duffy, we could get Anatoli. He actually ordered the hit, right?"

"As far as I know. He's the one who usually takes care of those types of situations."

"And with my father, we could get Slava. I know he helped launder the money and cook the books for Slava. Then we'd just have to figure out a way to get Ivan. And if we could have enough to make a racketeering case, like my brother has been planning all this time . . ."

Dmitry walks to the window and pushes the curtain back enough to look out at the parking lot and the surrounding area. The small gesture might have seemed innocuous to anyone else, but I know him well enough to know he's troubled. "What is it, Dmitry?"

"You know, I always wanted more from this life. I never thought I'd be this old and still smuggling, living the life of a criminal. I should've gotten out sooner. I should've taken the risk, like your father."

"Dmitry, after this is over, I'll help you get out if that's what you want to do. I have money. Quite a bit, actually. I've saved almost everything I've made over the last seven years. It's in an offshore bank, earning money. Once I get this behind me, I can give you a fresh start."

Even in profile, I can see that his smile is sad. "I could never ask you to do that. You are young. There is much life for you to enjoy. You have a future. A man like me? I have little left. What's most important now is how I live the rest of it."

"What do you mean?"

"The reason I know Ivan is because we worked together many years ago. Before even your father and I met. That's how I got into this part of the business. He's the one who runs the smuggling operation."

Oh shit! Oh shit, oh shit, oh shit!

All the pieces click together. I know what this means. What it *could* mean, that is.

I don't want to get too excited. If Dmitry won't testify or if I'm overlooking something, this could all be for nothing. But there's a chance that it could be big. Like free-us-all-from-this-hellhole-of-a-life kind of big. Contract killing, money laundering, providing guns to terrorists—it's enough for a RICO case. If I understand it accurately, anyway. And, if prosecuted right, it's enough to put them away for life.

And the unexpected twist of it all? The kicker that makes it that much sweeter? Duffy's testimony would free my father. All this could finally be over. For good. We could finally get back to being a family, to having lives and a future. We could be nearly whole again.

"Dmitry, I know it's a huge risk for you to take, and—"

"It's time, Nikolai. After all these years, I'm tired. And you were the only good thing in my life. With you gone, it's just . . . empty. No, it's time to see this through, once and for all."

"I meant it about the money, though. I could—"

Dmitry interrupts me again, coming to put a hand on my shoulder. "What have I spent my money on? Who have I ever had to buy presents for? What kind of a life have I ever had that requires much money? I have savings, too."

True. All true. I've had a glimpse of his life. For several years now. And it's no kind of life. Not for a decent person. And, for all his faults and flaws and mistakes, Dmitry's a decent person.

"Does that mean you'll do it?"

I hold my breath as I wait for his response. But it's not long in coming. And it changes everything.

"Yes, I'll do it."

"Then let's go talk to Duffy."

TWENTY-SIX

Marissa

I'm just getting out of the shower when my cell phone rings. The twist of my stomach and the twinge in my heart tells me I hope it's Nash. But, conversely, every rational part of me hopes that it's not. I've got to start being realistic about him. About us.

When I woke up, he was gone. I shouldn't have been surprised. But after last night, my expectations rose too high, leaving me feeling shattered this morning when I found he'd left without a trace.

How many times do I have to remind myself that we're too damaged to work? We would only scatter the pieces of what's left, scatter them so far that we'd likely never be whole again. And, as much as what lies ahead scares me, what scares me worse is that I might in some way hinder Nash from ever finding peace, from making his way to a place in life that he can live with—live with his past, with his future, with himself.

The best thing we could do is stay away from each other. I know this. But can I manage to resist the pull of him? Can my heart shut up long enough for my head to take control? I don't know the answer to that, so the best I can hope for is for him to stay away from me. Take the decision out of my hands.

Foolishly, I'm more than a little deflated when I don't recognize the number. It's local. And Nash isn't local.

"Hello?"

"Marissa?"

"Yes."

"It's Jensen. Jensen Strong."

"Oh. Hi, Jensen." I try to inject some pleasure and enthusiasm into my voice so he doesn't hear how much I wish he were someone else.

"I hope you don't mind, but I got your number from what's on record with the courts. Just between us, I totally bribed one of the clerks into giving it to me. I figured my firstborn wasn't too much to offer."

I chuckle. "Well, at least it wasn't your soul. And I'm duly flattered." Which I am. It's nice to have someone so interested in me that he'll go to that much trouble just to get my private number. Hopefully it's *me* he's interested in and not who I am or who I'm related to.

"I hope 'duly flattered' means you'd be willing to go to dinner with me as a show of appreciation."

"It might mean that. What did you have in mind?"

"How about tonight? Seven thirty. Someplace swanky with candlelight that will make you look even more ethereal than you already do."

I'm really not interested. Not at all. But I should be. Jensen is a great-looking, smart, successful, well-respected guy who is charming and interested in me. I'd be a fool not to at least explore the possibility.

And I feel like a fool.

Because I don't want to.

Even though he has all those things going for him, he lacks one crucial element—he's not Nash.

It has nothing to do with his looks or his job or his personality. It's just that I'm in love with someone else. And he's not him.

But I can't have Nash. Nash is unattainable. A loner. A wild card with no interest in me other than for some temporary distraction and a good time. He might care for me in his own way, but it's not a way that's healthy for me, a way that I can live with. And I can't pine away for him forever, which is exactly what would happen if I started waiting around for a guy like him.

He'd always be leaving.

And I'd always be waiting.

But that's just Nash. It's who he is. I knew it all along. He's hard and thoughtless and broken. Not on purpose. Just because. And I can't fix that. I can't fix *him*.

"How about lunch instead?" I say impulsively. Lunch is less intimate, which is good, and it also gets me out of the house so I'm not forced to sit around and think about Nash all day, which is also good.

Because that's exactly what would happen. I'd mull over every word and every subtle nuance of last night while waiting for him to show up or call or text or . . . something.

Always waiting.

But this will be good for me. Plus, it's work-related. I can pick his brain and try to figure out how to go forward with this case. And with my life.

I can't be on "vacation" from work forever. And if I'm not going to go backward, back to everything I knew before, then I have to move forward. Today feels like as good a day as any to take the first step. And it doesn't hurt that my lunch companion is a prosecutor. Spending some time with him might be helpful to me in several ways. And an innocuous lunch won't give him the wrong impression.

I hope.

"Well, it's not the venue I'd choose to charm you with my jazz flute, but I'll take it," he says teasingly. I don't have an overabundance of movie knowledge, but *Anchorman* is one that I've seen. Several times. And I loved it. It goes a long way toward warming me up for my lunch date. Maybe I might have enough fun to take my mind off Nash.

Maybe.

"Ohmigod, I love that movie!"

Jensen laughs. "I knew there was something special about you."

I wish I could say the same, but what it feels like is that I'm embarking on a great friendship. Nothing more.

I refuse to let loose the sigh of hopeless disappointment that's lingering in my chest. This is still a step in the right direction. All I can do is take things a day at a time. Maybe even a meal at a time.

"Where are you?"

I bite my lip, a little embarrassed to admit it. "Um, I'm still at home."

"I'll pick you up in an hour. Is that all right?"

"How 'bout I meet you there? I've got some things to do afterward."

I can tell it's not what he really had in mind, but he agrees and tells me when and where.

"Okay. See you then."

I'm still holding the phone, deep in thought, long after Jensen has hung up. The ring of my phone startles me, causing me to jump. Reflexively, I answer it.

"Why did you leave? I cooked a huge breakfast this morning and you missed it."

It's Olivia. I smile.

"Good morning, old woman. How does it feel to be a whole twenty-two years old?"

"It feels like cotton mouth and a headache." She laughs.

"That means you sent twenty-one off in just the right way."

"Well, if that's the case, I sent it off in an epic way. Ack!"

"Sorry I cut out on you last night. I, uh, I wasn't feeling all that well, so I just came on home. I didn't want to be the resident wet blanket."

Olivia is quiet, thoughtful. "Are you feeling . . . better now?"

"Ummm, some."

"Would this have anything to do with a certain asshole that looks a disturbing amount like my boyfriend?"

"Ummm, it might."

"Uh-huh. As I suspected. I hate that he's not more like Cash. I think all that time at sea warped his brain."

I know she's trying to excuse his behavior, and she might be right. But I don't think so. I think some people are just incapable of very much emotional depth. And Nash is probably one of them. All he feels is anger. It might be all he'll ever feel.

"Maybe," I say simply.

"So what do you have planned today? Wanna do some shopping?"

"I'm sure whatever plans you'd had that caused you to skip class were better than shopping with your cousin."

"Skipping class wasn't the plan. This hellacious hangover sort of made that decision for me."

"Then I'm sure you don't feel like spending hours going from store to store and trying on clothes."

"For you? Anything."

"Why are you so good to me?"

"Uh, because you're family and I love you. Duh," she says playfully.

"Family or not, I don't deserve it."

"Marissa, stop saying that. When are you going to realize that you're not the monster you think you are. You might have been at one time. Sometimes things happen that change us. Completely. Sometimes it's something good, like finding your soul mate. Sometimes it's something bad, like being kidnapped and being afraid for your life. Stop beating yourself up for the past. Look ahead. And know that you deserve to be happy. And to be treated well. Everyone deserves a second chance. You're no different."

"But what if I blow it? What if I can't be this person?"

"You already are. The fact that you're worried about it is proof. Marissa, a month ago you wouldn't have given a shit about this kind of thing. You didn't think there was anything wrong with you, and you certainly never considered for a second that you might actually fail at something. Like it or not, that girl is gone. Forever. You just need to find the strength to let her go and be who you are *now*."

"What if I can't?"

"I don't know the answer to that because it's not going to happen. You can. And you will."

"I wish I had your faith in me."

"Surround yourself with people who do. Kick those plastic people you called 'friends' to the curb and find yourself some real friends. Good ones."

I think of Jensen. He's definitely not the kind of person I would normally have spent my time with. His type of law is frowned on in my circles. Maybe that's a good thing. "You're right. And I'm taking the first step today. I'm having lunch at Petite Auberge with someone who isn't my normal kind of friend."

"Good for you!"

I'm glad she doesn't ask any more questions. Although I'm sure she'd wish me luck, for some reason I don't want her to know I'll be meeting Jensen.

We chat a little more, but I have to get off the phone to freshen up for lunch. Even though my heart's not really in it, I try to strike a good balance between friendly lunch and professionalism. I don't want to give Jensen the wrong impression about where I see "us." I figure a pencil-slim skirt that nearly touches the floor, a thin peasant shirt with cap sleeves, and some strappy sandals will keep things in perspective.

I arrive at the restaurant a few minutes early. Jensen is already at the table, wearing his work clothes, of course. Surreptitiously, he looks me over and his pale eyes sparkle with appreciation. That feels nice. Nice in a complimentary way, not nice in an exciting way. Not like when Nash would look at me.

Damn you! Stay out of my head.

Even as I think it, I smile pleasantly at Jensen as he pulls out my chair.

"You look amazing, as always."

"Thank you."

Jensen immediately launches into an effort to entertain me. Surprisingly, he does a good job. He's witty and smart, and he has a great sense of humor. I find myself laughing quite often, enjoying a lighthearted, casual lunch.

Until I look up and see Nash standing just inside the door of the restaurant, watching me.

My heart skips a beat and then picks up to a much faster pace. I feel warm and flustered. And I'm certain I've never seen a more handsome, more welcome sight than him.

He doesn't move. He doesn't smile or nod or wave me to the door. He doesn't approach the table. He just stares at me with his black, fathomless eyes.

"Nash's brother, right? The one you're helping?" Jensen says, drawing my eye and my mind back to him.

"Uh, yeah. Sorry. Would you excuse me for a minute, please?"

"Of course," he says, standing when I do. Like a gentleman. Like someone I should be with. Like someone I don't want.

On shaky legs, I make my way across the room to Nash. The closer I get, the more flushed and flustered I feel. There's something about him today, something that makes me feel hotter than usual. Stimulated. Ravenous.

Something is niggling at the back of my mind. Like trying to dig up bones from a deep, deep grave, I wrestle it to the surface until I'm able to put my finger on what's bothering me.

"Your hair . . ." I say dazedly when I stop in front of him.

Nash reaches up to run his fingers through it. It's loose, the long bangs framing either side of his face. I've only seen it pulled back or tucked behind his ears. Never hanging loose like this.

Yet it's so familiar.

"It was wet when I left," he says flatly, by way of explanation.

"What are you doing here?"

"I came looking for you. You weren't at the condo and you weren't answering your phone, so I called Olivia to see if she'd heard from you. She said you were here. Having lunch. She just didn't say you weren't alone."

The muscle in his jaw twitches as he looks over my shoulder at Jensen. But I'm not paying much attention to that. I'm busy digging up bones. Old bones that have never really seen the light of day.

Until now.

Until today.

But today they're out of the ground, battering me like a thousand tiny knives, penetrating me all the way to my heart, to my soul.

I can't stop the gasp. Or the pounding of my pulse. Or the crumpling of my lungs.

"It was you. In New Orleans, it was you," I whisper, feeling breathless and crushed.

Nash's brow wrinkles, but he doesn't ask any questions. Or make any denials. He's quiet as he waits. Waits for me to finally put two and two together.

All at once, every detail comes rushing back. I'd written that night off as part of my excessive drinking, especially when Nash (who was really Cash) had said he wasn't in New Orleans that weekend. I'd thought it was surely an erotic, drunken dream or hallucination.

Only it wasn't.

Standing here staring at Nash, feeling the way I feel about him, feeling the undeniable connection to him that I felt even back then, I realize that it was *this* Nash at Mardi Gras that night so long ago. It was *this* Nash who came onto the balcony and turned my body and my world upside down. It was *this* Nash who made every day and every kiss with his brother seem like . . . less.

After that night, I always felt like there was something missing when I was with the Nash I knew. It seemed that I was always searching for more with him. Yet I never found it. We never quite clicked.

Not like this.

And now I know why.

It was never him that I was supposed to click with. It wasn't him I was searching for. It was never him that stirred me to the point of complete abandon.

It was his brother.

And from the moment I saw the real Nash, from the moment he took my blindfold off in the car when he rescued me, I was drawn to him. I didn't really know why, other than that he saved me, but I was. Inexplicably, undeniably drawn to him. And now I know why. Now, with his hair hanging loose to frame his pained face, I see what my memory has kept hidden from me.

I remember.

I fell in love that night. Almost two years ago. In New Orleans. On a balcony. Overlooking a crowd. With a complete stranger. I fell in love with a ghost.

As the details fall into place in my mind, clicking together like so many puzzle pieces, the inevitable question follows.

Why?

"But why? Why would you do that?" Nash has the decency to look ashamed. Deeply ashamed. But I don't care. I want to twist the knife. I want to hurt him. Like he wanted to hurt me. Like he *did* hurt me. Like he *is* hurting me. "Did you hate me that much?"

Much to my dismay, I feel tears well in my eyes. I'd thought my heart was breaking before, but nothing compares to the pain I feel now. He used me just like my father used me. I was nothing more to him than a pawn, just like I was never anything more to my father than just a pawn. Maybe I just moved on from one bastard to another.

"It had nothing to do with you," Nash says simply, quietly.

"But it did. You . . . you touched me. And kissed me. And you . . ." I trail off, embarrassment stinging my cheeks as I think back to what I let him do to me. What I enjoyed him doing to me. "Oh God. You . . . you . . ."

I look around for somewhere to run, for a place to hide. I've never been more hurt and humiliated.

Perceptive as he is, Nash takes my arm before I can bolt and leads me back through the front doors to the sidewalk outside. He pushes me toward the end of the building, but I jerk free of him. "Don't touch me."

He looks wounded and I feel the tiniest bit of gratification that he can be reached, that he's not completely impervious to pain. But the small amount of guilt I might be able to inflict upon him is a raindrop in the ocean compared to what he's done to me.

My stomach twists and I bend slightly at the waist, fighting the urge to double over completely, to somehow protect my vital organs from the unbearable pain of it all. "Oh God, oh God, oh God. I let you do those things to me."

I feel nauseated.

"Let me explain."

"What is there to say? I get it. You hated your brother so much. You wanted to hurt him and you thought abusing his girlfriend would be a nice way to do that. You don't care about anyone but yourself and your stupid revenge. What else is there to know? To understand?"

"For the most part, you're right. All I could think of when I saw you on the balcony that night was that you were my brother's girlfriend, that you were the beautiful woman who should've been mine. Only you weren't. You were his.

"I went up there with the intent of getting back at him, with humiliating him. Humiliating both of you. I won't deny that. But from the moment you kissed me, I wasn't thinking about my brother. Or revenge. Or anything. Except you. I'm a bastard for wanting to use you, yes. For going through with it. But I'm the one who paid the price for it."

"Oh, and just how, pray tell, do you think you've paid the price for it?"

"For all the fury and bitterness I feel, there's one thing that's always been at the back of my mind. One thing I've never been able to forget, no matter how much I tried. That night. With you. I've never been able to forget you."

The pain is too fresh, the wound too deep to listen to one more word. The sincerity in his eyes isn't enough to penetrate the cloud of shrapnel surrounding my heart.

I shake my head and close my eyes against him—against his face, against his words, against the love that just won't die, not even under the sword of such betrayal. "I'm done. This is too much for me. You warned me and I didn't listen. That's my own fault.

The only thing I can do now is keep from making the same mistake again."

"Marissa, please."

That one word is another excruciating slice to my heart. It nearly takes my breath, this star-crossed love I feel. In many ways it feels so right, but, in reality, it is so terribly, terribly wrong.

Without turning to look at him, I speak the hardest words I think I've ever spoken. "Leave me alone, Nash. Just go away and leave me alone."

Squaring my shoulders and raising my chin, I swallow the devastation and make my way back into the restaurant, pretending to be the partly whole person I was five minutes ago before I was torn apart by Nash.

But it's all a façade.

I know, deep down, I'll never be the same again.

TWENTY-SEVEN

Nash

For the first time in seven years, I have to dig deep to find the anger I've lived with every day for so long. It's buried beneath whatever this is I'm feeling for Marissa and that horrible guilt and pain I feel for what happened in New Orleans.

I know I hurt her. Badly. I feel it in my chest, in my gut, in my bones. It's a deep, aching, nagging pain. Like a boxer took to me with nothing on his fists but fury. With nothing more than a few words and the devastation emanating from her, she beat the shit out of me. And, somehow, in the process, she stole the only thing that's mattered to me for all this time, the only thing that's kept me alive—rage. She took it the night she stood in front of a mirror and watched me ram my body into hers from behind. She stole it from me and I just didn't know it.

Until now.

I can find enough of the anger and determination to see this through, but I know the driving force of my life is gone. And what the hell I'll replace it with, I have no idea. I guess I'll have plenty of miserable time to figure that out.

But first there are some things I have to take care of. First, there are loose ends to tie up.

Speeding toward the interstate, away from Atlanta, I dial Cash's number. He picks up after one ring.

"Where are you?"

"We're stopped getting gas. On our way back to the club. Why?"

"I'll meet you there. I've got a few things to tell you. I'm bringing an end to all this, once and for all."

He doesn't ask questions, although I'm sure he wants to. But on the phone, a cell phone no less, it's just not smart to talk in too much detail.

"Okay. We'll be there in probably half an hour."

"I'll be a while longer. There's somewhere else I have to go first."

"I'll wait," he replies.

For the first time since seeing him again, I have the urge to hug my brother. To look him in the eye so he can see that I really have missed him and I really don't hate him.

Maybe there'll be time for that before I go.

We hang up and I take the familiar path to the prison. To see my father one last time. And then I'll be gone.

The setup is a little different this time. It's like the kind of prison visitation you see in the movies—two long rows of cubicles with a glass panel between them and dirty, black phones on the wall.

If my first trip to the pen hadn't made the consequences of a life of crime seem very real to me, this one certainly does.

They bring Dad out shackled and cuffed, like the violent criminal they think he is. He looks older than he did a few days ago. I know that's not possible, but that's how it seems. I wonder if asking us to give up on getting some justice and freeing him from prison is taking its toll.

Obviously he doesn't know me very well, I think. Or else he'd have known that I'd never give up. Not until my dying breath. He'd know that I'll see the bastards responsible for wrecking our lives pay. If it's the last thing I do.

Even as I think about my lifelong mission, the fire is a little more muted than it has been in the past. I guess something other than hatred and revenge has finally taken up some of the space in the vacuum Mom's death left inside me.

Dad sits down in front of me and picks up the phone. I do the same.

Finally, he smiles. "It's still so good to see you. I just can't get over how much you've changed."

"Not all of it has been for the better, Dad."

Even though it's impossible through the glass between us, I can almost feel his sigh, like a heavy breath settling down around me.

"You're strong, son. You always were. Stronger than you knew, even. You'll overcome this. I know it."

I nod. "For the first time in a long time, I'm beginning to think I can. I guess I finally realized that there are some things more important than revenge. Even for a man like me."

"Don't say that like you're some kind of monster. Deep down, you're still the same good kid. Smart, kindhearted, driven. I think you just had a little more of your brother in you than any of us realized. And he had a little more of you than I ever gave him credit for. That just makes you both even more perfect in my eyes. The key is learning to live with all that in a balanced way."

"Nah, that's not the hard part. Finding someone else who can live with it, *that's* the hard part."

Dad frowns. "What's that supposed to mean?"

I shake my head, for a moment wishing I could rid it of thoughts of Marissa, but knowing that if I ever manage to do that, I'll be a lesser person in the very next breath.

"Nothing." Dad's perceptive gaze makes me so uncomfortable I have to look away. "Look, the reason I came today—"

"Let me say this before you go any further. Son, whatever it is you think is so wrong with you, it's nothing that the love of a good woman can't fix. And if she's good enough and strong enough and *worth* your love, she'll stick right by you. Life has dealt you a shitty hand. *I* have dealt you a shitty hand. And I'll never forgive myself. But don't live out the rest of your days miserable and alone and blaming yourself for the past. You'll end up wasting the very bright future you have ahead of you.

"Just because it doesn't look like what it did when you were in high school doesn't mean it's not a future worth having. Find a new dream. Chase a different sunset. It doesn't have to involve a degree and a suit and tie, although it can if that's what you still want. You're young and smart and capable. It can be anything you want it to be. The only thing you have to do to see it happen is to make peace with the past. And with yourself. Let it go and move on. That's still the best advice I can give you. The past is like quicksand. It'll suck you in, and you'll die there if you're not careful."

"What if I don't know how to move on? What if I don't have a direction now?"

Or what if the direction I want to go doesn't want me? What if I'm not good enough for her?

"Find one. It's there. You just have to look for it."

I don't want to talk about moving on or think about impossible futures anymore. I came here for a reason. I need to see this through and get the hell out of here. Out of Atlanta. Off dry land.

I take a deep breath before I say what I have to say. I know Dad won't like this tactic; it's in Davenport blood to resist being extorted, which is essentially what I'm doing. If guilting someone into action can be considered extortion, that is.

"We've all made some sacrifices, Dad. I think you'll agree with that." My father nods. His expression is one of profound contrition. I feel bad already. "I think you'd also agree that I've had to do some pretty extreme things." Again he nods. He won't meet my eyes. "I have something to ask in return now." He raises his gaze and narrows his eyes on me. "You'll be getting more visits soon. I want you to promise me that you'll do exactly what's asked of you. That you can and you *will* trust me enough to just do it. Your sons are grown now. Let us handle this."

I look long and hard into his eyes. If I could put a message in his brain, I would. But I can't. The best I can hope for is to keep him alive in here long enough for Cash to do his thing and get stuff in order for Dad's appeal and the trial of the mafia.

I've done all I can do. I've arranged for two of the three testimonies that could put these men away for life, and Dmitry's taking care of getting some new leadership in the *Bratva*, leadership that will see to Dad's safety and to that of my family in exchange for putting Slava and his men in prison. The rest is up to Cash.

And maybe Marissa. And, of course, Dad. He has to testify or the RICO thing won't work.

He still hasn't said a word. He's thinking, wondering.

So I continue. "You don't need to understand anything yet. You just need to promise me you'll do what's needed. For me. For us. For all of us." I can't say much more. I don't want to tip off whoever is listening. It could put Dad's life in danger. Well, even *more* danger, I guess. "Prove to me that I'm all the things you think I am. Prove to me you still have faith in me. And then maybe I'll believe it."

That's low. But it's necessary.

And it's working.

I can see it on his face.

He nods. "Okay." A pause and a sigh. "Okay."

I feel an ache of emptiness in the pit of my stomach that's not usually there. Maybe it comes from getting a little time with Dad and then having to give him up and leave again. Maybe it comes from being reunited with my twin, then having to turn around and let him go. Maybe it's just leaving in general. This was home for a lot of years.

I'm leaving. Leaving family. Again. Leaving town. Again.

I guess I could stay.

But really, I can't. This isn't the life for me. There's no place for me here. Not yet; anyway. Maybe eventually. Someday. But not now.

A little voice in my head says I'm forgetting one thing that could be causing this feeling, one person.

Marissa. Maybe leaving her is what's making me so miserable.

I grit my teeth.

If that's the case, then I'm on the right track. Leaving is the best thing I can do for her. Get away from her, leave her alone. And there's nothing else I can do to help Dad or Cash with what's about to happen. I've done all I can do. I've served my purpose. And I'm getting Mom some justice. I should be on cloud nine.

It's just a little more of a hollow victory than I thought it would be. Than it would've been before I met her.

Marissa.

I push her out of my mind for the thousandth time as I pull into Cash's garage. This is my last stop before I head back to the coast.

I'm heading there as a favor to Dmitry. He asked that I do something for him in return for his testimony. It sounds like a small price to pay for his help in getting justice for Mom and freeing Dad, so of course I agreed. But first I get to deliver some good news to my brother. Finally.

Even though I'd say Cash heard the garage door, I knock before entering. No sense in starting things off on the wrong foot because I see him and his girlfriend in a compromising position.

He answers quickly. Fully clothed.

The first thing I do is hand him the keys to his car. He frowns as he takes them.

"Thanks for the loaner. I won't need it anymore, though."

"You getting your own ride?"

"Nah. I'm heading out today."

As perverse as it sounds, it pleases me that he looks a little dismayed. "What? Just like that?"

I nod. "Just like that."

"So no justice for Mom, then? That was all just bullshit? You're just gonna go back to that hellhole of a life you've been living?"

"Oh, there will be justice for Mom, but my part is done. The rest is up to you."

"What's that supposed to mean?"

I know my smile is smug. "I'm bringing you your racketeering case, wrapped up all nice and neat. All it needs is a bow."

If an expression can be equated with someone holding their breath in anticipation, Cash's is. "What?" I smile even wider at his question. It's little more than a reverent whisper.

"In exchange for his life, Duffy has agreed to testify." Cash starts to speak, and I'm sure I know what he's going to say, so I hold up my hand to stop him. "He was also much more agreeable once he realized that all three top men in this cell of the *Bratva* would be gone and the new person in charge will be . . . friendly to us." I can see that eases Cash's mind a bit. "He'll testify to contract killing. For immunity, of course. He'll go into witness protection afterward, just in case Slava has reach from prison. But I still think the new leadership will squash a lot of his influence. Anyway, Dmitry, the man I've spent the last seven years getting to know and who knows Dad, has agreed to testify against the guy in charge of smuggling. It should be considered an act of terror since the people *Bratva* sells to are enemies of the United States. Dmitry also knows the number four guy, the one who should step up to take charge. Thinks he can get his cooperation in all this for a chance at being top dog. I tend to agree. Dmitry can be very persuasive."

"How the hell—"

"You don't need to know the details. Leave the unsavory parts to me."

"Nash, I—"

"I know. I know."

"No, I don't think you do. I never wanted your life. I never wanted this. And to know what you've had to do, how you've had to live . . ."

I can see the pain and regret on his face. And I believe him. We both got thrust into this against our will. We did the best we could with only the minimal guidance of our father to go on. Makes me see the wisdom in what Dad just told me. Letting all this go would be a good thing all the way around. And we will. After.

"The past is the past. Let's leave it where it belongs and move on."

I can tell he has more to say, wants to make sure I understand. I reach out and clap my hand on his shoulder. I nod as I look into his eyes.

So much of our family's communication over the last years has had to be unspoken. We've had to believe in each other, to trust each other, even when it didn't seem like the smart thing to do. We had to believe in the unseen, hope in the unlikely.

Now, standing right here in front of him, I know Cash can see that I understand, and that it's all in the past.

Finally, he nods, too. Yes, he knows.

"The only thing you have to do is get the case together and keep Dad safe for his part of the testimony. Money laundering and cooked books ought to be the nail in the coffin for Slava and his boys. They're all three involved in different aspects, but all three were knowledgeable about the entire show. Each person's testimony will show that."

After a few seconds of digesting what I've said, Cash laughs. It's a lighthearted laugh, a pleased, nearly gleeful one. "Holy shit! You did it!"

I get the feeling he wants to let out a whoop. And that makes me smile again, too.

"I just did my part. The rest is up to you and whoever else needs to be a part of this to make sure it goes off without a hitch. You're the legal eagle. I'll leave that stuff to you."

"Does Marissa know? She's got contacts that could be very helpful."

"No, I didn't tell her. I'll let you do that. You two can get a plan going. I've got some things I need to take care of."

Leaving now, when things are looking so good, feels more like exile than it did seven years ago. I feel like I'm leaving happiness behind, rather than fighting for it in the future.

"I wish you could stay."

"I do, too, but I just . . . I can't."

Cash nods. "Will you be back? Ever?"

"Yeah. Someday. I hope."

"At least say you'll come back the day they let Dad go. That'll be a good day."

I can imagine it, and I know that it will. "I think I can manage that."

I feel relieved at the prospect of coming back, at the hope of it.

"And don't forget your promise to me," he reminds.

I smile.

The wedding.

"Never."

"How are you getting where you need to go? You know I can take you."

"Nah, that's all right. I'll leave just like I came. In one pretty damn expensive cab ride."

Cash shakes his head and smiles. "What the hell kinda cabbies are you using?"

"The desperate kind."

"Sounds like it."

"But they make good money."

"Sometimes desperation pays off."

And sometimes it doesn't.

Visions of Marissa settle over me like a cloud. The hurt look on her face when she remembered New Orleans will probably haunt me forever.

"You gonna say good-bye to Olivia?" Cash asks.

I nod. I guess I'd better. She'll likely be my sister-in-law one day. I'd better make nice.

"I'll be in touch with a number where you can reach me. I'll be wanting all the gory details on how you botched a proposal."

"Shhh." Cash shushes me as he looks behind him. "She hears everything. Be careful what you say."

"Who hears everything?" Olivia says, as if right on cue. Cash and I both bust out laughing. "What?" she asks from the doorway, looking confused.

"Nothing, babe," Cash says, reaching out to draw her to him. A little stab of envy pricks me, but I refuse to dwell on it. It's time to stop being jealous of my brother and his life. It's time for me to find my own version of bliss, whatever that might be.

TWENTY-EIGHT

Marissa

I sit, stunned, with my phone in my lap. I find myself doing this a lot lately.

I don't know what is making me feel short of breath—the fact that Cash just told me everything Nash has done to secure the RICO case, the fact that I'm going to have to make some very tough career and life choices in the very near future, or that Nash is gone.

Gone.

Without a good-bye.

Without another word.

Just gone.

He left things like they were.

Like I demanded he do.

I don't know what I would like for him to have said, or if there was really anything left *to* say. But I wish he had. I wish he had tried. I wish he had fought. For me. For us.

But he didn't. He respected my wishes and he left. Now he's gone. Forever. Never to be a part of my life. Ever. In any way.

I didn't expect it to end this way. I mean, I'm no idiot. After the things that happened over the last day or so, I figured it would end sooner or later, that we didn't stand much of a chance. Even after our one beautiful, surreal night, I knew we were a long shot. But I guess I thought there would be more time or more words or more . . . something. But, instead, there was nothing.

And that's where I am. Here. Now. With nothing.

And Nash is gone.

I close my eyes. The tears spill between my lashes and down my cheeks. I don't even try to stop them. There's no point. These are the first of many that will fall, I feel sure.

There's no doubt my life is getting ready to become much more difficult. There's no doubt there's a hard road ahead. There's no doubt the day-to-day details of my existence will be dramatically different, as will the people who fill them. But I won't shed tears over any of that. I feel no sense of loss; only dread and anxiety.

For the most part, I'll be going it alone. I will have the support of Olivia, of course. And Cash, such as his support will be. And maybe one or two more people, but in the end, I'm alone. When the dust settles and I've alienated all the horrible people in my life and I've abandoned the only career I've ever known and thought I ever wanted, I'll be left with the fallout.

There may be a great guy who will cross my path one day, but even then, I'll still be alone. He won't be Nash. And I'll never be satisfied with less. There will always be a hole in me, one that no one else can fill.

And that's the cold, bitter truth. The harsh reality of falling in love with a man who doesn't want to be held and who can't be tamed or contained.

The thing is, I never really wanted to tame him or contain him. I just wanted to be a part of his freedom, to fly with him. *I* wanted to be more like *him*, not try to make *him* more like me. I'm trying to escape me, not drag someone into my hell.

Maybe that's what I did, anyway, by making him a part of my escape. I pulled him into my struggle.

Maybe I expected him to save me. I know I *wanted* him to. But he did all the rescuing he was going to do the day he brought me home from a Russian mafia prison of sorts. Anything more than that would have to be his idea, something his heart is in. He'd have to come to that conclusion on his own. There's no swaying or forcing or convincing Nash to do anything. He's his own man. One hundred percent.

Maybe one day I can be my own woman. One hundred percent.

Maybe today, I'll be taking the first step.

Cash doesn't want to be involved in the prosecution because he'd have to assume Nash's identity again, which he's opposed to now for some reason, but also because of his father's involvement. But he wants to be in the loop, so he asked me to request to be a special prosecutor on the case so I can sit second chair and be involved every step of the way.

I think he knows what he's asking. He knows my father, knows the kind of life I've led. He knows that taking on a criminal case would be the social equivalent of moving to the ghettos. It's something I'd never be forgiven for, that would never be forgotten, and that would change the course of my life irrevocably.

But it's also just what I need.

And I think it's what I want.

There's nothing for me in my old life anymore. I'm not even sure law is where my future is. But I know this is important and it would be the most personally courageous, definitive thing I've ever done. And I need to be courageous. I need to embrace the new me. Fully. Publicly. Proudly. If I can't do that, the new me will shrivel and die in the shadow of the old me. That's my only other option—to go back to the life I knew, the life I had.

But that's no option at all.

I think of Nash. He goaded me, as though he thought I couldn't do it. Or wouldn't. But in a way, I think he was prodding me to do it, like he wanted to see me succeed and be the different person that I so longed to be. And if he were here, maybe he'd be a little bit proud of me for doing it, for being strong. Maybe stronger than he thought.

My heart speeds up.

I'm really gonna do this. I'm really gonna be the person I want to see in the mirror, the woman I can live with and be proud of.

I'm looking at a fragile, onetime opportunity to put away three upper-level members of a Russian criminal organization that operates out of Georgia. Not only that, but I have the opportunity to see justice served to the men who kidnapped me. At least I *hope* we can get them in the process. I don't even know who they are, but maybe I'm one step closer to finding out. At least we'll get the guy who ordered it done. Cash assured me the man responsible is one of the three targeted. There will be some satisfaction in that.

As I think of what's to come, legally speaking, I feel relieved to have something so consuming to focus on. Something other than Nash. Or the lack thereof. I also feel a little overwhelmed. I'm smart enough to realize when I'm out of my depth. And I am.

As I consider what my first step needs to be, I scroll through my list of recent calls. I stop on Jensen Strong's number, my thumb hovering there. As a prosecutor for the DA's office, he seems like the perfect place to start.

I press the square and hold the phone to my ear, listening to it ring. A shadow of dread overcomes the determination of my new endeavor. I know that after I talk to Jensen, I'll have another call to make.

Daddy.

TWENTY-NINE

Nash

I didn't sleep much last night, so I'm a little groggy as I thumb through some bills to pay the cabbie who brought me from the motel to the docks. The fare isn't nearly as exorbitant as the one I paid last night to the guy who brought me from Atlanta to Savannah. But I expected that. He drove me a long, long way.

The cab pulls away and I glance down at the envelope again before I begin my search. The boat name that Dmitry scrawled across the front is the only thing I have to go on. *Budushcheye Mudrost*. My Russian isn't perfect, but it translates roughly to "future wisdom."

Dmitry said I could find the boat at port here in Savannah. He gave me the letter to give to the captain, a man he called Drago. He asked that I hand-deliver it. That's all. That's the only thing he wanted from me. He's giving up so much to help me, to help my father and my family, and the only thing he asked in return was that I deliver a letter for him.

Of course, I agreed.

He can't deliver it himself. The only thing he's leaving the motel for is to meet Konstantin, the man who will hopefully rise into leadership with the local *Bratva*. Otherwise, he and Duffy will be hiding out at the motel until Cash and Marissa can get the ball rolling, get indictments going, all that technical shit. After that, I'd say Dmitry and Duffy will be deposed and then put in witness protection or something like that. I think that's how it works, anyway. I wouldn't know for sure. I'm not the Nash that attended law school.

It takes me nearly an hour to locate the boat. I was expecting a commercial vessel, something similar to what Dmitry and I have worked on all this time, not the private yacht I'm staring at. The *damn fine* private yacht I'm staring at.

I see one person walk by on the upper deck. I call out to him and ask for permission to come aboard. I get no smile or friendly greeting, only a very short, very clipped "yes."

I climb onto the deck and wait. In less than a minute, the same guy is standing in front of me. He's frowning and looks annoyed, like I'm an unwelcome interruption. Physically, he looks like a washed-out, nondescript version of Dmitry.

"I'm looking for Drago."

"I'm Drago," he says abruptly. His accent is thick and his disposition is surly at best.

"I have a letter for you from Dmitry," I say, holding up the envelope.

His frown deepens and he snatches the letter from my fingers. I watch him run his thumb under the sealed tab of the envelope and remove the piece of paper from inside. He unfolds it and, from between the creases, takes out another sheet of paper. Holding the second piece in his other hand, Drago begins reading the first.

He looks up at me several times as he reads. I don't know what that means, but I assume Dmitry is explaining who I am and why I'm delivering it. That or he's telling the other Russian something he doesn't like.

I hope it's not bad news and this asshole doesn't go all Boondock Saints *and shoot my ass.*

When he finishes the letter, Drago glances up at me again, narrowing his eyes on mine. After staring at me for God knows how long, like he's trying to figure something out, he hands me the second folded piece of paper, the one from inside the first letter.

I'm a little surprised that it's for me. If Dmitry'd had something to say, I would've thought he'd have said it to my face, when I was there yesterday. But looking at the page, with its sharp creases and wrinkled edges, it's easy to see this was written some time ago.

I unfold the paper and read Dmitry's neat print.

Nikolai,

Many years ago, I met a teenage boy. He was the son of a friend and one of the strongest young men I've ever known. He gave up his life, his future, and his family to honor his father and to one day find a way to bring justice to his dead mother.

I grew fond of this boy. I loved him like a son, like my own family. Over time, I watched him grow and struggle and become a most trusted friend, a man any father would be proud of.

I feel I've played a part in your hardships, Nikolai, even though indirectly. More than anything I want you to find happiness and peace.

I pray there will come a day when you can escape this life. If you're reading this letter, today is that day. Most likely, Drago is giving you this note. It has been hiding safely inside the instructions I wrote to him today. I don't know how many years have passed until you're reading this, but know that I've been planning this gift to you for a long, long time.

I bought this boat to one day take me to retirement, somewhere far away, but I want you to have one year of freedom on it. Freedom to find yourself, find your place in life, find happiness. And peace. Dearest God, I hope you find peace, my friend.

The crew and the captain are paid annually. That is taken care of through an account I keep for them. They do some small yet legitimate importing and exporting for me. But for this year, for your year, you need only tell them where you want to go and they'll take you. I suspect I know your first destination and I've told Drago as much in his letter. If you go there, give my best to Yusuf's wife. Tell her I'm deeply sorry for her loss.

Go, Nikolai! Take this gift and turn your life around. You deserve a second chance. More than anyone I know.

Sem'ya.
Dmitry

Stunned, I look up at Drago. He's watching me with suspicious eyes. Regardless, he honors Dmitry's letter. I'm not surprised. Dmitry inspires that kind of loyalty in those who know him.

"We leave in two days. You must give me your first destination tomorrow morning. Supplies must be bought."

With that, he turns and walks away.

For a few seconds, I stand and watch him go, still shocked, before I snap out of it and move to follow him.

"If you'll just show me which room is mine . . ." I say loud enough to stop him before he can get out of earshot.

Drago pauses, turning his head just enough that I know he heard me. He grunts once and then starts off in another direction. I follow him inside, through a lush living room to a staircase leading to the lower deck. He turns left down a short hallway and stops in front of a closed door. He opens it and steps aside.

"It's clean," he says gruffly before he walks away.

Obviously, I don't have to worry about him talking my ear off during the trip.

The trip.

I admit I'm a little relieved to have this as an option. When I left the restaurant yesterday, I just knew I had to get away from Marissa, that she deserves to have someone better than me in her life. I didn't really consider where I'd go. I mean, I'd never willingly go back to running guns. But staying in Atlanta wasn't an option. I'd be too tempted to pay Marissa a visit. At least now I have a place to go. For a year, anyway.

It's not exactly what I'd always dreamed. I figured once I put an end to all this shit with my family, I'd end up back in Atlanta. I never really considered what I'd do—maybe open a club like Cash or . . . or . . . Hell, I don't even know. I guess I never got that far. Maybe on some level I didn't think it would ever be over. This anger, this hunger is all I've known for seven years. I'm not sure how to plan a life without it. It's been my purpose for so long, I feel a little lost without it.

But now I have this. This gift from Dmitry. All I have to do is be on this boat in two days and I'll be sailing away from my problems.

But I'll also be sailing away from Marissa.

Damn! How the hell did I let her get under my skin?

After another few minutes of thought, I walk back the way Drago brought me. It takes me a little bit of exploration to find him. He's in the galley with two other men.

"I'll be back. I need to get some things straightened out before I leave."

I don't wait for any kind of response. I don't owe them any more explanation than that. And from what Dmitry's letter says, these guys are hired hands, so their only task is to do as they're told.

Making my way from the yacht, I head into downtown Savannah. Since this is where I most often came ashore to do any kind of business, I've always used a bank here to access my offshore investments. I'll need some money before I leave.

If I leave . . .

I push the thought aside. Leaving is the only real choice I have. The only one that's not something only a selfish bastard would do. And at some point, I guess I'll have to stop being a selfish bastard, especially if I ever plan to reintegrate back into polite society.

It gives me hope that one day I will.

One day. Maybe in a year.

THIRTY

Marissa

I'm taking a chance that Daddy won't be too busy to see me, to take a short face-to-face meeting. What I *want* is to take the coward's way out and just call. And I might have chosen that route if it weren't for the text.

When the elevator doors inside my office building slide shut, I press the button for my father's floor and I pull out my cell phone for the hundredth time. The instant the screen lights up, it shows the text. I imagine that it will be the most recently viewed item on my phone for a long time to come.

It's not from a number I recognize, but that didn't stop me from instantly identifying the sender. It's from Nash.

> Maybe there was a time when I hated you, but only
> for dating my brother who was pretending to be me.
> All that changed the night I held you in my arms on

the balcony. I knew you were more than what other
people saw. I still believe that. You're brave and
strong in ways most people aren't. And at the end of
the day, know that there's at least one person in the
world who believes in you. That's the last thing I want
to leave you with other than this: I could've taken
care of Duffy my way. I had the chance. The only
thing that stopped me was you.

Every time I read it, I'm torn between feeling like I can conquer
the world and feeling like I'm drowning in sorrow. I knew after
talking to Cash that Nash was gone. That was bad enough. But
then to hear from him . . . something like this . . . after he disappeared into thin air . . .

I responded to the text, hoping I could have one more chance
to talk to him, but all I received was an error message telling me
the number was no longer in service. It must've been a burner
phone, which Cash also warned me about. Nash had told him he'd
be getting rid of his phone, but that he'd be in touch. And he did.
Then he got rid of that phone, too. So fast. Just like that.

Much like his presence from the very first time we met, Nash
rocked my world, then turned around and walked out of it, leaving it in shambles.

At least he left me with something valuable, though—his support. I know enough about him to know he doesn't give it easily,
nor does he give praise or compliments easily. That's why his words
mean so much. I can close my eyes and see them behind my lids,
like he typed them on the surface of my brain rather than on a
digital screen. There and somewhere deep in my soul, like a tattoo
that will forever make all the difference in the world to me.

The elevator door opens with a hushed *ding*!

Nash is the reason I'm here right now, getting ready to face the bear. It's time to grow up and live my own life. My way. It's time to cut ties, whether Daddy likes it or not. And I've come here to look him in the eye as I tell him so.

I straighten my suit jacket and stop in front of his secretary's desk. I smile down at her when she looks up at me.

"Is he in?" I ask.

"He's on a conference call, but I'm sure he'll have a minute for you afterward if you don't mind waiting. Can I get you some coffee? Or would you like me to buzz your office when he's finished?"

I don't really want to answer any questions or talk to anyone else in the office before I tell Daddy, so I figure it's best to just wait.

"I think I'll take some coffee while I wait. I'm sure he won't be long."

She smiles and nods as she stands. "Cream and sugar?"

"Black, thank you."

She nods again and walks toward the kitchenette behind her work station. Within two minutes, she's bringing me a piping hot cup of expensive coffee. My mouth waters before I take one sip.

"Thank you, Juliette."

"My pleasure."

She takes her seat and resumes typing whatever it is she's working on, giving me plenty of time to focus on my nerves. I think it's a credit to how much I've changed that I don't talk myself out of this approach. Confronting Daddy or doing anything to displease him was never something I would've considered before. I was happy being a blind, well-trained monkey, mindlessly following his commands. It makes me a little sick to think that I might've lived the rest of my life that way, being his pawn, never following my own path.

I'm so immersed in thought, I jump when Juliette speaks.

"His call just ended. Let me tell him you're here."

She gets up and crosses to the wide, mahogany double doors and slips inside one. A few seconds later, she reemerges and waves me in, holding the door until I'm inside then closing it quietly behind me.

Daddy glances up at me, then returns his attention to his desk. "It's good to see you out and about, finally back at work. I was beginning to worry about you."

Bullshit, Nash's dry voice says from inside my head. It makes me smile. Because he's right.

I clear my throat. There's no reason to go through the motions of all these perfunctory niceties. They're not genuine and they're not necessary. I'm wise to his game. And since they were always for my benefit, nothing more than a polite ruse, I'll cut to the chase.

"Daddy, I'd like to work on a case with Jensen Strong at the DA's office."

That gets his full attention. He looks up at me, whipping off his reading glasses to narrow his eyes on me. "You're joking, right?" When I don't respond, he continues. "Why?"

As far as reactions go, this one's not as bad as I thought.

"It involves Nash's father," I say simply. I don't want to explain to him all the details about the Davenport subterfuge, nor do I have any intention of telling him about my kidnapping.

"I thought you said that was over."

"It is. But I still want to help. I owe it to him."

"You owe him your career?"

"I didn't say that."

"Yes, you did. You just told me that you want to work with the DA's office to prosecute a criminal. That's not what you do, which means you must want to give up your work here."

"It's not a permanent change, Daddy. It would only be until the trial was over."

"It's not the timing I'm concerned about. Marissa, you know as well as I do that the people we represent expect us to uphold our sterling reputation. It's unfortunate, but it's a reality."

Bullshit, the voice says again. He doesn't think it's unfortunate. Not for one second do I believe that. It's yet another manipulation, something he's saying just for my benefit, to elicit a certain kind of reaction.

"It is unfortunate because this is something I'm committed to."

"Marissa, honey, don't be ridiculous. Let the professionals handle this. A man's life is at stake."

"I *am* a professional, Daddy. Or did you forget that I graduated law school summa cum laude?"

"That's not what I meant and you know it. Regardless, this is just not something I can allow."

I straighten my spine and tip my chin toward the ceiling, glad that I didn't sit down when I came into the room. I want him to see me strong and tall. Standing on my own two feet, both literally and figuratively.

"I didn't come to ask your permission. I came to tell you out of courtesy and respect."

He slams his fist onto his desktop, his face growing instantly red with fury. "You call this respect? Throwing everything I've given you, everything I've worked so hard for our family to have, right back in my face, as though it means nothing to you?"

I take a deep breath and try to remain calm in the face of his anger. "I'm grateful for everything you've ever done for me, Daddy, every opportunity you've ever given me. But this is something I have to do. Maybe it's just time for me to live my own life, to come out from under the roof you've built."

My father gets to his feet. "You're doing this because you 'owe Nash'? You don't owe him one damn thing! You owe *me*!"

"I've done everything you've ever asked of me, Daddy. I've never questioned you or hesitated to follow your direction. Can't you just give me this one thing?"

I know before he speaks what the answer will be. This is as much a personal insult as it is a professional affront. This will forever, irrevocably change things between us.

"Wives of leaders don't dabble in criminal law, and they don't wallow with commoners or felons. You're throwing away everything I've ever groomed you to be."

And there it is. The truth.

"A politician's wife. That's what you groomed me to be, isn't it, Daddy?" He says nothing. "Law school was a formality, a social experiment. You never intended to give me one ounce of control or responsibility here. You just planned to find me the 'right' husband and pass me off to be a sidekick, didn't you?" His continued silence angers me almost as much as it hurts me. Suspecting I was right is much different than having my own father confirm it. "Well, I'm sorry to disappoint you, Daddy, but this is something I've got to do. For me. For my friends. For the people who love and care about me. About the real me, not the person you've created. I honestly hope one day you can meet her, and that you'll be proud of her. But if you don't, I'll understand. Because for the first time in my life, I can see beyond my own selfishness, beyond the curtain. I always thought what was outside the walls of our family and our lifestyle were ugly, that we had the good life." I walk slowly to my father's desk and set my coffee cup down on the edge before I look up to meet his handsome yet livid face. "I was wrong."

My insides are shaking as I turn and walk to the door. My father's voice stops me, but I don't look back.

"If you walk out that door and pursue this, you're no longer a part of this firm." His pause is filled with hurtful things, like the unspoken sentiment that I'm no longer part of this family, either. While it breaks my heart for him to act this way, it doesn't really surprise me. It's why I've never challenged him before. On some level, I knew he'd be this way. It's either his way or the highway, both personally and professionally. If I choose to walk my own path, I'll have to walk it alone.

As if to drive home his point and the finality of it, he adds, "Whatever's left in your office by the close of business will be thrown out with the garbage."

I give him a single nod as I reach for the doorknob.

He's throwing me *out with the garbage.*

Opening the door, I walk through it, walk away from everything and everyone I've ever known. And not once do I look back.

THIRTY-ONE

Nash

From my position on the stern, I can watch as the brightly lit Savannah skyline disappears on the horizon. I can't remember being this homesick since the day I shipped out and left home for the first time seven years ago.

I'm not running for my life or going into hiding this time. I'm not sailing into the unknown this time. Not really. No, this time I know how long I'll be gone and I know I'll be safe on this luxurious boat. It'll be like a millionaire's vacation, every man's dream.

Only it feels empty and lonely. Not much has changed in my life, so it doesn't take a genius to figure out what's bothering me so much. Or, rather, *who* is bothering me so much.

It's Marissa.

I hate leaving her, especially right now, with everything a disaster between us. I hate the thought of her thinking I'm such a bad guy, of leaving her with the impression I did. I mean, I'm not the best guy, but I'm not the horrible monster she saw at the restaurant the other day. I haven't been that guy since the day I met her, not truly.

Little by little, she's made me feel again, and monsters don't feel. They just damage and destroy and wreak havoc. That's the reason I left, so I wouldn't damage and destroy and wreak any more havoc. She deserves more than that, better than that.

But it sure makes me feel like shit to be watching land, and the possibility of going back to her, disappear right before my eyes.

Swallowing the sensation until it sits in the pit of my stomach like a bag of rocks, I turn and walk away from the railing, away from the view.

Away from her.

THIRTY-TWO

Marissa

Two weeks later

"So everything is ready and the depositions are scheduled?" Cash asks.

"Yep. And after that, Dmitry and Duffy will both go to safe locations with witness protection teams until the trial starts. Luckily, Jensen got the attorney general to help speed things along since this is such a big case. We were afraid the feds would try to take it over since it involves acts of terrorism as defined by U.S. federal law, but he's agreed to let us prosecute it. It helps that I have 'special knowledge,'" I tell him.

"I was hoping they wouldn't see it as a conflict."

"If I had to testify, we'd have a problem, but since Duffy's testimony will be enough to get the only other people involved in my kidnapping, I'm clear to sit on this side of things."

Just saying the words out loud still causes a flash of anger and bitter disappointment to course through me.

"Look, I know that bothers you. Duffy going free bothers the shit out of me, too. Trust me. He hurt us both. He hurt *all of us*. But his life will be over, just in a different way. He won't spend it in prison and he won't be dead for his crimes, but he'll never be a truly free man. He'll be hunted as a traitor for the rest of his life. Even in witness protection, wherever they stick him when all this is said and done, he'll spend the rest of his days looking over his shoulder, wondering if someone's coming for him."

"But all the bigwigs will be in prison."

"Yeah, but Duffy will always worry that they've somehow managed to hire someone to kill him, or that they've paid off some law enforcement to give them his location."

A fear that has steadily grown more powerful over the last couple of weeks rears its head. "Technically we have to worry about the same thing."

"No. And that's because the new leadership with this cell of *Bratva* has agreed to our protection. Even Slava and his cronies aren't stupid enough to test the entire Russian mafia. They have ties, but their power is insignificant compared to that of a sitting head honcho."

"God, I hope you're right."

I feel sweat break out on my palms.

"Besides, evidently my brother made quite the name for himself during his time at sea. And from what I understand, he's put the word out that if anyone lays a hand on you, three hundred and sixty-five days from that moment, they'll be dead a year."

It takes my brain a few seconds to process that and laugh. But it's an automated response. I'm still stuck on the fact that Nash has put out some kind of warning to anyone who might think to harm me.

But then common sense kicks in.

"I guess he needs to protect the people who are finally bringing him the justice he's waited so long for." I can't keep the hurt and disappointment from my voice.

"I'm sure he wants to do that, too. But that's not why he did it." After a pause, Cash clears his throat. "Look, Marissa. I misjudged you. It took me a while to see the person you are deep down. But not Nash. I think he saw it right away."

"Thanks, Cash," is all I can manage past my wobbling vocal cords.

My heart aches. I want so much to believe Nash cared about me as much as I cared about him, as much as I still do. But if he did, he'd be here. With me. Where he belongs.

But he's not. He sailed away. Out of my life. And one of these days, I'll have to let him go.

THIRTY-THREE

Nash

Two months later

The balmy Caribbean air ruffles my hair as I stare out at the wide expanse of sea. As far as the eye can see in every direction, there's nothing. I should feel relaxed and safe and satisfied after getting such an encouraging update from Cash. Everything is going along as planned, moving in the right direction. Marissa's kicking ass and taking names. With that jerk-off Jensen's help, of course.

I feel my lip curl at the thought of him cozying up to her over some law books. Just as it does every time I think of her with someone else, rage fills me. For a few seconds, I close my eyes and visualize throwing Jensen down on a fancy courtroom floor and beating the shit out of him, not stopping until his face is unrecognizable and my knuckles are a shredded, bloody mess.

I open my eyes and look to my right, to the satellite phone that's lying on the glass table beside my deck chair. It's for emergencies only—I make calls from ports whenever I just want to check in—but every day that I don't call and talk to Marissa, tell her I'm coming back and I'm going to be a part of her life whether she likes it or not, feels like an emergency, like I'm lost at sea with no compass and no life preserver.

She's starting to feel more and more like an anchor, like a North Star. Like *my* North Star. With every week that passes, it seems my direction just feels . . . wrong. Like I'm going the wrong way. Like I'm sailing away when I should be sailing toward.

Toward Marissa.

THIRTY-FOUR

Marissa

There's no question that the man brought into the room is Greg Davenport. This is the first time I've actually gotten to see him since this whole thing started. Jensen talked to him alone here at the prison the first time.

If I were passing him on the street, I think I'd recognize him. He looks like an older, slightly paler version of his sons. The resemblance is striking. But for the softer brown eyes and lighter blond hair, and the fact that he's older, of course, Greg Davenport could be a brother to Nash rather than his father.

His eyes flicker to mine and he smiles. It's a pleasant smile, but it seems a little tired and a lot worried. I wonder if he's sleeping. If I were in his shoes, I doubt I would be.

We've taken every precaution to keep things quiet until we can get Slava and the other two indicted and in custody. That won't guarantee Greg's safety, but it sure can't hurt.

His first question lets me know that if he's losing sleep, it's not over worry for his own safety. "How are my sons?"

Jensen looks to me for an answer. He doesn't keep in regular contact with Cash like I do. For obvious reasons.

I clear my throat and smile pleasantly at Mr. Davenport. "They're both fine, sir."

He laughs and I get a glimpse of what Nash might've looked like in his carefree days. I'm sure he was breathtaking! Now, there's only bitterness and anger. But even so, he's still the most handsome man I know.

Well, *did* know.

"And who might you be?"

"I'm sorry. My name is Marissa Townsend. I'm working with Jensen as a special prosecutor."

He shakes his head, looking duly impressed. Neither Greg nor Jensen knows the truth about my involvement in the case. I'm sure they both think my rich father called in a favor. But that's not the case at all. In order to be appointed to the case by the attorney general, I had to tell him about my involvement. I had to convince him that my intimate knowledge of some of the events and players would be a help to the case. I explained about being kidnapped and spending time in the presence of some of the suspects, about learning things from listening to them. Thankfully, he didn't require me to get specific. If he had, he'd have seen that I'm not nearly as important as I made it appear. What I have invested in this is heart. And what the attorney general doesn't realize is that *that's* what makes me most valuable.

Greg's voice brings me back to the present.

"You must be the one Nash knows."

"Yes, I know Nash."

He nods and smiles. "So you're the one."

I frown, my stomach flipping over at something I see in his eyes, in his smile.

"I'm not sure I understand."

"There comes a time in life when every man meets the woman who changes the game, who changes *him*. You're the one." I feel a blush sting my cheeks. I look nervously at my laced fingers where they rest on the table in front of me. I'm aware of Jensen's curious gaze on me. I do my best to ignore it. He doesn't know that the Nash we're talking about isn't the Nash he thinks he knows. And Jensen also thinks that relationship is over. Very much over. Which it is. I just wish it weren't.

"I think you must be mistaken."

"Oh no. I'm not mistaken. I'm not surprised it's a woman like you. You remind me of Lizzie. In all the ways that matter."

His look turns sad.

"I'm sure you miss her. This won't bring her back, but maybe bringing her justice and being able to watch your sons grow old will ease the pain."

"Nothing ever eases the pain of losing your soul mate. You're not as smart as you look if you think different."

He's not trying to insult me. I can tell from his earnest expression. He's trying to tell me something. Something I already know.

He's trying to tell me I'll never be whole without Nash. Never.

But I already knew that.

THIRTY-FIVE

Nash

Three months later

I take one last look around the tiny apartment before I say good-bye to Sharifa and Jamilla. It's not a great space, but compared to the shack-like structure where they lived in their village of Beer-nassi, this place is like the Ritz.

The walls are painted a cheery yellow and the furniture, while not exactly new, is a pale green and in good shape. The kitchen's white appliances are clean and there's even a microwave now, which Sharifa thinks is the most extravagant part of all.

But not Jamilla. If I had to guess, I'd say she would say her playroom is the most extravagant part of all.

It consists of a thick plastic play kitchen, complete with a pink table and four tiny chairs, each one currently occupied by a different stuffed animal. She's serving them the meal she just cooked in her little plastic skillet. The sun is streaming in through the window, turning her raven hair to glistening waves of black silk.

In the three weeks since I took them away from their home to bring them here to Savannah, the change in her diet is evident. Her skin and hair look healthy, and her cough has almost completely disappeared.

Not having to worry about someone bursting through the door to gun them down and not having to wonder where they'll get money for food is showing, too. Sharifa is more relaxed, and her calm spills over into her daughter's smiles and laughter. Maybe one day the memory of her father's brutal murder will be a vague memory.

I doubt Sharifa will ever fully recover from the loss of Yusuf, but this move is helping as much as anything can. Every time Jamilla giggles, Sharifa smiles. It makes me think there might be hope in the world after all.

I've been able to honor my friend by giving his family freedom they've never known before. And stability. All their basic needs will be met. I set up an account for them. It's funded by a substantial savings that's constantly generating money. Most of the dividend will go into Sharifa's checking account. A small portion will go into a college fund for Jamilla and an even smaller portion back into another savings account for emergencies. I've also already hired an immigration lawyer to help her become a naturalized citizen so she can work here, so that's been taken care of, too. All in all, they should be all set for a long, long time to come.

"My cab's here. I need to get going. You have my phone number, right?"

I bought a phone. One to keep permanently. Sharifa and Jamilla deserve to have an emergency contact. One that doesn't change from day to day or month to month. It's my first step toward laying down roots. I figure it's about time.

"Yes. But I will only call if emergency," she says in her stilted English.

"I told you that you can call anytime. I may not be local, but I can find someone to get you the help you need in an emergency."

She shakes her head vigorously. "Too much already. I can't thank you enough."

"You don't have to. It's what Yusuf would've wanted. You're never a bother. Call me anytime."

Sharifa steps closer to me and reaches up to lay her hand on my cheek. "Bless you, Nikolai. May every day for your wife and children be blessed. Peace be with you."

Her words cause a pang in my chest. I don't have a wife. Or children. I may never have. And if I do, will I have a family with the woman I love? Or will I settle for something . . . less? "Thank you, Sharifa. I pray the same for you."

I tell Jamilla good-bye and give her tiny shoulders a squeeze. She turns into my chest and throws her arms around my neck. She gives me a big, smacking kiss on my cheek then leans back to look at me. She's smiling broadly.

It's with a heavy heart that I make my way out the door and down the steps. My only wish is that Yusuf were here to see his family smile, to see them happy and safe here in the United States.

I'm preoccupied during the cab ride back to the hotel. This morning when I went for coffee, I saw on the news that the trial against the Atlanta sect of the Russian mafia is well under way. Because of all the sensationalism surrounding it, the judge closed the courtroom. There is no close coverage or photos or anything, really. The media is simply updated periodically with information they can release to the public. It's pretty vague stuff, just talking about crucial testimony of former employees, but never going into specifics.

But then I saw a short press conference held specifically for legal counsel to give statements. The balding lawyer for the *Bratva* gave his brief spiel, proclaiming that he was even more confident after this week's proceedings that his clients would be proven innocent. And then there was a statement from the prosecution.

And Marissa gave it.

She was practically glowing in her dark blue suit and pale pink blouse. Her voice was strong and confident as she spoke.

"With the ironclad evidence presented by our team and the irrefutable testimony of eyewitnesses, we have no doubt justice will be served."

She took a few questions and answered them deftly, like she'd been fielding them all her life. It's easy to see this is what she was born to do. And that she enjoys doing it. And I'm big enough to admit that it's bittersweet.

She's doing great. She's happy and driven, and she found her place in life. Her peace. She took life by the balls and came out on top. And of course I wish her well.

I just wish we could've found that together.

It took me a couple of months to realize I was in love with her. Well, probably not to *realize* it. More like to *admit it*. And when I did, I knew that was why I had chosen to stay away from her. I love her enough to want her to be happy and safe and successful, and all that other shit. I want her to have everything she wants in life.

And she can't have all that if I'm around. I'm a criminal. Or at least I was. Either way, I'm not worthy of her. And I'd probably ruin her career. Especially after this. She'll be a star in legal circles by the end of this trial. She'll have the world in the palm of her hand.

And I'll always have to watch from afar.

That's just the way it is.

I close my eyes so I can more clearly see her. I picture her first as I saw her this morning, in the suit and light pink blouse. Smiling. Confident. Happy.

But quickly, she loses her clothes and I picture her like I saw her the night before I left. She's looking back at me over her shoulder, her luscious lips parted in a moan as I slide in and out of the tight glove of her body.

Damn, why did it have to work out this way? Why couldn't it have been different? Why couldn't I have been different?

I'm grouchy by the time I unlock the door to my room. I feel alone and far removed from everyone who means anything to me, and I don't like it. It makes me angry.

I push the button to bring up the lighted screen on my new phone. I punch in Cash's number. The display only requires a light touch, but my mood is not conducive to a light touch. It's there in my desire to stab my finger through the glass cover of the phone, and it's there in the ache in my jaw from gritting my teeth.

"Yeah," comes Cash's voice, short and clipped.

"It's me," I say simply.

"Where are you?" he asks. In those three words, I can hear the change in his tone. If I didn't know better, I'd say it sounds like he's glad to hear from me.

"I'm in Savannah. Pulling out tomorrow."

I feel my lips thin just saying that out loud. I should be looking forward to sailing the rest of the world. But I'm not. There's only one place I want to be. And it's the only place that I can't go. That I shouldn't go.

"You still on Dmitry's tugboat?" he asks wryly. I called him a couple of weeks after I left and told him where I was and what I was doing. I described the yacht to him. He knows it's nicer than most houses.

"Yep."

"Have you been able to keep up with the trial?"

"Some. I take it it's going well?"

"Hell yeah, it is! I really think we're gonna pull this off, man!"

His excitement is obvious. And it only makes me feel worse for some reason.

"Considering all the people who have sacrificed so much to make this happen, I sure as hell hope so!"

Cash is quiet for a minute. "You know you can come back, right? No one's making you stay away."

"You think I don't know that?" I snap. I regret my reaction immediately. Sighing loudly, I pinch the bridge of my nose, hoping to ease the throb that seems to have come out of nowhere. "Sorry, bro. I'm just a little on edge today."

"No problem. I just wanted you to know that you're welcome. We'd all love to have you back. I think Dad would be thrilled."

"Dad, huh?"

"Not *just* Dad, but yeah. Dad would."

"Hmmm," I say, unwilling to ask about Marissa specifically.

"I'm sure Marissa would. She's miserable without you."

"I doubt that. I saw her at the press conference. She looks like she's doing great."

"She is. I mean, the trial's going great. She's doing a good job. But . . . she just isn't . . . I don't know. Maybe I'm wrong. What do I know about women?"

"Good point," I say playfully.

"Like you're much better."

"I know more about women than you *ever* will."

"You wish," he teases right back. "Hey, speaking of women. You still game to be my best man?"

"Sure. You popped the question yet?"

"Not yet, but it won't be long. The trial should be over in another month. I'll do it then. When all this is behind us. She'll be ready for a fresh start. We all will."

"Just tell me when."

"How long will you have this number?"

"I plan on keeping this one."

"Really?"

"Yeah. I'm betting on this working out so none of us have to hide anymore. Ever."

"I am, too, man. I am, too."

"Well, keep me posted. It's a satellite phone, so you should be able to get me most of the time, even after I ship out."

"Where you headed to this time?"

I shrug. I don't know why. Cash can't see me. I guess I just feel apathetic all over.

"Europe, I think. I've been to the Caribbean, Central and South America. And Africa, of course. I think it's time to spend some euros."

"Damn, what a hard life you have," Cash says dryly.

"Hey, you don't want to get into a pissing contest with me today, man." I laugh to take some of the bite out of my statement. I meant every word of it, but I didn't mean to sound like such an asshole.

"I know, dude. It can't be easy."

I grunt. I don't know what to say. If I get started, I'm liable to start whining like some lovesick loser about the unfairness of it all.

"It's gotta get better eventually, right?"

"It will. Just know you're welcome back here any time. And that I do expect you here for the wedding. And all the before and after crap, too. If I'm gonna do it, you're suffering through it with me."

"Don't make it sound like you're not on cloud nine to be marrying the girl of your dreams."

Cash laughs. "Yeah, who am I kidding. It'll be the best day or week or month of my life. Well, until the honeymoon. And every day after that."

"All right, all right, all right. Enough already." My tone is teasing and I'm sure he knows it.

"Call when you can," he says lightly.

"I will."

"I, uh, I miss you, man. It's been a long time since I've had a brother."

I have the sudden urge to smile, which isn't exactly an everyday kind of thing for me. "Me, too. Me, too."

After we get off the phone, I allow myself a few minutes to fantasize about what it would be like to be in Cash's position, with what looks like a great life all out ahead of me, just waiting to be lived. It takes no more than a few seconds for me to abandon the scenario. Without the girl in my arms, none of the rest of it works.

THIRTY-SIX

Marissa

I circle my shoulders as much as I can within the confines of my seatbelt. The tension of the day hasn't quite drained away yet. Sometimes it takes a couple of hours of being at home to fully relax. Sometimes it takes a couple of glasses of wine, too. Or a hot bath, a little time, and a little wine. I've discovered that's like the distress trifecta. And tonight may require those more extreme measures.

The trial is going well, but it's incredibly intense. Much more so than what I ever expected. In the beginning, it was more procedural, nothing exciting like you see on television. But now that we've gotten into testimony and cross-examination, it's not only more interesting, but it also calls for a deft touch when it comes to strategy.

Needless to say, I let Jensen handle most of that.

He's doing a great job. It's easy to see how he's risen so far so fast within the DA's office. He's exceptionally bright and intuitive when it comes to the law and how to finesse witnesses. It's pretty impressive to watch.

After I park and drag my briefcase from the passenger seat, I make my way to the front door. I slide the key into the lock and push the door open. A little sliver of fear skitters down my spine. It's not nearly as bad as it used to be. But it's still there. I wonder if it always will be.

That's one of two things that has refused to leave me since the time around my abduction. The echo of fear is number one. Nash is number two. And not necessarily in that order.

The fear of someone grabbing me abates within a few minutes of being in my house, with it settling quietly around me. Missing Nash—seeing his face, hearing his voice, smelling his clean, manly scent—that sometimes haunts me all night long. When I'm here, in the place I knew him so intimately, I don't get very many peaceful moments. His memory is with me almost constantly. It's one of the many reasons this case has been so cathartic. In a way, I dread for it to be over. But, like all good things, it must come to an end.

With a sigh, I start peeling off clothes as I make my way to the bedroom. I've just slipped on some silky pajama shorts when the doorbell rings.

My pulse stutters and I hurriedly pull on the matching shirt and grab my robe from the back of the bathroom door as I rush to see who's calling at such a late hour.

Several of us met for dinner and drinks after court tonight. It's well after nine now, an odd time for anyone to visit unannounced.

I lean in to look through the peephole to see Jensen's face looking comical in that walleye way.

I pull the chain and open the locks.

"What are you doing here? Is everything okay?"

Jensen is smiling broadly. Maybe too broadly.

"I just had a thought. May I come in?"

I pull my robe more tightly around me. "Of course."

I step back and let him pass me, then close the door behind him. He doesn't walk far, which puts me practically right on top of him when I turn toward him.

"What's up?" I ask, leaning back against the door so I can get some extra space.

"You *do* realize that we're going to win this, right? And that our careers will skyrocket, right? And that the world of Georgia law . . . hell, the world of law *period* will be our oyster, right?"

I smile. "How many drinks did you have tonight?"

"I'm not drunk," he says happily. "Well, maybe a little, but not *too* drunk." Jensen takes a step toward me, the look in his eyes changing to something I'm unfortunately familiar with.

He looks like a man who's not here to take no for an answer.

"Jensen—"

"Shhh," he whispers, cutting me off with a fingertip to my lips. "Let me show you how good we can be together *outside* the courtroom." He brushes the hair away from my face, his eyes boring hot holes into mine. "I know you feel it, too. We've got some kickass chemistry."

"Professionally, yes."

"But not *just* professionally. I think you're incredibly beautiful, Marissa. You're smart and funny and so, *so* sexy."

As if to accentuate his point, he lets his finger trail down my chin and into the valley between my breasts.

"Um, I think it's probably time you left," I say, trying to keep my composure. I can't risk harming the case in any way by making waves with Jensen. He's right. We *are* good together. And we need to keep being good together until this is done. It's too important to screw it up now.

"One kiss. Give me one kiss and if you tell me you feel nothing, I'll go." I really don't want to, and I'm afraid kissing him will only further inflame him. But if he's the nice guy he normally is even when he's drunk, he might honor his agreement and just go. Peaceably.

So I chance it.

It's worth it.

For Nash.

I nod and Jensen smiles. Slowly, he runs his hands up into the hair at the back of my head and leans in closer to me.

Like a ghost that refuses to leave, Nash's face flits behind my eyes as my lids drift shut. If only the kiss of another man could make me forget. If only . . .

Jensen's lips are warm and firm. He's not too aggressive or too slobbery or too . . . anything. He's actually a very good kisser. But, as adept as he is, it makes no difference. There's just no sizzle, no bang. No fireworks. There's only one pair of lips that can bring those. And they don't belong to Jensen.

I feel the pressure of his tongue trying to get past my lips. I resist until he becomes really insistent, and then I part my lips, allowing his tongue inside for just a minute before I have to turn my head away.

That was way *too much*!

"Jensen, I think you've made your point. Now, how 'bout you go sleep it off and, come Monday, we'll pretend this didn't even happen, okay?"

From my peripheral vision, I see him pull his head back a little. I turn just enough to meet his eyes. They're dark with passion, the pupils huge inside the pale blue irises. In them, I see a debate. He wants to press me, to press the issue. But something is holding him back.

"That was a great kiss, Jensen. It's not that. And it's not you. It's . . . it's . . . someone else."

That gets his attention. He pulls back further, frowning. "Who? Nash?"

"N-no," I say, only because it's not the Nash he's thinking of.

"Then who?"

I can't think of a convincing lie quickly enough, so I go with the truth. "His brother."

"You're kidding, right?" When I don't respond, he laughs, a short, bitter bark. "Oh my God. The guy that looks like he spent time in the same cell with his dad? That guy?"

"Jensen, don't be mean."

"Are you telling me I'm wrong? He looks like a career felon."

That gets my ire up. I push at his chest until he moves back, giving me some space. "Well, he's not, so maybe you should keep your shallow opinion to yourself."

I slide out from between Jensen and the door, walking into the living room before turning to face him.

"You can do so much better than him. For God's sake, Marissa, come on!"

It's my turn to laugh. "You know what, Jensen? You couldn't be more wrong. He's one of the greatest men I've ever known, long hair and all. Why do you think I'm fighting so hard to win this case?"

"I heard you had some personal interest in it, like *really* personal. But it was hush-hush and I figured you'd get around to telling me eventually."

I'm so glad now that I didn't.

"Oh it's personal, all right," I say, letting the statement sound suggestive, hoping that will be enough to kill his attraction to me. Maybe if he thinks I've got a thing for slummin' it, he'll deem me unworthy of a man like him and leave me alone. "I happen to like a man with some ink and some scruff. I think it's pretty hot."

All right, that might've been laying it on a bit thick.

I cringe inwardly, praying it wasn't too much.

With an exasperated shake of his head, Jensen gives me a look and backs toward the door.

"I guess you're right. Looks like our good chemistry stops on the courthouse steps."

I raise my chin a notch, but say nothing.

"Good night, Marissa."

"Good night, Jensen," I say, waiting until I hear his footsteps on the sidewalk before I go and snap the deadbolt closed on the door. "Good riddance, Jensen," I whisper, cutting off the light and heading for my bedroom once more.

Twenty minutes later, as I'm sliding between the sheets, the bed has never felt bigger. Or colder. Or more empty.

And neither has my heart.

THIRTY-SEVEN

Nash

Another month later

She's very attractive, the girl who's dancing for me. And she's very obviously attrac*ted*. Clubs in Italy are not much different than they are anywhere else in the world.

This girl is blond, which isn't as common in this country. That's probably why I continue to watch her. She reminds me of what I miss most. Of *who* I miss most.

I'd give anything to stop thinking about Marissa. This is the umpteenth time I've attempted to drown out her memory in someone else. So far, it hasn't worked. And judging by the halfhearted reaction in my jeans, this time won't be any different.

I'm sure I could do the deed. I'm a guy; that's not normally a problem unless there's too much alcohol on board. No, it's not the physical inability to go through with it. It's the emotional one. Everything else gets in the way. My head, my heart, and the fact that I just don't really want to.

Willfully, I bring my attention back to the action on the dance floor. The girl, the blond one I've been watching, runs her hand down her friend's arm, pausing just long enough at her plump breast to be suggestive. Her eyes are on mine, though. And the invitation is clear. Even when I look at her friend, the dark-haired one, I know I could have them both if I did so much as nod my head toward the door. I sigh into my drink.

But I won't. I won't motion for them to follow me when I leave. And I won't be bothered if they turn their attention toward someone else. No, tonight the only company I'll be keeping will be a bottle.

THIRTY-EIGHT

Marissa

Olivia's eyes are wide with surprise. "Are you kidding me? That's great news! Why aren't you more excited?"

I shrug. I'm sitting with her at the club. It's the middle of the day on a Saturday, so we're alone. "I am, I just . . ."

When I don't continue, she reaches out and grabs my hand. "You just what?"

I feel my chin begin to tremble. "I just don't know what I'm going to do now. It's almost over."

"But that's a good thing. We can all finally move on. And you, you'll have so many career options your head will spin."

"I know. And that's great, but I'm just not sure this is what I want to do."

"What? Prosecute huge cases and make the world a better place? Or practice law at all?"

I shrug again. I don't really mean to do it. It's almost automatic, as though my body can't resist an outward manifestation of the ambivalence that's churning inside me.

"Both, I guess. But it's not just that."

"Then what? What is it? Did something happen with your dad?"

I've been keeping Olivia up to date on all the drama with my father. He basically disowned me when he saw that I was actually going through with the prosecution. But then, once we started making good progress and the press started to get involved and people began to see how much good we were trying to do by locking these guys up, he changed his tune. Suddenly I was worth his time. Suddenly he sees a bright future in politics *for me*.

That was when I stopped taking his calls. He'll never want me just for me. He'll always see me as a means to an end. Or a project of some sort. Or maybe a family trophy. Who knows?

That is, of course, when he doesn't see me as an embarrassment.

"No, I haven't talked to him lately. It's . . . it's just . . ."

My eyes sting as the tears rush in. I look down at my hand where it rests in Olivia's, blinking as rapidly as I can to keep from having some sort of hysterical fit.

"Tell me," Olivia prompts softly.

"I feel like this is the last little bit of Nash I have, like once this is over, he'll be out of my life completely. Forever. I think I've been doing this for him more than anything else. I wanted him to be free of all that anger and bitterness. I wanted him to be able to move on and have a happy life."

Before I can continue, Olivia finishes my thought as if she could read my mind.

"And you thought he'd move on to that happy life with you."

To hear that hope spoken aloud and to know that, little by little, day by day, it has been disappearing is almost more than I can bear. It makes it too real, too final.

With one involuntary gasp, the floodgates open and all the pain I've felt over the loss of Nash comes rushing out in deep, soul-wrenching sobs.

"I-I-I thought he'd c-c-come back," I sputter as Olivia comes off her bar stool and gathers me into her arms. I lay my head on her shoulder and I cry. And I cry. And I cry. I cry until there's nothing left.

Olivia doesn't move a muscle, other than to stroke my hair. Finally, I pull back from her to reach into my purse for a tissue.

"I'm sorry," I sniffle before blowing my nose. "I guess that's been a long time coming."

Olivia sits back down, her expression sad. "To be honest, I thought he'd come back, too. I really, really did. It was obvious he had feelings for you. I think he's just too screwed up to know what to do about them."

"We just didn't have enough time. And now we never will. I just thought . . . I had hoped . . ." I swallow back the sob that rises into my throat. I've cried on Olivia's shoulder—literally—enough for one day. "But I'm a big girl," I say, sitting up a little straighter. I need to put on a brave face and put this behind me. At least outwardly. I'm not sure I'll ever be able to really do that on an emotional level. At least not completely. "It's time I figure out what I'm going to do with my life and get to it. I'm not getting any younger."

Olivia rolls her eyes. "Because twenty-seven is *so old*."

"Twenty-eight," I say automatically.

"What? Twenty-eight? I thought . . ." I see her forehead wrinkle as she thinks our ages through. Her eyes round when she realizes I'm right. "Ohmigod, ohmigod, ohmigod! We missed your birthday!"

She covers her mouth with her hands like she cursed in front of a priest. I can't help but smile. To me, this is no big deal. But to Olivia, it's tantamount to burning my house down.

"It's not a big deal."

"Of *course* it's a big deal! How could this happen? How could I not know?"

I shrug again. It's the story of my life lately. One big shrug of ambivalence. "I don't know, but it doesn't matter. I've been fussed over on my birthday for most of my life. You know, to keep up appearances and all." It's my turn to roll my eyes. "It was kinda nice to be anonymous that day. I didn't really feel like celebrating."

And I didn't. The only thing I really wanted was for Nash to come back. Or even to call and tell me he missed me. But that didn't happen. After that, no amount of presents or parties or birthday wishes could've salvaged that day. That being the case, I figured it was just best that no one knew.

The look on Olivia's face assures me that she understands all that I'm saying *and* all that I'm not. She gives both my shoulders a squeeze. "It'll get better, you know." It's not a question; it's a statement. And I *do* know that. I think. It's just that, at the moment, it doesn't feel like the dull ache in my chest will ever go away.

THIRTY-NINE

Nash

Another three weeks later

It feels strange to be worrying about my property. It's been so long since I've had anything of real value, anything much in the way of possessions. And now, leaving the boat at the dock in Savannah while I travel into Atlanta makes me nervous. It would suck buckets of shit if something happened to it. A huge chunk of my life's savings is wrapped up in that thing.

I smile as I think of how it all happened.

The morning after I left those two girls at the club in Naples, Italy, I decided to gather the crew and head out a little earlier than planned. They weren't as easy to find as I expected. It was while I was on the yacht, docked in the marina, waiting for them, that I was approached by a man interested in chartering a private yacht to take him and his wife on a two-week sail for their anniversary. I explained to him that it wasn't my boat. He was persistent, though. I don't know if he just didn't believe me, or if he thought I was trying to drive the price up, but he kept on. The amount of money he offered me was staggering. It wasn't enough to get me to take him and his wife on for two weeks—I knew I couldn't in good conscience make that kind of commitment until the trial was over—but it was more than enough to get me thinking.

Now, in just three short weeks, my life already feels different. I have roots. Sort of. And I have a profession. Sort of. And I have some kind of a future.

Okay, so maybe it's not quite the one I dreamed of as a kid, but it fits in with what my life has become, with what *I* have become. And maybe, it just might be enough to fill the emptiness that's been plaguing me.

Maybe.

As always, any time Marissa comes to mind, she takes over for a while. Sometimes it's harder than others to get her off my mind. The closer I get to her, the harder it's getting. And it was pretty damn hard, anyway!

The trial is coming to a close. Cash called to let me know that Marissa and her cohorts were preparing for closing arguments. After that, the jury would go deliberate. No one knew how long that might take, so he told me to get my ass back to the States as fast as I could. He and Dad wanted me there for the verdict. So that's what I did.

I'm making it just in the nick of time. The jury went into deliberation this morning. I could've missed it had they not decided to break for the day, have dinner, and go back into sequestration.

I'm trying not to see that as a bad sign—their inability to come to a quick decision. Instead, I'm grateful that I'm gonna make it in time to be with Dad and Cash.

Luckily, I was already on my way back to the States. I was heading back with the intention of offering to take Cash and Olivia as my first charters, sort of test the waters with them.

Pun intended.

I snort at the mental image I have of Cash rolling his eyes at my wit. The cabdriver looks back at me and I glare at him until he turns away. Then I smile. My anger isn't what it once was, but I still intimidate people for some reason. I get a kick out of it sometimes, just like with this guy. He probably thinks I'm a hit man or something. It doesn't help that I don't try to disabuse him of that notion. I guess old habits die hard. In my previous line of work, the image of being a dangerous man can save your life. If you're in it long enough, you *become* that dangerous man. I suppose a look like that never leaves you completely.

That's something you'll have to work on if you expect to get any clients. No one wants to go out to sea with a guy they think might kill them in their sleep and take all their money.

And here she comes again.

Marissa.

As usual, any time I think of the future, I think of her. And how she won't be a part of it. And why I even would want her to be. Sometimes, I don't fight her image. I just let her have her way for a while. I don't do it often. It always ends up with me either aching for that delicious little body of hers or aching for her in a soul-deep kind of way that I don't know what to do with. But every now and again, I can't resist the temptation of just thinking about her. And every now and then, of what life could've been like.

If only things were different . . .

My phone wakes me. I must've fallen asleep in the cab with a vision of Marissa dancing in my head like those damn Christmas sugar-plums. I pull the noisy rectangle out of my pocket and glance at the screen. It's Cash.

"I'm on my way," I say as a greeting.

"The jury called to come back after dinner. They reached a decision."

"Oh shit!" I sit up straight and look around for some indication of where I'm at. I see a mile marker flit by. "I'm still a good two hours away, man. How long until they're going back to court?"

"They're getting everyone back now."

I sigh.

Damn!

"Maybe they'll piddle around and I'll still make it. I'll be there as soon as I can. Keep me posted."

"Sure thing."

After we hang up, I feel the nervous energy start. I can't seem to sit still in the backseat. I feel like I should be doing something to hurry this god-awful ride along. But there's nothing I can do. All I know is that there's no way in the deepest part of hell that I'll be falling asleep again.

One hour and twenty-three minutes later, my phone rings. It's Cash again.

"What's going on?"

"Guilty. On all charges." He's about to bust. I can hear it in his voice. It takes a few seconds for his words to sink in. Then I'm flip-flopping between elation that we won and irritation that I missed being with them for the verdict.

"Holy fu—Holy crap, man! That's great news! Hot damn! Hot. *Damn!*"

Cash whoops into the phone and his excitement pushes me more toward elation and less toward irritation. There will be lots to celebrate tonight. Lots.

I hear him laughing. And, in the background, I hear feminine voices laughing, too. They're already celebrating.

"So what's next?"

Cash collects himself enough to answer me. "Sentencing. I don't know when that will happen yet, but Georgia state law set a maximum sentence of twenty years for a RICO conviction. I hope they get every day of it! We're already discussing civil suits, too. And then, of course, there will be Dad's appeal, since Duffy admitted to . . . what he did. I'll get Duffy's signed affidavit and start the process as soon as I can."

I know how Cash feels. It's hard to say it sometimes, to say out loud that our mother was murdered. Especially on a day like today, a day full of good things.

Cash is hurried and vague. And I know why. It's the same reason it's hard to talk about Mom. Today is a day for celebration. This was a huge victory. Tomorrow, there will be plenty of time for . . . everything else.

"Well, we can talk about all that later. Right now, we've got some celebrating to do. Where are you gonna be?"

"Just come to the club. We'll be taking over the VIP room tonight."

I like the sound of that. "Sounds good, man. See you in an hour or so."

FORTY

Marissa

I must admit, I can see why criminal prosecutors become obsessed with their jobs. Not only is the fight consuming, but the verdict . . . Oh God! There are few better feelings I've experienced in life than getting the conviction, none of which took place in a courtroom.

Velvety black eyes flash through my mind, and I push them out. *Not today. Let me just have this one day of peace and happiness.*

It was hard enough not seeing him for the verdict. Olivia had said he would be there, and the disappointment was pretty devastating when he didn't show up. But I'm past that. I'm trying to just enjoy the glow of victory. I know it won't feel complete without him, but that's something I'll have to get used to. I doubt anything in life will ever feel complete without Nash. I *hope* it will. I truly, truly hope so. But something in me doubts it ever will.

I take the next left, drawing ever closer to Dual. Rather than show up there in my work clothes, I opted to go home and change before heading over to join in the festivities. I have a feeling there will be drinking and celebrating into the wee hours and I wanted to be comfortable for it. The jeans and long-sleeved T-shirt—my nod to the early spring nip in the night air—have already put me at ease.

I walk through the front door of the club, speaking to Gavin as I pass.

"You working the door tonight?"

"Yeah. Evidently there's been an unexpected party upstairs that's left us a bit shorthanded. Maybe I'll get lucky down here with some young bucks that need a lesson in ass-kicking. Or maybe a beautiful attorney will need a ride home."

The wink of his blue, blue eye assures me he's teasing. He's an incorrigible flirt.

"Well, if it's calm, come up and have a drink. We've got a lot to celebrate today."

"So I hear. I guess congratulations are in order to you, as well. That's some show you must've put on out there."

I shrug, pleasantly flattered. "Well, it wasn't just me. There were a lot of people responsible for tonight's success."

"There's nothing hotter than a gorgeous woman who doesn't know how to take a compliment."

I laugh.

Incorrigible!

"Then I'll just say thank you and be on my way. How's that?"

"You don't have to rush off now."

"Cash might have my hide if I distract you from your work."

"Don't you worry about Cash, pretty little dove. I'll take care of him."

His smile is devilish and he wiggles his eyebrows suggestively.

I laugh again, shaking my head at him. "You could be dangerous," I say as I turn and make my way toward the stairs.

"Only in the best possible way," I hear him say before the ambient sounds drown out his voice.

Stopping on the top step, in front of the door, I smile. I can hear the wild celebration coming from inside the VIP room, even above the loud music from downstairs in the club. And that's saying a lot.

I open the door to find chaos. I give all the faces a cursory glance. Except for the bartender, whom I haven't seen before, I recognize everyone. Each was involved in the trial in some form or fashion, from Cindy, the paralegal who dug up some invaluable information for us on more than one occasion, to Stephen, the court reporter. We all got to know him very well over the past few months, too.

During a case like the one we just won, a bond is formed that gives you the feeling that this is your family-away-from-family. Or, in my case, my family-in-place-of-my-family. I learned to trust and depend on them in ways I've never felt comfortable doing with the people in my life, family or not. All in all, this was one of the most treasured, rewarding experiences of my life.

But where to go now?

The troubling thought sneaks in before I can stop it, stealing my smile for a second. But before I can start stressing over life questions like that, Jensen yells at me from across the room where he's waiting at the bar.

He grabs two shot glasses and starts toward me. All eyes turn in my direction and I feel my smile return. Just for tonight, I refuse to think of anything more serious than what to drink next.

Jensen stops in front of me and the room gets quiet. Well, as quiet as a room situated above a club filled with this many people can get. Jensen clears his throat.

"To the woman of the hour, without whom we probably wouldn't have been handed down a victory." He raises his glass, as does everyone else in the room. "To Marissa."

The glow of adulation is surpassed only by the lump of emotion in my throat. I toss back my shot, wondering for a second if the liquid can pass the obstruction. But it does. And it burns all the way down, making my eyes water.

"Marissa!" Everyone yells.

I feel a laugh bubble up just as Jensen wraps his arm around my waist and swings me around. I let the laugh go, thinking that this might be the first night in a long, long time that I can find some semblance of happiness.

Until he sets me on my feet and my eyes collide with Nash's.

FORTY-ONE

Nash

Of all the things I expected to see when I walked in, that shit wasn't even on the list. Jensen's arms wrapped around Marissa, her laughing and clinging to him. All their friends crowded around, cheering them on. A room full of people I don't belong with.

More than ever, I see that this is no longer my world. And it never will be. I don't fit in here. Buying the boat and planning for a life at sea was a good choice. I guess I just always thought that someday . . . Maybe . . .

Marissa's smile dies as I watch. Jensen sets her on her feet and I slide my eyes over to him. He's staring at me. I squelch the urge to walk over and rip his throat out.

I glance around the room. Everyone is staring at me. I know only a few of them. Not that it would make any difference if I knew them all. These aren't my people. This isn't my world. But it's hers. And it will forever separate us. A gulf. A chasm. An immeasurable ocean.

Turning away from her, I locate Cash. He's grinning from ear to ear. It reminds me to keep this all in perspective. Ultimately, we got what we wanted. The men behind my mother's death and my father's subsequent incarceration are going to prison for a long time. And Duffy, even though he was the actual triggerman and deserves a painful death, will be on the run for the rest of his life. He'll have to leave this country if he doesn't accept witness protection. Either way, life as he knows it is over. Maybe that's an even better punishment. I choose to look at it that way. It's the only way I can really let it go.

And I need to do that. I need to take this victory and move on.

To what?

I push the question out of my mind, reminding myself that I have a plan and that's that. I ignore the bright blue eyes that drift through my mind, the ones I can practically feel burning a hole through me.

I walk to my brother and stop in front of him. I stick out my hand and he takes it. He pumps it several times as we smile at each other. Impulsively, I pull him in for a hug. We clap each other on the back.

I lean away from him. He's still smiling broadly.

"It's over, man. It's finally over," he says, obviously relieved.

I nod. "Finally."

On what should be the happiest day, I feel bereft. And partying is the last thing I want to do right now. But I don't want anyone to see me struggle, so I ask Cash quietly, "Can I use your apartment for a little while? I need to clean up."

I see the crease appear between his eyebrows for an instant before it smooths out. "Sure."

I nod and turn, walking straight from the room and not looking back.

What the hell did you expect to happen?

I chastise myself as I make my way down the steps and across the floor of the crowded club. Evidently, on some level, I thought Marissa would be thrilled to see me, that she'd declare that she's been miserable without me, beg me to take her with me and we'd sail off into the sunset. As ridiculous as that sounds, that's the scenario that I had hidden somewhere deep, deep down.

You're a fuc—You're an idiot!

It infuriates me that I'm still censoring myself for her, like she gives a shit. Like she can hear me. Like she cares. I mutter a blistering string of raunchy expletives as I stomp into Cash's office and slam the door shut behind me.

I walk through to his apartment and slam that door as well, feeling infinitesimally better having gotten some of my aggression out. What would really help me is the opportunity to beat the hell out of that stuffed shirt that was wrapped around Marissa. But since that wouldn't win me points with anyone and would likely land me in jail, I settle for flinging my duffel across the room and heading for the shower.

I barely turn the cold spigot on. The burn of the hot water temporarily deadens the intensity of everything else. By the time I get out, my skin is on fire, but it calms soon enough, leaving me right back at square one.

Before getting dressed, I stretch out across the bed to let the air dry me. I concentrate on the dull throb of the music outside and will my anger away.

I make myself think of things I can control, or things that give me some small amount of peace, like Dad getting out of prison or watching the bright red sun set over the clear waters of the Caribbean.

I don't know how long I lie there. The noise from the club outside two closed doors seems less and I can't find a clock in the dark room to tell me the time.

I get up and get dressed, looking out into the office at the clock on the wall. I've been down here for almost two hours.

How the hell did that happen?

I head back out into the club. The crowd has thinned considerably. Looks like the night is winding down. Of course, it *is* a weeknight . . .

I glance up at the two-way glass that fronts the VIP room. I don't know if they're still up there, but I suppose I should at least make an appearance before I ask Cash for his car and get the hell out of here. The quiet of his condo will do just fine for the night. Anything to be away from here. Away from her.

I take the steps two at a time. Before I can reach the top, the door opens and Jensen appears in the opening, shuffling a wobbly Marissa toward the steps.

"I told you I'm fine to drive," she slurs.

"And I told you there's no way I'm letting you leave here behind the wheel."

"But you're drunk, too. Who's gonna drive?"

"I'm not *that* drunk," he's saying.

I stop in the center of the steps, crossing my arms over my chest. "Going somewhere?"

"Yeah. This one wants to go home, but she's had too much to drink."

"And you? Have you been drinking?"

"Not that much."

"*Any* is too much to be driving her home. I'll take her."

"That's all right, Cash. I've got her."

He starts to lead Marissa around me. I don't know what makes me angrier—him calling me Cash or seeing his hands on Marissa again.

Who the hell are you kidding? You know exactly *which one it is!*

"I'm gonna have to insist," I say through gritted teeth. I don't want to make a scene. Not because I'm personally opposed to kicking this guy's ass on the steps of a club, but because it would embarrass Cash and probably Marissa. And it's them that I care about. Not me. And certainly not this pompous piece of shit.

"Insist all you like, I'm taking her home."

His pale eyes are challenging me. For some reason, it strikes me as funny. He has no clue what I'd do to him if I let loose. No. Clue.

"You don't want to do this, lawyer boy. Trust me."

"Maybe I do," he says, his bravado increased by his alcohol consumption.

"Hey!" Marissa shouts. "Boys. Please. I'm driving myself home, so you can both put it back in your pants." She giggles at her words and pulls her arm out of Jensen's grasp.

She attempts to walk past me, stumbles, and falls against my side. I reach out to steady her and she melts against me. She looks up into my face and smiles. "Sorry."

"Let me take you home," I say quietly.

She stares deeply into my eyes, like she's trying to see . . . something. I don't know what, but evidently she finds it. She nods. "Okay."

"Marissa, I—" Jensen begins, but I cut him off when I plant my palm in the center of his chest, stopping him in his tracks when he would take a step toward her. I don't even bother to look at him; I keep my eyes trained on Marissa's sparkling blue ones.

"Last chance," I warn.

Marissa looks to her left. "Jensen, it's all right. I appreciate it, but we've both had too much to drink to be driving."

I hear him sigh and, perversely, I hope he keeps pushing it. I'm itching to teach this prick a lesson. But on the other hand, I wish he'd just shut his mouth and go away. Right now, what I'd like even more than smashing lawyer boy's face is Marissa. Just Marissa. And what I see when I look into her blue, blue eyes.

From the corner of my eye, I see him turn and stomp back up the steps. With him gone, my focus is complete. And so, for a few minutes, anyway, is my soul.

"Can you make it down the stairs okay?"

She nods and turns to take another step toward the bottom. She wobbles and I steady her.

"Whoa," she says.

Without asking, I sweep her up into my arms and carry her down to the landing. I'm sure I could safely put her down now. But I don't. I carry her out the door and into the chilly night.

"Where are you parked?"

"Over there," she says, pointing out and to the right, then laying her head on my shoulder. She loops her arms loosely around my neck and snuggles in. I pull her in tighter against my chest. It's like she was made to fit there. Perfectly. In my arms.

Holy shit, woman! What have you done to me?

When we reach her car, she digs her keys out of her pocket and hands them to me. I hit the fob and hear the hushed click of the locks opening. I set Marissa on her feet long enough to open the passenger door and get her inside without cracking her head.

On the drive home, neither of us says anything. I glance over at her several times to see if she's asleep. She's not. Each time, she looks back at me, holding my gaze but never speaking.

Anticipation is so thick inside the quiet interior of the car, it's almost palpable. It's made me diamond-hard behind my zipper.

I park at Marissa's and come around the car to get her out. She starts up the sidewalk, but I stop her, picking her up to carry her again.

"I can walk," she says, but still she nuzzles her face against my neck. She probably *can* walk, but she doesn't really *want* to walk. And I don't want to let her.

I don't respond, just carry her to the door, hand her the keys, and bend enough that she can unlock the knob and deadbolt.

Once inside, I kick the door shut behind me and set her on her feet. I don't want to be *too* presumptuous, so I wait to see what she's going to say. Or do.

In the low light spilling in through the glass panel at the top of the door, we stare at each other. Silent. Thoughtful. There's a lot I'd like to say, but I can't. I shouldn't. I won't. There's no reason to. It won't change anything. And if she doesn't feel the same, it would kill me. But if she does, it would be even worse, I think.

I reach up and rub the backs of my fingers down her satiny cheek. She tilts her head into the touch. When I bend down and take her lips, the kiss isn't as feverish and desperate as I figured it would be. There's something sad and . . . final about it. I don't know who is making it feel that way, her or me. But it has a definite "the end" ring to it.

For the first time in my life, I make love to a woman. I've had sex hundreds of times, with too many women to count. I've done dirty, wicked things to them. Hell, I've done dirty, wicked things to Marissa. And I'd like to do more. But tonight isn't about that. Not even if I wanted it to be. Tonight is about leaving her with the other piece of my soul, the small part she hasn't already taken.

With every article of clothing I strip from her body, more than ever, I'm aware of the smell of her perfume, the silk of her skin. It's as though all my senses are heightened and completely concentrated on her. Every soft place, every sweet sigh, every delicate shiver will be forever burned into my mind. I'm not sure that's a good thing, but it doesn't matter. No consequence is enough to stop me.

From the time I first slide into her warm body, all the way through the last squeeze of her orgasm, I'm aware that we're giving each other a bittersweet, wordless good-bye. For these few minutes, I'm happier than I can ever remember being. And sadder. And forever, I'll be a better man for just having known Marissa. She healed the breaks in me that I thought I'd die with, that I'd never live to overcome. Because of her, I have some semblance of a life to go to now.

My breathing is just returning to normal when I feel the first wet splash on my skin. Marissa is lying with one of her legs thrown over mine and her head on my chest. And she's crying. I feel each tear as it falls from her face. They're only slightly warm, but they burn nonetheless.

"Will you be gone when I wake up?" she whispers, her voice catching on the last word.

I think about her question before I answer it. I hadn't really made any kind of plan, but I know now what I have to do. "Yes."

I feel her shoulders shake as she sobs. Each one feels like a fist squeezing tighter and tighter around my heart.

Suddenly, she moves, levering herself off me and rolling off the bed. She doesn't turn to look at me. She just squares her shoulders and walks tall and proud across the room. "Good-bye, Nash," she says softly. Then she disappears into the bathroom, closing and locking the door behind her. I sit up in the bed, stunned, until I hear the shower cut on.

One thing runs through my head as I dress and call for a cab. *It's for the best. It's for the best. It's for the best.*

She still hasn't come out of the bathroom by the time the cab arrives. I know those are the last words she'll ever say to me.

FORTY-TWO

Marissa

I don't know why I'm still lying in bed. I know I won't be sleeping tonight. As much as I wish I could leave reality behind, even for a little while, the pain of letting Nash go is too excruciating to let me rest.

I turn my face into the pillow for the tenth time at least, inhaling deeply. Beneath my nose is the scent of Nash—man and soap. Beneath my cheek is damp cotton, my tears making an ever-widening wet spot.

I knew on some level that tonight was a good-bye. If I had one ounce of self-preservation, I'd have steered clear of Nash. But I don't. And, in a way, I don't regret it. As painful as it is to lose him all over again, it was worth it to have him back in my arms, even if it was just for a little while.

The sobs start again. They echo in the emptiness of the room, much like they echo in the emptiness of my heart. I almost don't hear the pounding at my door over my own agony.

My heart stops for a breath before it picks up again at a faster pace. A teeny, tiny part of me responds to the fear that it might be some dark figure from the past, coming to take me away again. But it's overwhelmingly overshadowed by the hope, the desperate hope, that it's Nash.

Please God, please God, please God, I chant in my head as I scramble to push my arms into my robe on the way to the door.

I look through the peephole and my breath catches. It's Nash.

I open the door and he takes my face in his hands, almost angrily, and crushes his lips against mine.

"What the hell have you done to me?" he murmurs against them. I don't care what he's saying and I don't answer; I only care that he's back. If only for a little while, he came back.

He kisses a trail across my cheek and jaw, down to my neck, and then he pulls me in tight to his body, holding me against him.

"I can't leave you again. Not like that. Ask me to stay," he says into my hair. "I'll be whatever you need me to be, whoever you need me to be. I'm not perfect, but I'll be perfect for you. Just give me a chance."

I try to lean back, but he won't let me go. "Nash," I say, pushing against his chest.

Finally, he eases up enough that I can pull back and see his shadowed face. When I start to speak, he lays his finger over my lips. "I've sailed all over the world trying to get away from you, trying to get away from what you make me feel. All I've found is that there's no ocean big enough to drown out thoughts of you, no place far enough to escape your pull. You find me. You always find me. When I was lost at sea, you found me. When I was lost in life, you found me. You found me and you saved me. And I know there's nowhere I can go that will make me happy as long as I'm sailing away from you. The best part of me is you. The only part that matters is the one you have, the one you hold in the palm of your hand."

"You'd stay? Here? For me?"

"I'd do anything for you."

"But what about the boat? Cash told me you bought a yacht to charter."

"I'll sell it. I'll give it up. I'd give it all up for you. Anything. Everything. Everything for us. If it means that I can keep you, that it will make you happy, then I'll do it. Whatever it is. Just say the word."

My heart is near bursting. I don't have words at first. I find myself wondering almost confusedly if this is real or if I've dreamed the whole thing. The only thing I know is that if it's a dream, I never want to wake up. Never.

"What if I don't want you to?"

He goes completely still and says nothing for a few seconds. "What if you don't want me to what?"

I know what he's thinking. I can see by the stricken expression on his face. He thinks I'm getting ready to tell him I don't want *him*.

"What if I don't want you to sell the boat?" He says nothing, just watches me. Finally, I smile. It's probably the happiest smile I think I've ever smiled in my life as I wind my arms around his neck and pull his head down to mine. I whisper into his ear, "What if I want to sail away with you?"

I hear him exhale right before he hugs me so tight, he nearly squeezes the breath from me.

"Damn, I love you, woman," he whispers into my neck. If I thought I'd been deliriously happy a few seconds ago, I was wrong. Never in my life have a few words made me feel so dramatically, wildly, indelibly changed. In this one short space in time, my life has gone from uncertain and unfulfilled to overflowing with hope and love and a peace I've never known. His next words mirror exactly what I feel all the way to the deepest part of my soul. "You make me feel whole."

"I was just thinking the same thing," I admit.

"You were?" he asks, a smile in his voice.

"That and one other thing."

"What's that?" he asks. When I don't respond, he straightens his head and looks down at me. "What's that?" he repeats.

I reach up and stroke his stubbly jawline with the tips of my fingers. "That I love you. That I love this stubble. And these lips," I say, moving my fingers over his full bottom lip. "And this face. And this hair," I say when I tuck a few loose strands behind his ear. "And that you're right. You *are* perfect for me. Already. You're everything I didn't know I needed, but everything I always knew I wanted."

Reaching up to wind his fingers around my wrist, Nash turns his face into my palm. "I'll spend the rest of my life making you happy, proving to you that you made the right choice. I promise you won't regret taking a chance on me."

"I'm not taking a chance. I feel like I can't breathe without you. I'm just doing what I need to do to survive. It's as simple as that."

"Then let me be your air," he says quietly. This time, when his lips meet mine and he sweeps me up into his arms, I feel like he's carrying me away to our future, to happiness, to wholeness. And I'm thrilled to go along for the ride.

FORTY-THREE

Nash

Four months later

The sun is streaming through the cabin window, turning Marissa's sun-kissed skin to glistening gold. She's on her stomach, facing away from me, her breathing deep and even. I could watch her sleep for a while longer. But not only would that be creepy as hell, I've got a raging hard-on that's got her name written all over it.

I peel back the sheet, the only thing that's covering her. The weather here in Fiji is balmy all the time, so we sleep in very little, which is perfectly fine with me. She stirs slightly and I press my lips to the center of her back and then drag my tongue down her spine and over to one butt cheek. I sink my teeth in and nip her lightly. She flinches and I hear her muffled gasp. I rub my lips back and forth over the spot, whispering as I do, "I love this ass."

Marissa squirms beneath me, shifting just enough to flatten out and spread her legs a little more. Reaching down, I run my hand up the back of her thigh and then to the inside, sliding up toward the heat I can already feel coming from her. When I slip my finger inside her, she's already wet and ready for me.

"What's this? Were you dreaming about me again?"

Gently, I move my finger in and out, holding her down with the weight of my chest.

"Mmm," is her only answer.

"It sure feels like you were," I continue quietly. "Care to tell me the details? I'd be happy to try and make them feel real. Very, *very* real," I say, driving another finger deep inside her.

"How 'bout I show you instead," she says, wiggling her lower body to squirm out from under my chest.

I love it when she demonstrates things for me.

The sun is much higher in the sky by the time we make it ashore. Cash and Olivia are lounging by the hotel pool with Gavin and Ginger.

"What's going on, lazy people?" I say when we're within earshot. "I thought we had appointments to get all pampered and shit."

Olivia scoots off her lounge chair, bends to give Cash a kiss, then grabs Ginger's hand and drags her to her feet. "We're off. You boys enjoy yourselves. We're going to get beautiful."

"Perfection can't be improved upon," I say, pulling Marissa in close for a kiss before Olivia can drag her off, too. She smiles up at me.

"Keep talking like that and you'll get another dose of this morning's medicine."

"I've got plenty more where that came from," I say, referring to my arsenal of compliments.

The grin she gives me is suggestive. "Oh, I know you do."

I swat her on her delicious butt as she turns to follow Olivia and Ginger. I watch her until she's out of sight, then move to sit on the end of the lounge chair Olivia just vacated.

"So, am I supposed to be talking you out of the wedding jitters or something like that?"

"I guess if I had any you could, but I think I'm looking forward to this more than she is."

"Ha! I doubt that. She practically floated outta here. I don't think her feet have touched the ground since we got here."

Cash proposed to Olivia a couple months ago, not too long after the sentencing on the *Bratva* boys was handed down. They talked about a big wedding, but once Dad was released, it seemed like it was pretty easy for Ginger to talk Olivia into a destination wedding. It was even easier once Ginger told her that both her dad and mine had agreed.

Olivia's mother was a nonissue. She refused to take part in any way with Olivia and Cash's "farce of a wedding" as she called it.

What a colossal bitch!

It sealed the deal when Ginger told her that Marissa and I had agreed to ferry everyone over here on the yacht. After that, it was just a matter of picking the ideal spot and making all the arrangements.

They decided on Fiji. The ceremony is to be a blend of traditional Fijian and Christian. The wedding party is small, consisting of Marissa and Ginger as bridesmaids; me, Gavin, and Dad as best men; and Olivia's father here to give her away. It starts at eight thirty p.m., Fiji time.

Cash's smile seems permanent. I'd say mine looks the same way. Never in a thousand years would I have guessed that our lives could turn out this way, not after the way they've been progressing since Mom's death. I guess it just shows what the love of a good woman can do for a man. It can fix all the broken pieces and heal all the old wounds. If she loves a man, scars and all, that is. And mine does. I think Cash's does, too. We're both lucky in that way.

"Well, if you've got nothing better to do, I need to talk to you."

I take a deep breath. This is step one.

Standing on the beach opposite Marissa, the setting sun glowing on the waves, the warm air ruffling our hair and the torches lit all along the path, I have to admit that it's a great place for a wedding. I should be watching for Olivia, but I can't seem to take my eyes off Marissa.

She looks amazing in her Fijian wedding attire. The thin white skirt is long, but it's slit to midthigh and shows off her legs to perfection. She got sunburned during her afternoon with the girls, so I don't think she's wearing a bra under the matching white top. Every now and then, when the breeze blows just right, I think I get a glimpse of her nipples and it's driving me crazy.

As though she can feel me watching her, she glances over at me and smiles. She takes my breath away.

Her cheeks are flushed with color, mostly from the sun today, and her hair is platinum after spending so much time at sea in the last few months. Her eyes are sparkling happily, and something tells me she's gonna be ready for some really aggressive sex tonight. That's my favorite mood of hers. At least sexually.

She tips her head toward the path as the drums start beating, and I make myself look at the bride. Some Fijian men dressed in humiliating outfits are carrying Olivia on some sort of bed . . . thing. They stop not far from her father and let her down. He takes her hand and tucks it in the bend of his arm, and they turn toward Cash.

I look back at him. He's not smiling, but he doesn't look mad or aggravated. He looks stunned. I bet he couldn't speak a word right now if someone held a gun to his head. I see my father clap a hand on his shoulder. I'm sure it's a very emotional time for him, too. In all likelihood, I'd say he never thought he'd see this day. Today, many of my family's dreams are coming true.

I hope one of mine will, too.

I look back to Marissa. I watch her as the man presiding over the wedding begins to speak. I still watch her as Olivia and Cash speak their heartfelt vows to one another. Only a few bits and pieces penetrate my preoccupation.

"You breathed life into parts of me I didn't even know were dead," Cash says solemnly. He finishes and there's a pause before Olivia begins hers.

"You're everything I could ever want in a man, in a mate. You're the father of my unborn children and the person I want to grow old with," she says shakily.

As I listen with half an ear, I watch as Marissa delicately wipes happy tears from her cheeks; they're streaming from her eyes.

Even the minister's words can't bring my attention fully away from Marissa. "You may kiss the bride."

I watch Marissa's eyes shift to mine. She holds my gaze rather than looking back to Cash and Olivia. I wonder what she's thinking right now, gazing at me across a sandy path, in the middle of paradise, as our loved ones tie the knot. Is she wishing I'd pop the question so she can have a wedding of her own? Is she disappointed that I haven't already? Would she be crushed if I never did? Or would she be relieved?

I don't see any answers in her eyes, only love. I see her lips move and can easily discern what she's saying, even though she isn't making a sound.

"I love you."

I smile and return her silent words. The moment is lost when Cash and Olivia walk between us, announced as Mr. and Mrs. Cash Davenport.

They both look like they couldn't be happier. And I couldn't be happier for them.

The celebration starts immediately. Rather than having the wedding inside the small chapel, they opted for the beach. And rather than having the reception at the resort, they opted to have the food and drink brought to tables outside. Not that we need much, anyway. We kind of bring our own party.

Much later, I'm getting antsy. I don't have a watch on, but I know it has to be past midnight, yet the others show no signs of wearing down. I look at the edge of the trees and see the horse tied there.

Rising, I walk to Marissa where she's talking with Ginger and I take her hand. Without a word, I tug her to her feet. She looks up at me questioningly, but she doesn't protest. She just follows me across the sand, to the edge of the trees, to the horse that's waiting for us.

I help her onto it, still neither of us speaking. I climb on behind her and guide the horse slowly along the path, the one I memorized today.

We make our way through the lush forest, uphill until we reach the clearing. A white blanket is laid out in the grass. The red rose petals strewn across it would be visible even if the moon weren't bright and full. The dozen or so candles lit and set around the perimeter see to that.

They flicker in the light breeze as I dismount and help Marissa down. I tie the horse to a tree and take Marissa by the hand to lead her to the blanket. We stand facing each other for a long while before I turn her toward the ocean. I step up behind her, wrapping my arms around her and folding her body in close to mine, enjoying the view over her shoulder and the smell of her hair.

The moon is reflected on the water, laughter can be heard from the beach below, and, off in the distance, I can see our boat floating on the gentle waves of the calm water.

"This night is just about the perfect way to end the last few months."

"It's been wonderful."

"No regrets?" I ask, resisting the urge to hold my breath until she answers.

"Are you crazy? I've never been happier."

"You don't miss your job or your friends or your family?"

"I have everything I need right here," she says softly. She tilts her head to the side to glance at me. I kiss the tip of her nose.

I feel an intense relief already. She never talks about her previous life. And I never ask. Until now.

Step two, check.

"See that boat out there?" It's the only one visible from where we are.

"You mean your boat?"

"No, I mean *our* boat."

"Well, just because I've been spending an inordinate amount of time in the captain's bedroom doesn't make it mine," she teases.

"No, but the ownership papers do." She leans away enough that she can turn to face me. "A few weeks ago, I had the title transferred into both our names. Well, sort of."

"What do you mean, 'sort of'?"

"Well, it's titled to Mr. and Mrs. Nash Davenport."

I hear Marissa's hushed gasp. "And wh-why would you do that?" Her voice is breathy.

"Because I want my wife to know that she is a part of me, a part of my life, a part of everything I have and everything I am. All she has to do now is agree to marry me."

Reaching inside my pocket, I pull out the ring that's been burning a hole in my clothes for almost two months now while I've tried to find the perfect place to propose. Dropping to one knee, I take Marissa's shaking left hand in mine.

Looking up at her, at the face I still dream about and the eyes that melt my heart, I feel the nerves disappear. I had wondered if there was any chance she'd say no. But looking at her now, the love she has for me bathing me as openly and completely as the huge moon above, I know she's already mine. And I'm already hers. I have been since the first time I kissed her on a balcony in New Orleans, and I will be until the day someone puts my body into the ground.

"Please say you'll be my wife. I want you tied to me in every way a man can be tied to the woman he loves. I can't live without you and I never want to try. Share the boat with me. Share your life with me. If you will, I promise to keep you safe and happy every day for as long as I draw breath."

She doesn't say yes, but I'm assuming she means it when she pushes her finger into the engagement ring I'm holding. About two seconds after that, she bursts into tears and drops to her knees, throwing her arms around my neck.

"Is that a 'yes'?"

"Yes," she cries.

There are fireworks. Not on the horizon or ones that can be seen with the naked eye, but they're there nonetheless. In all the places that matter, all the places that I can feel. "Welcome to our future, Mrs. Davenport."

"I love you," she mumbles into my neck.

"I love you, too, baby."

And I do. More than anything.

The End

A FINAL WORD

A few times in life, I've found myself in a position of such love and gratitude that saying THANK YOU seems trite, like it's just not enough. That is the position that I find myself in now when it comes to you, my readers. You are the sole reason that my dream of being a writer has come true. I knew that it would be gratifying and wonderful to finally have a job that I loved so much, but I had no idea that it would be outweighed and outshined by the unimaginable pleasure that I get from hearing that you love my work, that it's touched you in some way or that your life seems a little bit better for having read it. So it is from the depths of my soul, from the very bottom of my heart that I say I simply cannot THANK YOU enough. I've added this note to all my stories with the link to a blog post that I really hope you'll take a minute to read. It is a true and sincere expression of my humble appreciation. I love each and every one of you, and you'll never know what your many encouraging posts, comments, and emails have meant to me.

http://mleightonbooks.blogspot.com/2011/
06/when-thanks-is-not-enough.html

ABOUT THE AUTHOR

New York Times and *USA Today* bestselling author **M. Leighton** is a native of Ohio. She relocated to the warmer climates of the South, where she can be near the water all summer and miss the snow all winter. Possessed of an overactive imagination from early in her childhood, Michelle finally found an acceptable outlet for her fantastical visions: literary fiction. Having written more than a dozen novels, Michelle enjoys letting her mind wander to more romantic settings with sexy Southern guys, much like the one she married and the ones you'll find in her latest books. When her thoughts aren't roaming in that direction, she'll be riding wild horses, skiing the slopes of Aspen, or scuba diving with a hot rock star, all without leaving the cozy comfort of her office. Visit her on Facebook, Twitter, and Goodreads and at mleightonbooks.blogspot.com.

Read on for exciting bonus material . . .

Q & A WITH M. LEIGHTON

How did the idea for the series come about?

I guess it all started with Olivia. As I got to know her, got to see her struggle with what she *wanted* versus what she felt that she *needed*, I realized that her love interest would have to be two men. Polar opposites. One would have to encompass all that she desired, while the other would have to be the logical choice her head would make. That's when I realized that, to complicate matters, they would need to be brothers. Both handsome, both wanting her, and she would be attracted to both of them as well. It wasn't until I had begun writing that I decided to make them twins. Identical in so many ways, but for the few areas that she wrestled with so deeply. From there, the rest, as they say, is history.

Why do you think bad boys are so appealing?

I think it's human nature to want what we can't have, something we feel is slightly beyond our reach. And that's something every bad boy exudes – an attitude that he can never be tamed or contained. It makes us ladies want him all the more. But not necessarily to tame. I think we all like the idea of being the *one girl* who he can't live without, the *one girl* who makes him forget all others. To me, that is the single most appealing thing about a bad boy. Dangerous, yes. Sexy, yes. All the bad boy trappings, double yes! LOL. But, in the end, what we all want is to be desired above all else, to be the one thing a man can't survive without.

Who would you choose if you could: Cash or Nash?

Is it a cop-out to say both? LOL! To me, they are both a bad boy and a good guy, all wrapped up in an irresistibly gorgeous package. They just do it in different ways. They both make my heart race. They both came alive to me as if they're real men. They both have me completely devoted to them when I write. I don't think I *could* choose.

Do you identify with Olivia?

In many respects, yes I do. I didn't used to be, but now I'm somewhat clumsy. I blurt things out that I really shouldn't. I struggle with what I want versus what I need. And I'd also secretly love to be a bartender. I don't know why, but they fascinate me. Also, I have many of Olivia's weaknesses – the bad boy with the gilded tongue, the insatiable need to follow my heart. Yes, I can definitely identify with Olivia.

What is your advice for would-be writers?

Don't ever give up on your dream! I hung up my keyboard for a little while after I'd tried the traditional route in 2009. I didn't write for several months. But the fire was already in my blood. I found myself typing again before too long, and also willing to try again to get my stories out. Now, in retrospect, I'm so, so glad I did! If I'd given up, I'd have missed out on one of my life's most amazing, miraculous, magnificent experiences. And I wouldn't change what has happened for the world!

So I'd say to would-be writers, if you have a story to tell, tell it! If you have a dream to chase, chase it! Life is too short to pile up years and years of regret. Live it while you can.

Where do you go to write? And do you have any funny writing habits?

I always, always, always write in my office. I can brainstorm anywhere. I keep a notepad or my phone with me at all times, for that crazy, spontaneous moment when I have to jot down an idea, but when it comes time to actually construct my story, I do it in my office.

As for funny habits, as influential as music is to me and my writing, you'd think I would write while listening to music, but I just can't do that. I have to have complete and utter silence. No television, no music, no people talking. I have to be, for all intents and purposes, alone with the characters in my head so that I can better hear their voices. But before I type the first word, I always listen to some music. Throughout the day and night I'm constantly listening to it, letting the words and the melody inspire me and solidify the characters that are such a huge part of my life.

Also, I write in my pajamas. A girl has to be comfortable when she's writing about sexy men, don't you know.

Do you remember the first thing you ever wrote?

Book-wise, yes. It was an adult paranormal romance about vampires. He he. As for the first thing I *ever* wrote, I have no clue. I really had no idea that I might ever be interested in writing. My mother did. She used to tell me I should write because I was so good in English class and Advanced Composition. She said I could write a ten-page essay about a pencil. I guess she was right!

You're very prolific on Twitter and Facebook: do you find them a good way to reach out to your fans?

Yes, I really do. I love, love, love hearing from readers! They enrich my life more than I could ever say! In fact, many of them have actually become friends of mine. I just can't imagine *not* interacting with them!

Which actors would you pick to cast as your main characters?

CASH/NASH – In *Down to You*, I always envisioned Cash and Nash as the model Jessie Pavleka. But, for reasons I won't disclose here (they're spoilery!), I see them as Charlie Hunnam in *Up to Me*. The scruff and that rough look . . . *sigh*

OLIVIA – I picture her as Kendall Jenner. Her eyes are brown, but to me, her face still looks so much like how I picture Olivia. She's friendly and approachable, yet gorgeous and doe-eyed.

GINGER – I think the perfect Ginger would be Emma Stone. She's funny and pretty and spunky. I can just hear her delivering all of Ginger's insane lines with the perfect amount of pluck. ☺

MARISSA – Amanda Seyfried could be Marissa. She can be both cool and aloof, yet fragile and damaged when you look a little more closely.

TARYN – The best person I can think of to describe her is Angelina Jolie in *Gone in Sixty Seconds*. She is perfect! She's raw and in-your-face, and she's sexy yet rough. She's totally Taryn.

DARRIN TOWNSEND – I think Paul Rudd would be the perfect person to play Olivia's kind, mild-mannered father.

MARC – I could see Zac Efron playing him if he had dark eyes. His light and flirty personality would make for a great Marco, not to mention that he's hot!

M LEIGHTON'S TOP 10 ROMANTIC READS

1. *The Wolf and the Dove* by Kathleen E. Woodiwiss

2. *The Thorn Birds* by Colleen McCullough

3. The *Calder Saga* by Janet Dailey

4. The *Born In Trilogy* by Nora Roberts

5. The *Malory-Anderson Family* novels by Johanna Lindsey

6. The *Cynster* novels by Stephanie Laurens

7. *The Twilight Saga* by Stephenie Meyer

8. The *Haardrad Family Saga* series by Johanna Lindsey

9. *Shanna* by Kathleen E. Woodiwiss

10. *The Flame and the Flower* by Kathleen E. Woodiwiss

DOWN TO YOU

**A scorching hot love triangle you *do* want to
get caught up in . . .**

When college student Olivia Townsend returned home
to help her father run his business, she never imagined
a complication like Cash and Nash Davenport – twin
brothers different in so many ways but with one thing
in common: an uncontrollable desire for Olivia.

Cash is dangerous, sexy, and bad to the bone – a
man whose kisses make Olivia forget she is playing
with fire. Nash is successful, reliable and intensely
passionate – and already taken.

But Olivia is in for a surprise. These boys have a secret
that should make her run away as far and as fast as
she can. If only it wasn't too late. A sensual game
between three players has begun, and it's about to spin
deliriously out of control . . .

Ebook 978 1 444 78018 5
Paperback 978 1 444 78019 2

HODDER

UP TO ME

The delicious sequel to DOWN TO YOU

For Olivia, romantic bliss has never felt so right as it has with Cash. Unpredictable, except when it comes to satisfying her desires, Cash's 'bad boy' reputation is well-earned, but he's turning his life around with the one woman who accepts him for who he is.

Until strangers from the past turn Olivia and Cash's world upside down. What they want is something only Cash can give them. And if he doesn't deliver, then they're taking the one thing that Cash values the most . . .

Olivia always knew that falling for Cash meant she was likely to get burned. But this new threat is beyond anything she imagined. Now she has to trust Cash with her life – and for Olivia, that's much easier than letting go and trusting him with her heart.

Ebook 978 1 444 78020 8
Paperback 978 1 444 78021 5

HODDER